TO WED FOR DUTY?

The seventh Earl of Sachse has only recently gained the title, but he already knows his duty: to wed one of the debutantes thrust under his nose at every turn. But he is interested in one woman only: coolly beautiful, maddeningly remote Camilla. Known throughout London as a force to be reckoned with, she has made it clear it is her pleasure to tutor the dashing earl in the ways of society, even offering to find him the perfect bride.

TO WED FOR LOVE?

But he is determined that it is Camilla who will share his marriage bed. He tantalizes her with his caresses and soothes her with his kisses. But why does she resist him so, when she obviously yearns to surrender to his single-minded pursuit? Then, Camilla's hidden past comes to light, bearing consequences neither ever expected. Soon, he will discover the secret that haunts her lovely eyes and make a decision that will change their lives forever.

"LORRAINE HEATH IS AN INCREDIBLE TALENT."
Katherine Sutcliffe

By Lorraine Heath

LORRAINE HEATH

AS AN EARL DESIRES

AVON BOOKS
An Imprint of HarperCollinsPublishers

AVON BOOKS
An Imprint of HarperCollins*Publishers*
10 East 53rd Street
New York, New York 10022-5299

Copyright © 2005 by Jan Nowasky
ISBN: 0-7394-5326-2

Avon Trademark Reg. U.S. Pat. Off. and in Other Countries, Marca Registrada, Hecho en U.S.A.
HarperCollins® is a registered trademark of HarperCollins Publishers Inc.

Printed in the U.S.A.

For my mom,
my dear friend,
my biggest fan

~⟲ ○⟲ ⟳~

I hope heaven is filled with video poker machines and you're hitting the royal flush every time, but knowing you, you're still betting way too conservatively. I had so much fun whenever I was with you. Thank you, Mom, for the smiles, the laughter, the memories.

All my love
Always

Chapter 1

London
1879

"**H**onestly, Sachse, I don't know how you expect to find a suitable wife if you refuse to be fitted for new clothing."

Archibald Warner, the seventh Earl of Sachse, watched as Camilla Warner, his predecessor's widow, paced before him, clearly agitated, wringing her delicate hands, furrowing her youthful brow. While the previous earl had been older than any man Arch had ever known—not that he'd ever met the fellow, and based upon what he'd learned so far he was rather glad that he hadn't—his widow was two years Arch's junior. And the most beautiful woman he'd ever seen.

Today she wore a fashionable dress of the palest pink silk, which accentuated her trim figure and complemented her alabaster skin. She was quite at home in his residence—it had been part of her husband's holdings—and had removed her decorative hat upon entering his library. The sunlight pouring through the windows glinted off her upswept brown hair, touching upon it and causing it to glisten, making it appear that many of the strands had been spun from gold.

All Season, she'd been an exemplary hostess, accompanying him on most of his outings, introducing him to this duke and that earl, this marquess, that viscount. She knew the history of every aristocratic family and details about their lives that some might prefer she didn't know. Without looking in *Debrett's*, she could advise on the proper hierarchy and where one should be seated based on rank so as not to give offense to anyone else at the table.

He was truly amazed that she'd mastered all the etiquette and protocol, which he tended to bumble. He couldn't have been more grateful for her assistance . . . usually.

This afternoon being a rare exception.

She'd arrived at his residence only moments ago and before he could even offer a proper greeting, she promptly began to scold him because he had no desire to be fitted with new clothing. Rather he preferred to sit in his library—the only advantage he'd found so far to being the earl was the abundance of books at his disposal—and finish reading the novel he'd begun yesterday. He often wondered if he should advise Camilla when she went off on one of her tirades that he'd served for a time in Her Majesty's army and was quite skilled with a rifle.

"Sachse, have you listened to a single word I've spoken?"

He looked into her earnest brown eyes. She cared so much about things for which he cared nothing. And yet the intensity with which she cared intrigued him.

"Perhaps I should simply marry you; then I would not have to be concerned with a new wardrobe." *Or a good many other things come to think of it. The notion did have some merit.*

Although judging by the exaggerated rolling of her eyes, she disagreed. "You cannot marry me. I am barren.

You must marry a woman who can provide you with an heir."

She spoke with practicality, but as always, he heard her hesitation and her slight quiver over the word *barren*. She tried so hard to appear unfeeling, but he'd long ago deduced that it was simply a well rehearsed act. Much of her behavior was a performance, which more often than not irritated him because she did not trust him enough to reveal her true self.

Whatever had the old earl done to make her think that she was naught but an actress upon his stage?

"Therefore," she continued, "you must see your tailor when he arrives this afternoon and not find yet another excuse to leave the house before he gets here."

"I have very little interest in securing a woman who places such high regard on the cut of my jacket."

"It is not your jacket that will impress her, but rather what it tells her about you."

"Which would be what exactly?"

"You care not only about the latest fashions, but you have the means to purchase them. You are modern. You take great pride in your appearance. You will make an excellent husband."

"A woman can determine all that from a bit of clothing?" he asked, incredulously.

"One should never underestimate how loudly one's attire speaks to the world. Of course, in addition I will be touting the strength of your character, and it will make my calculated whisperings more believable if you are well turned out."

He set his book aside and rose to his full height. She took a step back. She always did. Kept her distance when he would like nothing more than to close the space separating them—the physical as well as the emotional. She intrigued him because she appeared to live within a tower of her own building, much as Rapunzel, and he wondered if he removed the pins from her hair if the golden brown tresses would fall to the ground.

"Why do you care so much that I marry?" he asked.

"I care that you have an heir, that you do not lose all that you've gained from the old Sachse—may he rest in hell."

Arch chuckled at the answer, which he suspected only touched upon the truth. She gained nothing if he gained an heir, and he'd learned that she never took an interest in anything that offered her no gain. If she wished to pretend her motives were as she'd indicated, he'd allow it for now. In time, though, he would discern her true reasons.

"Camilla, I will not lose any of this until I die, at which point, I will not care what happens to any of it."

She turned away from him, and the temperature in the room seemed to drop, causing a shiver to race along his spine. He didn't know how she managed so effectively to show her irritation with him, yet she did.

"How can you not appreciate all that you've gained?" she asked.

"I do appreciate it."

She spun around. "You do not. You mock it." She lowered her gaze. "And in so doing, you mock me."

He longed to console her with a touch, but he'd learned early on that she was not a woman who relished his touch, so he clutched his hands behind his back. "I would never dream to mock you, Camilla. I am merely uncomfortable with that which I've gained through accident of birth—or in my case through lack of other significant births."

Although his bloodline could be traced back to the third brother of the second Earl of Sachse, he was here only because so few males had been born between then and now, and those who had been born had subsequently suffered through the misfortune of death.

She lifted her gaze to his. "There are those who scheme, plot, and murder to gain what you have."

"A life of leisure."

"The life of a gentleman, an aristocrat, an earl."

He bowed his head slightly, conceding to her point. "I should be more appreciative."

"Indeed you should."

He released a weary sigh, determined to battle a bit longer for his right not to purchase more clothing. "I do not see the urgency in acquiring a new wardrobe when the Season is so near to being over."

"Have you hunting clothes?" she asked.

"No."

"What will you wear when you hunt?"

"I had not planned to hunt."

"Then how can you be an exemplary host when you entertain at the country estate?"

"I didn't realize that I would be entertaining."

She closed her eyes, as though losing patience with a dull-witted child. He was sorely temped to cross the distance separating them, take her in his arms, and demonstrate to her that he in no way resembled a child but was a man to be reckoned with.

But when she opened her eyes and pinned him with her hard-edged glare, he was grateful he'd not moved a muscle. Not that she intimidated him, but he was unaccustomed to dealing with a woman's wrath. He had a propensity for keeping the women of his acquaintance jovial and in the most accommodating of moods. With Camilla, he always felt a bit off-balance.

"Of course, we shall entertain. I have already issued several informal invitations, and once we are settled into the country estate, I'll formalize them. We shan't invite many people, as you are still new to your position, but we shall use the months between this Season and next to secure your place among those with influence."

"And find me a wife."

"To determine possibilities. People are more relaxed in the country."

"Will people not question you're living in the same house with a bachelor?"

"I'm a widow. I require no chaperone. Besides, I'll have my secretary with me to serve as my companion. Sachse Hall is large enough that you shall be in one wing and I in the other."

"Is that how it was with you and my predecessor?" he asked quietly, knowing it was none of his business but unable to resist inquiring and praying that it had indeed been that way. "You in one wing, he in the other?"

She lowered her golden lashes, and he watched as a faint blush crept up her ivory throat and onto her pale cheeks. He was accustomed to country lasses of hardier stock. She always seemed so frail until she spoke.

"He was my husband. I did as he asked."

"And what did he ask of you?"

She snapped up her chin, impaling him with her eyes. It always amazed him how quickly she could go from ice to fire. "*That* is none of your concern."

Of course it wasn't, but still he found himself brimming with curiosity. Before he could issue an appropriate apology for his inappropriate inquiry, the door opened quietly, and the butler stepped into the room. Arch still found having all the servants about a bit unnerving.

In spite of their discretion and quietness, he was never able to feel as though he'd obtained complete solitude. He suspected he was an inconvenience to them as well. Conversations and actions stopped when he appeared, which left him with an incredible need to apologize for disturbing them—which Camilla had warned him was absolutely unheard of. One did not apologize to one's servants.

"Yes, Gibson?" Arch asked.

"My lord, you have a visitor." The butler presented a card on a silver tray.

Arch gave it a cursory glance before nodding. "Send him in, Gibson."

As soon as Gibson had left the room, Camilla took a step forward. "Who is it?"

"Mr. Spellman."

"The solicitor? Whatever does he want?"

She looked toward the door as though she expected Dr. Frankenstein's monster to waddle in. He'd read Mary Shelley's *Frankenstein* to her only last week. He'd read a good many books to her since he'd met her. As much as she seemed to take delight in his reading to her, he was disappointed he never could convince her to return the favor.

Although he supposed he shouldn't be. Camilla preferred to be waited on rather than to be the one doing the waiting. One of her more irritable charms.

"He has come to discuss finances," Arch told her. Mr. Spellman had sent word the day before that he needed a moment of the earl's time.

"Whatever is wrong with your finances?"

"As far as I know, nothing."

She rushed over to him, brushed imaginary lint from his shoulders, straightened the lapels of his jacket, which needed no straightening, and patted his shoulders. "Remember, you are in command of your affairs. Your money is yours to spend as you will, and expenses are incurred that a common solicitor cannot possibly understand."

He grabbed her wrists, stilling her fluttering hands. An expression of fear crossed her features, which she quickly masked, and he decided to ignore. Whether she realized it or not, in whatever manner the old Sachse had treated her was indeed Arch's business, because he couldn't undo what he didn't fully comprehend.

"What expenses?" he asked.

"Archie, you're hurting me."

He didn't fathom how he could be, but the fact that she'd slipped into an informal address alerted him that she was truly upset. He released his hold on her, not at all surprised that she quickly stepped beyond his reach.

She began to adjust her own clothing, and he knew she would not answer his inquiry regarding expenses she seemed to know about that he didn't. The woman was a continual mystery. Fortunately, he enjoyed the challenge of solving a good mystery.

A sound at the doorway caught his attention. Carrying a well-worn leather satchel, Lawrence Spellman walked into the room. "My lord."

"Mr. Spellman."

Spellman bowed his head toward Camilla. "Countess, I did not expect you to be here."

She angled her chin. "I spend a good deal of time with the earl. How else can I educate him regarding his responsibilities?"

"Quite commendable, but I assure you that I am up to the task of telling him all he needs to know."

"Then you were aware that Lady Jane Myerson was seen in public without gloves?"

Arch pressed his lips together to keep himself from smiling—not only because Camilla considered bare hands scandalous, but because Spellman seemed at a loss for words, so the first round of their constant battling would go to Camilla.

Spellman angled his head like that of a thoughtful dog. "I was not aware of that fact, but it is hardly condemning behavior."

"Of course it is. A true lady doesn't display bare hands in public except when she is eating or playing the piano for an audience. Lady Jane Myerson has let it be known that she has an interest in the earl. If not for me, he might make the mistake of actually considering her as a suitable wife when she is anything but."

Spellman released a sigh as though ready to accept that victory wouldn't be his today. "Then the earl is fortunate to have you to guide him."

"He is indeed."

"Mr. Spellman, I believe you came here to discuss my finances, not my social life." Arch had no recollection of Lady Jane Myerson. Perhaps he'd seek her out simply to irritate Camilla.

"Yes, my lord. However, I must restate that I do not believe it is appropriate to have the countess present during our meeting."

"Where's the harm?" Arch asked.

Spellman darted his gaze around the room as though he was searching for the harm, or perhaps he simply wished to avoid looking anyone in the eye. "The matters I'm here to discuss concern the countess."

"So you prefer to speak ill of me behind my back rather than to my face?" she asked tartly.

And Arch wondered why she'd immediately assumed the worst: that Spellman would be speaking ill of her rather than complimenting her.

"I believe that a woman's place is not among gentleman," Spellman said.

"I must disagree, Mr. Spellman," Arch said, before Camilla could issue her retort. "If you are here to discuss matters that concern the countess, then I think she should be present to hear what is said."

"My lord, I must insist—"

"No, Mr. Spellman," he cut in. "It is I who will be the one to insist. Let's get to the business at hand, shall we?"

"Yes, my lord, as you wish." With a final glare at Camilla, which she haughtily returned, Spellman crossed the room, stood behind the desk, placed his satchel on top of it, and indicated the chairs opposite him.

Once Camilla had taken a seat, Arch joined her. Spellman sat, releasing another drawn-out sigh.

"It is time, my lord, for you to determine if you wish for the countess to have an allowance and if so what amount would be appropriate. However, I must advise you that you are under no obligation to provide her with anything, not even a roof above her head."

Arch was acutely aware of Camilla stiffening beside him, thought he could actually see the hairs on the nape of her neck bristling. He, on the other hand, assumed a casual pose, leaned back in his chair, and stretched out his legs.

While Camilla's strategy when facing an opponent was to reveal her arsenal, Arch's was to keep his hidden until the precise moment it was most needed. He realized he often gave the impression that he wasn't up to the task of seeing to his affairs, but he felt he gained an advantage by not revealing all his strengths—or his weaknesses. "Why in the world would I not wish to see to her comfort, Mr. Spellman?"

"The previous earl didn't deem her important enough to mention in his will."

"An oversight I'm sure. The earl was up in years. Did he alter his will at all after he married the countess?"

"No, my lord."

"Did you mention the oversight to him?"

"No, my lord. It was not my place to question the earl's actions."

"Yet, here you are seemingly questioning mine."

"Because I fear matters are getting out of hand." Spellman reached into his satchel and retrieved a stack of papers. "These are lists of items bought thus far this year from various establishments throughout London. Each month the countess purchases at least two dozen dresses, nearly as many shoes, a dozen hats, cloaks . . . the list is endless—"

"Will you be unable to pay for these purchases when the time comes?" Arch asked. He knew the elite shops—which he was fairly certain were the ones Camilla would make use of—expected their influential clients to be bothered with paying for purchases only at the end of the year.

Spellman's face turned blotchy as it reddened. "Of course, I shall be able to pay for them."

"Then I fail to see the problem."

"The problem is the abundance of items bought. The old earl was an extremely frugal man, but since his death three years ago, expenditures within the Sachse households have gone up tremendously. Thus the reason that I thought I should make inquiries now, rather than waiting to be shocked at the end of the year as I have been each year before you arrived to take the helm. The countess is prone to making unnecessary purchases, my lord, and in truth is no longer entitled to spend the earl's money. A fact that I generously overlooked in the past, because a woman must have some means with which to live. But the matter is now in your hands."

Arch looked at Camilla. He could understand the increase in spending within the last year as Camilla came out of mourning, but he was baffled that expenditures had increased during the first two years following the old earl's death. He'd had numerous people remark on how faithfully she'd observed the two-year mourning period. None seemed to fault her for quickly dispensing with the half-mourning attire. After all, she was young and a favorite among the Marlborough House Set. Within their eyes, she could do no wrong. They all seemed to want her happiness as much as Arch did.

Based on rumors he'd heard, he wasn't certain the same could be said of the old Sachse. Perhaps she'd purchased items she couldn't yet use simply because her husband's death gave her a measure of freedom she'd not had while he lived. Arch wondered how many times the previous earl had taken her to task for purchases such as these. As Spellman had also worked for the man, Arch assumed he was familiar with the way the old earl had managed things. But now there was a new earl in London, and it was time everyone began to accept and grow accustomed to *his* ways.

"Are they necessary purchases, Camilla?" he asked quietly.

She turned to him, and he could see the worry lines deepen within her brow. "Yes, Sachse. You see—"

He held up a hand to silence her explanation. If he determined that a problem regarding the expenditures existed, they would discuss the matter in private, not with an audience. He gave his attention back to Spellman.

"Have I the means to pay for them?" He knew Spellman had answered the question earlier, but he thought it bore repeating. He knew the answer, but was making certain that Spellman knew it as well. It was a habit from the days when he taught lessons at the Haywood School for Boys—determining someone's knowledge by testing.

"Yes, my lord. You are quite well-off, but you will not remain so—"

"Then, pay the accounts when they come due, Mr. Spellman."

Spellman folded his hands on top of the papers. "I had every intention of doing so. But I think it would behoove you to set a limit on how much the countess can spend yearly, if you are so inclined to allow her to spend at all."

"The countess has already stated that she is purchasing *necessary* items. One does not limit necessary purchases."

"But two dozen dresses—"

Silencing Spellman with a practiced, hardened gaze that had never failed to bring under control a roomful of unruly boys, Arch slowly unfolded his body and came to his feet. "It is not your place to question the countess or her purchases. Nor should you be running about London looking into her activities. You are simply to pay the bills that come your way and send me an accounting. If you are unable to manage that task, then I shall find someone else to handle the affairs of this estate."

Spellman stood, a visible shudder running through his body as though he were attempting to unruffle his own feathers.

"The previous earl understood that a woman must be

given boundaries, or she will take advantage and lead a man to ruin. I advise you to take the reins and limit her spending."

"Why?"

"*Why?* Because, my lord, she spends frivolously."

"Which I've already stated is none of your concern."

"But it is my responsibility to advise you so that mistakes may be avoided."

"And I appreciate your advice when it pertains to business or the running of the estates. Where the countess is concerned, however, I keep my own counsel, and you would do well to remember that if you wish to remain in my employ."

Leaving the papers where they rested, Spellman picked up his satchel. "Very well, my lord. You won't be the first to have been brought down by a woman."

"Mr. Spellman, I am not too proud to admit when I have made an error in judgment. However, I have carefully reviewed my financial status, and I do not see any cause for alarm. I know you had the best intentions, and I do appreciate your bringing your concerns to my attention."

"That is what I am paid to do, my lord. I bid you good day." He angled his head toward Camilla. "Countess."

Spellman strode from the room. Arch didn't think the man was at all satisfied with the outcome of his visit, but then it wasn't Arch's goal to please his solicitor. He was more interested in pleasing Camilla. He turned to her.

Her luscious lips were parted slightly, her brow knitted. She looked to be momentarily stunned, as though she could hardly believe what had transpired. Then, like someone wiping a slate clean, she blanked her expression.

She rose from the chair, walked to the window, and gazed out on the garden. "I have always found Mr. Spellman to be a most unpleasant man. I thought you handled him admirably."

Arch sat on the edge of his desk and folded his arms

across his chest. Ah, yes, he'd handled the man admirably. But how best to handle the countess was something he had yet to ascertain.

"I believe you have earned the right to spend the earl's money more so than I have."

"You are more generous than he ever was. I had fully expected you to take the larger of his two London homes when you first arrived. Instead, you took the smaller residence. You are a constant source of amazement to me."

"I could say the same of you."

She shook her head as though she didn't wish to travel in the direction of his comment. "The old earl would have required an accounting and explanation for each purchase."

"I am not the old earl."

"So I am slowly coming to realize."

Slowly? He wondered what he could do to hasten the process along. In spite of his best intentions not to do so, he rose, crossed over until he stood only a hairbreadth away from her, inhaled her sweet rose perfume, and said with a low voice, "I wish I had known you before he ever possessed you."

Watching her delicate throat as she swallowed, he desperately wanted to press his lips against her fluttering pulse.

"You would not have liked me," she whispered.

"What was there not to like?"

"I was ignorant . . . poor . . ."

As though suddenly realizing that she was revealing too much, she managed to dart away from him without meeting his gaze. "I would die before I returned to the life of a commoner. I have established a place for myself among the Marlborough House Set and am in a position to achieve anything I want, and I want a good deal. While we search for a wife for you, I shall be searching for a duke for myself."

"You say that as though the most important aspect to a man is his title."

She arched a finely shaped eyebrow. "Because I believe that a man's title is *all* that matters."

He shook his head in denial of her words. "You can't mean that. What of love?"

"What of it? It has no power. It garners no attention when one walks into a ballroom. It doesn't provide servants, or fine clothes, or a large residence. It doesn't earn one favor with the queen. It doesn't keep you out of the street or the gutters. I have been a pauper, and I have been a countess. Now I seek to be a duchess. As such, I shall garner respect—"

"You don't need a title to have respect."

She scoffed. "How little you know. If it were possible, I would strive to be a queen. Then there would be no one more important than I."

"If you were to search for love, rather than rank, then to one man there would *be* no one more important than you."

"Spoken like a poet, rather than a realist."

He was not a man usually prone to violence, but he thought he'd find great satisfaction in plowing a fist into the old earl's face, because he'd managed to strip Camilla of her ability to dream, and Arch thought that might have been the old Sachse's cruelest legacy. "You have never known the reality of being *my* countess."

"And we both know that I never shall. Not that it matters. As I've said, I have goals. I shall help find you an agreeable wife, and in the process, I shall find myself a satisfactory duke."

"You think a duke will make you suddenly fertile?"

She blanched, and he regretted the harshness in his voice and the callousness of his words immediately. He didn't know why he'd been unable to prevent the anger from forcing them out of his mouth. "Camilla—"

She sliced her hand through the air, effectively silencing his apology. "I am not stupid, Archie. I shall target a duke who already has an heir and a spare."

"Which means he will no doubt be old."

"And I shall be burdened with him for fewer years."

"Why would you knowingly go into a marriage that you hoped would be brief?"

"My dear Archie, obviously there are subtleties to the aristocracy that you have yet to fully comprehend. I require rank, and I shall pay whatever price I must to achieve it."

What he did *comprehend* was that it angered him beyond all reason that she sought something that mattered so little.

"When searching for a wife for me, do not apply your standards in acquiring a duke. I want a woman I cannot live without, a woman whose death would cause my heart to break."

He stepped toward her. "I require a woman who makes me smile and causes me to laugh with abandon. A woman with whom I may be comfortable in silence, but whose voice will delight me and whose conversations will bring me joy. A woman who will stir my blood to the point of boiling. She must care deeply about all things and not shy away from revealing that she does so." Another step.

"She will be compared to fire, not ice. She will embrace all that life has to offer, not hold it at bay. She will love me with every fiber of her being, hope for a thousand years to be held within my embrace, and mourn my passing as though she truly regrets that I am no longer by her side."

"You have unrealistic expectations regarding a wife."

"I know of a queen who loved her prince exactly like that."

"I find that sort of love to be cruel. I think it better not to experience it. Then one never has to deal with the depth of loneliness and despair that comes from mourning so great a love."

"But then one must also live with never knowing so great a passion."

Before she could argue further or he could convince

himself that he was making a terrible mistake, he took her within his arms and lowered his mouth to hers. She released a tiny, muffled squeak. Her arms were stiff, wedged between their bodies, but her lips were pliant, urging him on. But he had no desire to rush this moment that he'd waited months to experience.

She'd taunted him with her constant nearness, her faint rose fragrance teasing his senses, her sultry voice whispering etiquette and protocol near his ear, her warm breath wafting along his chin and neck. He'd watched her eat countless meals, studied the way she ran her tongue over her lips as though she feared wasting a bit of sauce. He'd reveled in the dreaminess that came to rest within her eyes whenever he read to her—and had imagined the emotions flitting across her face were for him rather than the story.

Slowly he deepened the kiss, exploring the confines of a mouth that was quick to issue a tart response with a voice cold enough to freeze water. But he found no chill. Only heat. Shimmering between them as their tongues welcomed the dance of seduction.

He relished the taste of her. Sweet and so . . . salty. He became vaguely aware of the warmth pooling around his lips, seeping into the kiss. He drew back.

Tears welled within her eyes, washed along her cheeks, gathered at the corners of her mouth. He'd never seen her appear so young, so vulnerable, so terrified.

Her gaze dipped to his trousers, the tight cut revealing the unmistakable evidence that he'd not only desired her, but had been prepared to go well beyond a kiss. She was panting, trembling as though she could find no air to breathe.

"Damn you, Archie, damn you!" she rasped.

Before he could respond, she spun on her heel and dashed from the room. Frustration bit into him because he was hardly in a condition to give chase. And even if he were, what good would it do him?

He turned to the desk, grabbed the inkwell, and flung it with all his might, sending it crashing through the window and into the garden. Grabbing the edge of the desk, he bowed his head.

What in God's name had just happened?

He'd never in his life lost control of himself, of his emotions, of his desires. And yet in the space of a heartbeat, he'd managed to do all three.

Worse yet, now that he had tasted the sweet nectar of her mouth, how in God's name could he ever forget that he had?

Chapter 2

⁓◦◦⁓

Camilla continued to tremble as her carriage clattered along the London streets. Whatever had possessed Archie to kiss her?

Certainly she'd sensed a spark of anger in him as he'd rattled off his expectations for a wife, but it was the passion in his voice that had held her mesmerized. His words had seemed to flow from his heart, as though he truly believed that love such as he'd described not only existed, but should be available to him. His determination to possess it left no doubt that one day he would. A man who cared so deeply about love was a rare occurrence, and she found herself envying the woman he'd take as his wife.

But why had he placed his mouth against hers after speaking about great love and great passion when she was a stranger to both? What had she done to give any indication that she would welcome his advances when she tried so hard to keep a wall in place so he wouldn't realize that she was fascinated by him?

There had been no love lost between her and her husband. And there most certainly had been no passion. He'd acted as though he could barely tolerate being between her legs, and she'd certainly never enjoyed his presence there. Often the pain had been unbearable, but she'd stoically endured it because not to do so resulted in worse consequences. She'd learned the hard way that displeasing him in the least was to be avoided at all costs.

Shuddering with thoughts of her late husband, she shoved them back into the corner of her mind where nightmares dwelled and concentrated instead on the present earl and the flavor of his kiss. He tasted of mint. Or perhaps she'd only imagined that he did. She could barely remember the specifics. Only that his arms had been like taut rope, not flabby like her husband's, which had always reminded her of bread soaked in milk. She should have been frightened by the strength she felt within Archie. But she wasn't. From him, she felt no threat of physical harm. But the harm to her heart?

She dared not contemplate the possibilities there. Because they did exist.

Archie was undoubtedly the most kind and generous man she'd ever known. When he looked at her as he had just before he pressed his mouth to hers, she wished that she was anyone other than who she was, that she was deserving of a man such as he.

She fought not to remember how her stomach had quivered and her heart had fluttered. He unsettled her. He caused her to want things she couldn't have, to be willing to risk discovery of the truth for a few moments in his arms—for surely a man such as he would discern the truth with ease. When in his presence, she was forced to keep her guard up, to remain ever vigilant against revealing her weaknesses.

How was she to have known that he would become a weakness, like a box of chocolates that once opened was impossible to close until its contents had been devoured.

"My lady, are you all right?"

She glanced over at her secretary, who'd been waiting in

the earl's foyer. Everyone knew Camilla didn't believe that a lady of her status should be bothered with the mundane tasks of her position, and so she kept her secretary near as much as possible to handle inconsequential matters.

Lillian was only a little older than Camilla. The fifth daughter of a merchant, Lillian had been educated, but all the education in the world couldn't alter her appearance. Camilla didn't like to be cruel or speak ill of those she favored, and she was fond of Lillian, but the dear woman was little more than bones and points jutting here and there. No matter how much she ate, she never seemed to gain weight so she rather resembled a stick walking along the street, but refused to pad her clothing. She had an angular face. A pointed nose that held her spectacles in place. Even her front teeth came together to form an unattractive angle that led one's gaze down to her sharply pointed chin.

Camilla forced herself to smile and hoped that Lillian couldn't tell that Camilla's lips were swollen, tingled, and carried the intoxicating taste of Lord Sachse upon them.

"I'm fine, Lillian, thank you for inquiring."

"You seem unsettled, and I saw Mr. Spellman lurking about. His presence usually doesn't bode well."

Camilla smiled softly. "Hardly lurking. He wanted to speak with the earl about my expenditures."

"I feared they would get you into trouble again."

"No, not with this earl. He told Spellman they were none of Spellman's concern, and even after Spellman left, he failed to ask me why I would purchase so many clothes."

Archie had surprised her by standing up to Mr. Spellman, defending her right to spend as she chose. Yes, she'd earned that right, but she'd not expected a man to understand what it was for a woman to be berated constantly, never to measure up to her husband's expectations.

She'd been only sixteen when the old earl had taken her as his wife, believing that his aged seed could more easily find root in a younger girl. He was desperate to replace the son lost to him when his first wife had taken the boy to America for a holiday. The child had fallen ill and died there, and the old Sachse had never forgiven his wife for taking so little care with his heir. Camilla wouldn't have been surprised to discover he'd poisoned the dear woman.

He'd been a horrible, horrible man. Camilla had come to loathe him with every fiber of her being. But she had been powerless to control her destiny.

That was no longer the case. Now she was in complete control. She had paid dearly to acquire power and influence—and she would do anything to hold on to all she'd gained and if possible to climb higher.

She was not by nature greedy, but she'd learned through harsh experience that wealth was preferable to poverty, beauty favored over ugliness, confidence better than doubt, holding a title more advantageous than being a commoner. She'd attained all and looked back on her life with no regrets, except on the most lonely of nights when she would undoubtedly find herself staring at too many regrets to count.

But then ciphering had never been one of her strong suits, so it was quite possible that her regrets were not as numerous as she feared. But neither were they as dangerous as the truth, for if revealed it would cause her to lose her influence more quickly than anything, so she kept it well hidden. Even Lillian, who spent the most time in her company, didn't suspect.

Manipulation of facts and appearances was a part of whom Camilla had become, and although it reeked with dishonesty, it was the only way she knew to protect herself. As Charles Darwin had theorized twenty years earlier with *The Origin of Species*, survival was dependent upon adaptation to one's environment. And if she was nothing else, she'd determined she was a survivor.

"Perhaps you should explain to the new earl what you do with all these purchases."

"No, as generous as he appears to be, I have no way of knowing if his generosity will extend beyond me. I'll not risk having my good works stopped."

"So the possibility exists that he could withdraw his generosity at any time," Lillian mused. "What will you do under those circumstances?"

"For security, I must find myself another husband. I've not given up on snagging a duke simply because one got away from me this Season." For a time, she'd been betrothed to the Duke of Harrington, but Rhys had fallen in love with a Texas heiress, which had caused scandal and near ruin for all involved. Still, *she'd* managed to survive the fiasco.

She would find herself another duke with the ability to elevate her status to that of duchess. After all, she had turned thirty only recently and was extremely skilled at managing her assets: her face, her figure, her ability to appear confident and in control, when she was anything but.

"Finding another duke will be a bit of a challenge when Lord Sachse seems to take up an inordinate amount of your time."

"Lord Sachse is no bother, I assure you," she responded hastily, not understanding her need to defend him when she'd never felt a need to defend any man. "He is nothing like the old earl."

Which makes him oh so much more dangerous.

She returned her gaze to the window. Archie was indeed nothing like the old earl. He was handsome beyond measure. Young, energetic, fit. She loved the way his eyes sparkled when he discovered something new, and she'd been able to share so many discoveries with him in London. They'd attended concerts at Albert Hall and seen Madame Tussaud's wax figurines. They'd strolled through art museums and gone to operas.

She'd never met anyone who possessed as much curiosity as he did. He asked questions about everything, studied all around him as though unable to be fully satisfied with any explanation, as though there was always more to discover.

And when his inquisitive gaze fell on her, his eyes would darken, causing her to quiver with anticipation—of what she didn't know, but it hovered just beyond reach, a silent promise as yet unfulfilled.

He did more than watch her. He studied her as though she were a butterfly housed beneath glass. What did he see when he stared at her so intently? What was he able to discern from his constant perusal? Obviously he did not see her true self, or he never would have pressed his mouth against hers.

And what a marvelous mouth he had. So skilled at eliciting pleasure. She'd found the movement of his lips, the sweep of his tongue incredibly tantalizing. As much as she'd wanted to retreat, she'd been forced to stay, because she'd never known anything as sweet or enticing. Or hot. The heat had seared her blood, had warmed her throughout. Then the tears had come because for the first time in her life, she experienced the rising tide of passion. She couldn't give in to it. He would discover her secret then.

And with the discovery, he would cease to look at her with interest because she had little doubt that what he valued most, she lacked. She'd faced rejection countless times throughout her life, but she had an odd feeling she'd not survive a rejection from him.

"Lillian, have the driver stop the carriage. I wish to walk in the park."

While Lillian saw to the task, Camilla kept her gaze on the grassy green knoll that had come into view. Children scampered over it, and she imagined the games they were playing. Their laughter and cries were filled with innocent joy. She hated that a time would come when all that would be stolen from them, when the realities of life would shove aside hopes and dreams.

The carriage rolled to a stop. The footman opened the door and helped Camilla climb out. She knew Lillian would no doubt join her, but she had no desire to wait.

She began walking along the path, enjoying the rustling of the leaves in the breeze. She preferred the bustle of London to the slow waltz of the countryside. If not for Archie's need of a hostess and the fact that it would be unfashionable to do so, she would remain in London after the Season came to an end.

She stopped walking and studied the children dashing hither and yon. They were the one thing in life that no matter how diligently she worked or conspired, she would never attain. She would never know what it was to feel a child growing within her, to see love reflected in a man's eyes because she'd gifted him with a son or a daughter.

The old Sachse had taught her that a woman who couldn't bear children was not one worth having. She'd thought she might die from the lessons he gave.

Instead, like delicate skin constantly chafed, she'd grown tough and hard. She'd found other things within herself to value. And while they might be shallow, of little consequence in the grand scheme of the world, they gave her a measure of satisfaction and allowed her to fool everyone around her. No one knew of her heartbreak, shame, or regrets.

She would do whatever it took to keep things that way.

Chapter 3

My dear Camilla,

I must begin by seeking your forgiveness for my inexcusable conduct this afternoon. Your actions clearly indicated that you were appalled by my behavior. I must admit that my actions took me by surprise as well.

It is not my place to find fault with the things which you've come to value or the choices you make in your life.

I was not angry with you. Rather I was lashing out against my new situation, which forces me to consider aspects to a woman beyond love. As you were quick to point out, I am in need of a wife who can provide me with an heir.

I had always considered love to be the one and only criterion that I would use when selecting a wife. Although even that isn't quite true, because I'd never viewed the finding of my soul mate as a selection, but rather more of a quiet recognition that would slip upon me at an unexpected moment: that this one person was mine and I was hers.

I know you think me a silly romantic, but I grew up surrounded by such a love. To know that it can exist, and not to seek it out, seems rather sad to me.

I shall not give up on the notion entirely, but I shall take your concerns to heart and keep in mind that there can be nothing between you and me other than friendship.

Rest assured, dear lady, that I'll not overstep the boundaries between us again. I shall sacrifice the warmth of your lips against mine, the scent of your perfume filling my senses, the press of your curves against my chest, the sound of your whimpers, and the feel of your arms around me. I shall sacrifice them all because it is what you desire.

You have been most kind to me since I have come to London. I didn't mean to reward you by making you unhappy. I understand my place in your life. And I will not seek to make it more.

I need you, Camilla, to help me find a wife. And I will do all in my power, little though it may be, to help you secure your duke.

Your devoted servant,
Archibald Warner
The 7th Earl of Sachse

Camilla sat within her library, gazing out the window, while Lillian sat nearby reading aloud the latest batch of correspondence. A countess received an ungodly amount of letters, was required to send an abundance of replies. When Camilla had hired Lillian, she'd explained that she believed her eyes should be spared the constant squinting necessary to read all that came her way. She also had no desire to get ink upon her fingers, so left the task of writing to Lillian as well.

She and Lillian had devised a workable solution. Lillian first read the letter aloud. Camilla skimmed over it later if she determined it held any significant information, then provided the response that Lillian dutifully wrote.

Camilla was going to have a dreadful time responding to each of today's inquiries because she could barely remember what each person had written. It was so unlike her not to remain focused on the task at hand. Whatever would

Lillian think when Camilla stumbled along instead of providing her usual confident responses?

How could Camilla explain that her mind kept drifting to the afternoon and the kiss that Archie had bestowed on her? Even after her refreshing walk in the park, she found that his bay rum scent still lingered, and memories of the passion simmering between them wouldn't be put to rest, but remained to taunt and tease her with the possibilities of what might have been if she weren't so fearful of the consequences.

She'd never considered herself a coward, but where he was concerned she certainly was.

A sound at the doorway had her turning her attention there, grateful for the distraction from her morbid musings. The butler stood patiently, holding a silver tray. Like all the servants in her residence, Lillian, too, for that matter, he technically worked for Archie because it was the Earl of Sachse who paid the salaries. She fully understood that if it ever came down to it, their loyalty would have to go to him rather than to her. She was really no more than a guest, and she feared a time would come when Archie would realize that.

"Yes, Matthews?"

"A letter has arrived from his lordship."

Her heart kicked painfully against her ribs, and she had trouble drawing in a breath. "From Lord Sachse?"

The high tone of her voice surprised her, sounding very much like the squeak of a mouse when cornered by a large and ferocious-looking cat.

The butler, as befitted his station, gave no indication that anything was amiss in her response, and stated levelly, "Yes, madam."

She felt as though her ability to think clearly had stepped out of the room as Matthews stepped farther into it. What could Archie possibly want? Why would he send a letter? Had he written about their encounter that afternoon? Described it in detail? Asked for another session? Demanded another kiss, or she would indeed find herself with an allowance?

It was as though she watched through a dark tunnel as Lillian, reacting from years of habit, took the letter from Matthews and, using an intricately carved silver letter opener, unsealed the envelope in preparation of reading its contents aloud to her mistress.

"No!" Camilla jumped to her feet, then fought to regain her composure as both her employees stared at her as though they didn't quite know this woman who was acting so unlike herself. She held out her hand. "I'll take the letter."

Lillian furrowed her brow, which caused the pointed tip of her nose to appear more pointed. "You don't wish for me to read it to you first?"

And risk the possibility of revealing my very personal and private encounter with Lord Sachse this afternoon? I think not.

Although she knew that Lillian was the soul of discretion, she also believed it was imperative to keep secret that Archie had kissed her—and worse, that she'd kissed him back—until she'd regained her senses. It was so much less embarrassing that way. Deigning not to answer Lillian's question, she snapped her fingers impatiently. "The letter, Lillian, if you please." And even if she didn't.

"As you wish, my lady." Lillian handed the envelope over to Camilla.

"Leave me now," Camilla ordered. "I wish to have a moment of privacy."

Once the servants had departed, and the door was closed, Camilla returned to her chair by the window. She removed a single sheet from the envelope, unfolded it, and held it toward the late-afternoon sunlight.

In spite of her apprehension regarding what he might have written, she smiled. She'd known that he'd write with neat, yet bold, sweeping strokes. Slowly, she trailed her fingers over the marks he'd made. So beautiful, so elegant, so perfect.

She'd known it would be so. He was a teacher after all, and she'd known he'd teach by example.

Tears filled her eyes. At that precise moment, she'd have gladly given up her hard-earned title to be able to read what he'd written.

With letter in hand, Camilla retreated to the sanctuary of her bedchamber. She was desperate to know what Archie had written, but not desperate enough to risk asking Lillian to read her the letter—especially after she'd broken from their usual habit. How would she explain her sudden reversal without appearing flighty? She certainly wouldn't reveal the truth: that she lacked the ability to read.

It was her most shameful secret: her inability to decipher the complex maze of scrawl that resulted in words that allowed people to communicate through writing rather than voice.

She envied those with the ability to read, to open a book and bring forth a story that had once existed within someone else's mind, to know with a single glance over a newspaper everything of importance that was happening within the world, to see a sign on a shop window and know immediately what was being advertised even though no drawing was provided. People who could read took for granted the possibilities that existed because they could share others' experiences and thoughts. Even a stranger's. They didn't appreciate the largeness of their world, while she was left to flounder within the smallness of hers.

She'd spent the early years of her life in poverty on the streets, clutching her mother's skirt while her mother sold her skill with a needle . . . and sometimes herself. The memories were not pretty.

She'd been eight when her mother had taken her to the children's home. Had she been younger, she might have had more success with the schooling they'd offered, but she'd been too proud to let on that she hadn't a clue as to how to read or write. Her gift was memorization. She could have someone read to her and repeat what she'd heard almost verbatim. She'd thought if she pretended that she could read and write, that eventually both skills would take root and the pretense would become reality.

Instead, she'd simply learned how to pretend extremely well and convince people to believe whatever she wished them to. She made herself indispensable at handling chores, so she was often called upon to work rather than to study. She became like a magician, providing distractions that hid the truth and manipulating the performance so that it seemed true magic had taken place.

They thought she was oh so smart—and so had she— until she realized that in her cleverness she'd sacrificed all hope of ever mastering the ability to read. By then, it was too late.

But then her world again changed. The Countess of Sachse had taken to volunteering at the children's home to lessen the heartache she'd experienced after her son had died in America.

She'd liked Camilla. Camilla had liked her. And when she'd made the offer to take Camilla on as her companion when Camilla was fourteen, Camilla had seen an opportunity to better herself. Certainly, the countess had never required that she read. It was conversation that interested her, and so Camilla had learned how to speak like a lady, with a lady's intonations and an educated woman's choice of words. Words she couldn't spell, words she would never recognize when presented in print.

But speak well she could, fool the world she did. Then she became a countess and achieved the means—a secretary—to keep forever her most humiliating secret buried deeply where none would find it.

She walked to her dressing table and opened the large gold-inlaid box in which she kept her precious jewelry. She removed a tray, then the one beneath it. Carefully, she took out the remaining pieces of jewelry and set them aside. Then she slipped a fingernail into a spot between the side of the box and its apparent bottom. The slot was invisible to the most discerning eye. She worked free the covering that hid the false bottom.

She set Archie's letter on top of another she'd received and never read. As she lay dying, the countess had given it to Camilla.

"Show it to no one," she'd whispered. "And do not read this until my husband is dead and buried, because I never want him to look into your eyes and see the truth. Although I would find some satisfaction in knowing that I'd bested him—I would not have all that I've done undone until it is time. I trust you and you alone. I know that you will see that my wishes are carried out."

And Camilla would indeed see that they were carried out—if she only knew what they were. Countless times since Sachse had died, she'd considered taking this letter to Lillian and asking her to read it aloud, but the countess had written something she wanted no one else to know, and she'd trusted Camilla with whatever it was.

So she was left to wonder and unable to carry out the dear woman's final request. She couldn't even fake doing so, as she had no earthly idea what the countess might have asked of her. She'd provided nary a hint of what she wanted. Perhaps to spit on her husband's grave. Although Camilla had done that anyway. Twice. Once for herself and once for the previous countess on the off chance that it had indeed been her request. She knew the old earl had been no kinder to his first wife than his second.

She'd assumed his first wife had wanted to exact some sort of revenge, but she had no idea what it might actually entail. Still, Camilla took satisfaction in knowing that regardless of what it was, she *would* have carried out the request to the best of her ability had she known what it was.

The knock on her door nearly had her leaping into her jewelry box. She swallowed hard to get her rapidly pounding heart lodged out of her throat and back into her chest. "One moment please."

She scrambled to reassemble everything and put all the items back where they belonged. She always felt so guilty about letting down the earl's first wife. The woman's ignorance concerning Camilla's inability to read was a testament to Camilla's success at convincing everyone that she was indeed well educated. She would have told her predecessor the truth, but it seemed a cruel thing to reveal when death had been hovering in the shadows. Camilla had determined it would be kinder to allow the countess to believe that her final wishes would be handled to her specifications.

Closing the lid on the jewelry box, she released a sigh before straightening and turning to face the door. "Enter."

Her lady's maid, Frannie, stepped into the room. "Lord Sachse has arrived for dinner."

"Lord Sachse?" Again, that irritating squeak. She really needed to stop letting thoughts of him affect her so.

"Yes, my lady. He indicated that you were expecting him."

"Of course I'm expecting him." Only she hadn't been. She'd forgotten that she'd invited him to dine with her this evening. Or perhaps she'd only hoped that he wouldn't come after the blistering kiss he'd delivered that afternoon. Perhaps that's what his letter had told her—that he would still come for dinner.

Damnation! He would expect that she'd read his missive and was well aware of what he'd written. Oh, the tangled web she'd woven was threatening to suffocate her.

"Assist me in changing for dinner."

She selected a cream-colored satin dress with deep purple vertical stripes. She'd discovered that vertical stripes made her appear taller, and tonight she had a need to appear not quite so small. The flounces were edged in purple and fringed. The square neckline stopped just short of revealing the barest hint of her bosom. She decided against wearing a false hairpiece to give buoyancy to her hair. She felt false enough. Around her throat she wore a length of purple velvet from which dangled an intricately carved silver medallion. On her wrist she placed a simple silver bracelet.

She considered but decided against more jewelry. This evening called for casual elegance. While Frannie assisted her, Camilla began mentally to prepare herself for the manipulation that would soon take place. She had to give the appearance that she knew exactly what was in the letter that she'd hidden away.

An apology, of course. She was fairly certain the gentleman in him would apologize for taking advantage that afternoon. But what else? There had been very little remaining space on the page, so he'd either apologized ridiculously profusely or had gone on to another subject entirely. Discerning the answer to that riddle would require that she remain vigilant and alert during the evening.

She studied her reflection in the looking glass. She hardly appeared to be a spy on the verge of uncovering information, but then she supposed that was the whole point. Someone ferreting out facts wasn't supposed to let on that she was doing exactly that.

She took a deep breath to steady her nerves. She'd carried out this ruse with far more sophisticated men. But then she'd never cared about a single one of them, and she did care about Archie. He'd somehow managed to create a crevice within the ice surrounding her heart, then worked his way into it. She couldn't allow him to burrow any further. Tonight she would shove him out and repair the barriers.

But she would take no delight in doing so.

That, too, made the exercise much more daunting. As a general rule, she always enjoyed fooling people, getting the upper hand. She found no satisfaction where Archie was concerned.

She inhaled another deep breath. "Well, I suppose I am as ready as I shall ever be."

"You look lovely, my lady," Frannie said. "As always. Lord Sachse will no doubt be mesmerized."

That was the plan. If he were mesmerized, he could be manipulated more easily.

Ignoring the quivering of her nerves, she strolled out of the room, along the hallways, and down the stairs.

She found him in the library. It was her favorite room because she believed the smell and look of all the books lining the floor-to-ceiling shelves gave the impression of wisdom coupled with power. She'd always considered books intoxicating. She found pleasure in simply opening one, inhaling the musty scent, and looking at the letters printed on the page. She took special delight in books that had illustrations. A picture could often portray what words couldn't.

She watched as he turned back the cover on a book that was set on a high table. He looked particularly handsome this evening, in gray tailcoat and trousers, with a blue waistcoat, and a red silk cravat. She wondered if he'd gone to greater lengths than usual to impress her.

As though suddenly aware of her presence, he looked up and met her gaze. "Is this a new book?"

"Yes." She'd purchased it because she'd liked the way it looked.

"I didn't know you read French."

She didn't. She didn't read at all. And she certainly hadn't realized the blasted book was written in French. She hated continually lying to him, but she'd carried the deception too far and for too long to give up on it now. She finally responded. "A bit."

Taking a step toward her, he looked to be a man who suddenly found himself standing on the edge of a precipice, unable to decide whether or not he should jump. "I wasn't certain I would be welcomed."

"Of course, you would be welcomed. This is your home after all. I am not one to forget that I am here only out of the goodness of your heart."

"And if that were not the case, if I didn't technically own this residence, would you welcome me then?"

Always. Her throat knotted, preventing any words that might make her vulnerable from being uttered. She merely nodded.

"You received my letter?"

Another nod. Where had her quick-thinking mind run off to?

"And you read it?"

"That is the purpose of a letter is it not? To be read?" Ah, at last, some semblance of wit.

"Indeed it is. So you found my apology acceptable?"

So he had indeed written to ask for forgiveness. He'd certainly used a lot of ink to do it.

"Our encounter this afternoon is already forgotten," she assured him.

He seemed utterly disappointed, until a corner of his mouth curled up slightly, almost teasingly. "Not by me."

His gaze darkened and intensified as though he were remembering every sweep of their tongues and the hard press of her body against his. She would fight his heat with ice.

"As I assume you are here for dinner, I suggest we get it over with."

"Get it over with? That hardly sounds as though you're looking forward to it. If you'd rather I not be here—"

"No, of course, I welcome your presence. I simply meant that I see no point in continuing to discuss this afternoon or the letter."

He took a step toward her, and she moved quickly back.

The other corner of his mouth hiked up, so that he was bestowing upon her a warm smile. "I thought only to escort you into the dining room . . . as is my usual practice."

She gathered her courage around her, relaxed her hands, which had fisted at her sides, and placed one on his offered arm. "Of course."

"As I said in my letter, I understand my place in your life."

Oh, he'd said that, too, had he? And where exactly did he think his place was?

"You need never fear me," he continued.

Well, she did fear him. She couldn't help it. He terrified her. Even as she wanted him to move to the far ends of the earth, she wanted him to step closer to her.

"You don't frighten me."

"Can you say the same of the attraction that shimmers between us?"

"I wasn't aware of any attraction."

"And here, I'd always considered you to be an astute woman."

The challenge in his eyes infuriated her. Why couldn't he be as easy to manipulate as every other man in London?

"I believe you are delusional," she said, hoping to turn his observations away from her.

He chuckled, and she remembered that he favored having a woman who would make him laugh. This encounter was obviously not going in her favor.

"Am I delusional regarding your being astute or there being an attraction between us?" he asked.

She gave him a haughty look. "Well, as I am obviously astute, then it stands to reason—"

"That you would feel nothing if I kissed you again?"

Feel nothing when her lips had already begun to tingle in anticipation of his mouth against hers? "Please don't test me."

She thought she sounded pathetic and weak. She detested both impressions. They left the hardiest woman vulnerable.

He bowed his head slightly, lifted her hand to his mouth, and kissed the tips of her fingers. "As you wish."

She stared at him, unable to believe the ease with which he'd given up the pursuit—and a bit disappointed as well.

"I promise you that what happened this afternoon will never happen again," he said.

Had *that* been in his letter or was he just now adding it? How was she to respond? She finally decided to settle for, "I'm quite relieved."

"Are you?"

"Undoubtedly."

"Why are you trembling?"

Because you are near. Because it is foolish to want you when your occupation had once required you to determine who had mastered a lesson and who hadn't.

"I'm feeling faint because I've yet to dine," she said, instead of offering the truth.

"Then we'd best see to dinner."

"Yes, we had."

With a measure of relief, she allowed him to escort her into the dining room. She'd managed to keep the truth from him, but her success was bittersweet. She'd never regretted more that she had secrets to keep.

Chapter 4

She was hiding something. Arch was certain of it. She'd seemed uncomfortable, on edge when first meeting him in the library, and she'd not relaxed since coming in to dinner.

If she hadn't told him that she'd read his letter, he would have thought that she hadn't. He believed he'd been forthright in his apology as well as his explanation regarding what he expected future encounters between them to entail, but she was acting as though she wasn't quite certain of where she stood . . . or more precisely as though she was unsure how to tell him exactly what she thought of him.

He sat at one end of the long table, while she sat at the other, eating with precise, concise movements, never taking her eyes from her food as though she feared if she so much as blinked, it would dash off her plate. He was accustomed to her delighting him with silly gossip about one person or another. She seemed to care little for England's political affairs, but she knew a great deal about the personal politics *and* affairs that affected the aristocracy. Who was seen with whom. Who *should* be seen with whom. Which ladies had unblemished reputations, which had demonstrated questionable behavior and should be viewed with suspicion. Such as Lady Jane Myerson and her scandalous absence of gloves.

"I did not realize that Lady Jane Myerson had an interest in me," he said quietly, trying to bridge the river of silence separating them.

She set down her fork, signaled to the nearby footman for her plate to be removed, and dabbed delicately at each corner of her mouth. He truly wished she wouldn't draw attention to her lips. He so wanted to kiss her again.

"All the ladies have an interest in you," she finally responded. She pierced him with a glare. "That is one of the reasons that it is so very important for you to be measured for hunting attire. I received word from the tailor that you were not available to him once again."

"Shortly after you rushed out I went for a walk to gather my thoughts. I saw you standing on the knoll at a nearby park."

"I didn't see you."

"I was too far away. By the time I reached the spot, you'd left. You seemed very lonely up there."

"I wasn't lonely. I was watching the children."

"I would think that would be a painful undertaking."

"Why?"

He was wishing now that he'd simply told her that he'd gone for a walk. He'd not meant to traverse this uncomfortable ground. "I would think it would be difficult to look upon what you cannot have."

"As we've gone to the art museum twice, I assume you enjoy looking at paintings."

"Indeed, I do."

"But you cannot purchase them all."

He fought back his grin. "No, I cannot."

"Does that dim your enthusiasm for them?"

"No, rather it makes me appreciate them more."

"There you are." She signaled for more wine to be poured.

"You don't like pity, do you?"

"Not particularly, no. Nor do I like informing the tailor that you will be in your residence when you will not."

That again. The blasted clothing. "In the morning I shall go round to his shop to be measured," he assured her.

"I devoted a good many hours and went to great lengths to select the fabrics that would complement your coloring. Many people do not realize that the shade of fabric can enhance one's appearance as much as the style of the clothing. I do not appreciate feeling as though my efforts were wasted."

"I assure you, Camilla, I'm grateful for everything you've done for me. I don't know how I would have managed without you." And then because he could no longer stand the distance separating them, he shoved back his chair, picked up his plate, utensils, and wineglass, and began walking toward her end of the table.

She looked positively terrified. "What are you doing?"

He set everything down at the place beside hers, pulled out the chair, and sat. "*Joining* you for dinner."

"It's improper."

"What does it matter when it is only the two of us? My father sat beside my mother every day of his life so when they spoke neither had cause to raise their voices. When I'm sitting at that end of the table, I feel as though you are upon a stage, and I am in the audience. This nearness is preferable, don't you think?"

"I think if you become lax, that you will fall into bad habits."

"It is a risk I think worth taking."

"If I am to educate you, I must educate you on all matters."

"Educate me on this then. Mr. Spellman left his documents on my desk, and I looked them over very carefully. They provided descriptions of the items purchased. I was surprised to discover how plain much of the clothing was."

She reached for her wineglass, her hand shaking. She took a longer swallow than usual, before saying, "I have occasion to wear plain clothing."

"And how do you explain the dolls?"

"My hobby. I collect them."

"I've never seen any here."

"I keep them in a room for my private enjoyment."

He studied her, trying to determine why she seemed so incredibly nervous, and what reason she could possibly have for lying to him. "I thought the purpose of a collection was to display it—"

"The purpose of a collection is simply that—to collect."

"What are you afraid of?"

"I'm not afraid of anything."

"Everyone is afraid of something."

"What of you then? What are you afraid of?"

"I'm afraid of never finding love, of living a lonely life, and at its end finding myself with nothing except discontentment."

She looked at him as though she'd never seen a sadder creature. "Do you not understand that you shouldn't reveal so much of yourself?"

"If I don't, then how will anyone truly come to know me? To trust me?"

"Why can you not be content to gaze upon the surface?"

"Because it isn't the surface that draws me to you."

She came up out of the chair as though someone had suddenly lit a fire beneath her. "I have no desire to discuss so private a matter where servants can hear. You may join me in the drawing room as soon as you've finished with your dinner."

She swept from the room as though she were a woman scorned. He hardly knew what to think, how to react. He was not a stranger to women. On the contrary, he'd enjoyed the company of his fair share over the years, had been left with the impression that they'd enjoyed being with him as well. But then none of them had been married to the old earl, and from what he'd been able to ascertain from those who knew him, few had liked the man.

With a sigh, he shoved back his chair and stood. Perhaps she thought all earls of Sachse were cut from the same cloth.

He walked out of the room, down the hall, and into the drawing room. Standing before a window, she was gazing out into the night. The firelight from the nearby hearth played over her golden brown hair, the delicate slope of her neck, her narrow shoulders. At moments like this he found it difficult to envision her as the haughty woman she so often came across as being.

"Would you prefer for me to leave your home?" he asked.

"It is not my home." She glanced over her shoulder at him. "All of this is yours. Do not think for a single moment that I forget that fact. I know it is only your generosity and kindness that allows me to live in this house. You may ask or demand of me what you will, and I have no choice except to follow through on your wishes—until I have found another husband to see after me."

"You are not my slave, Camilla."

"But you provide for me, do you not? The old Sachse, may he rest in hell, made no provisions for me—as Mr. Spellman was only too quick to remind you."

And perhaps that was a good deal of the problem. He couldn't imagine being in her situation when she never knew from one day to the next if his generosity would be withdrawn. If so, how would she live?

As though sensing the direction of his thoughts, she continued, "This afternoon you asked why I was so keen on finding you a wife. The truth is, that I thought if I could influence you, if I could select your wife, I could ensure that she would be an agreeable sort who wouldn't kick me out before I'd found my duke."

He watched as she blinked back tears before facing him fully. The withering of her pride nearly brought him to his knees.

"Dukes are rare," she rasped. "Those who have secured their heir and their spare and are widowed are even rarer. You are more likely to take a wife before I take a duke. And then what becomes of me?"

"I would never turn you out."

She gave him a sad smile. "A promise easily made, but not easily kept when you have another woman to keep happy."

"I would *never* turn you out," he repeated through clenched teeth.

A corner of her smile crept up higher, and a sparkle seemed to be fighting to return to her eyes. "Although considering all the qualifications you were rambling off earlier this afternoon, I'm not certain you will find a wife as quickly as I expected."

"No, I don't imagine I will." He wanted to take her in his arms, not to kiss her, but simply to hold her, to give and draw comfort. But it was not emotional or physical comfort that she required. Rather she needed to feel financially safe.

An idea began to take shape in his mind. The old Sachse hadn't provided for her, but Arch could and, in so doing, he could set her mind at ease. "How much would you require in order to live comfortably?"

She looked suddenly defeated. "You've decided that Mr. Spellman is right. I need an allowance."

"No, not at all. But I have recognized that I've taken advantage. You have graciously taken me under your wing, and I have done little to show my appreciation. You do not owe me this service, nor should I expect you to give me your time. I was paid to teach. You've been teaching me and, therefore, you should have a salary as well, money which is yours to spend as you see fit, without Mr. Spellman questioning how you use a single penny. Would a hundred pounds a month suffice?"

She opened her mouth, closed it, opened it. "That is more than generous." She shook her head. "But there is very little more that I can teach you."

"On the contrary. You are exceedingly familiar with the ladies of London. I want you to help me find a wife, but I prefer that you help me find one who meets *my* requirements rather than *yours*. I shall pay you a monthly stipend until I marry."

She gave him a suspicious look. "You don't strike me as a fool, but certainly you must realize that if I find you a wife, I cease to have income. I could find fault with every lady who comes our way."

"I trust you not to be that unscrupulous."

He could fairly see the wheels turning in her mind.

"And in return," he continued, "here is what I propose. Since your concern is that my wife might convince me that I should turn you out with nothing, and you doubt my promise not to, we shall strike a bargain. Find me a wife who meets my requirements rather than yours, and I shall pay you a final stipend of"—he considered the last set of ledgers he'd looked over, determining an amount he could easily afford—"twenty thousand pounds."

She stumbled back, and he thought that if the window hadn't been behind her, she might have fallen. "That is a princely sum, and I would be able to bring more than myself to a marriage."

"And if you didn't marry, you'd still be provided for. If you invest that money, you will have a nice yearly income."

"Indeed." She shoved herself away from the window and began to pace. "However, with your standards, you have set me an impossible task." Abruptly she stopped and faced him. "What if I find you a wife, but she doesn't meet all your requirements?"

"Yes, I suppose I do have quite a few, and some may seem unreasonable at that. When all is said and done, I require only that she make me happy, but I ask that you keep all my requirements in mind."

She smiled, and it seemed to him that something had changed within her, for it was a warmer smile than he'd ever seen coming from her. "I should like very much to help you find a wife of your choosing."

"Then our bargain is struck."

"Indeed."

"I don't suppose we should seal the bargain with a kiss," he teased.

"Indeed not. Nor is a written document which must be signed necessary. I believe that a handshake will suffice."

She extended her hand. Because they'd been eating dinner, neither wore gloves. He swallowed hard before sliding his hand around hers. Her eyes widened slightly as though she were surprised by the intimacy of so informal a touch. Always when going to dinner, her bare hand had rested on the sleeve of his jacket, and he'd never had the audacity to place his hand over hers.

Her skin was soft, the warmth of her palm complementing the warmth of his, the heat radiating up his arm to settle low in his gut. He wondered if she was experiencing the same sensations. For a single heartbeat he imagined the fire that would ignite between them if bared flesh from shoulder to heel was pressed together. As though suddenly aware of the direction his thoughts had turned, she gave his hand a quick shake and pulled her own free.

"May we both never regret the bargain we've made," she said.

But her voice was low, raspy, and reminded him of whisperings that should be made beneath sheets during the late hours of the night, leaving him with the realization that his touch had affected her as hers had him.

He gave a brisk nod, fearing that the hoarseness of his own voice would reveal that he already regretted many of the promises he'd made this day.

Chapter 5

Women adored him.

They *absolutely* adored him. Young and old. Beautiful and plain. Married and unmarried. Mothers and daughters. Wives and sisters.

Standing within the National Portrait Gallery, Camilla watched in amazement as lady after lady stopped to speak with Archie.

They seemed to be drawn to him as hummingbirds to nectar. Not that she had ever seen a hummingbird, but last night he'd taken her to a lecture on the tiny American creatures, and she'd seen illustrations of them sipping from blossoms. She'd been intrigued with the notion of their existence, and she thought surely the little birds darting in and out among the flowers were like these women vying for a bit of his attention.

She wasn't surprised by their behavior, only baffled by the fact that she'd failed to notice it before now. Although she supposed she shouldn't have been. They'd both been rather occupied throughout the Season with the Duke and Duchess of Harrington—but then that was another story entirely, a situation she preferred not to reflect upon.

She knew the ladies weren't blind to Archie's handsome features. Still, she thought it was probably his quick
smile that initially drew them in, his warm eyes that held
them spellbound. Whenever he looked at her, she often forgot that anyone else existed. It was his way to give a person
his complete, undivided attention, as though for that single
moment in time no one was more important to him.

He was tall, slender, usually in need of someone putting
him back to rights: straightening his collar, adjusting his
jacket, combing his thick brown hair back off his brow. He
always gave the appearance whenever he arrived anywhere
that he'd rushed to get there.

No doubt because he would stop to study something
along the way to wherever he was going and lose track of
the time—then have to hurry to catch up. He looked at all
things as though if he scrutinized them diligently and long
enough, he could come to understand every aspect of their
being. Part of the reason that he was so dangerous to her.

She needed to find him a wife and find one quickly. She
was striving to make certain that Archie was seen about
London in these final days of the Season. She was gathering
impressions of the ladies, looking at them a bit differently
than she had before, trying to determine who might be best
suited for him.

He would no doubt look upon his wife with the same
intensity that he looked at all things. Therefore, it stood to
reason that Camilla should focus her attentions on the most
comely of women. Flawless complexion. Unblemished.

She thought perhaps a woman with blond hair would
do well for Sachse. Because he was so dark, they would
complement each other, like twilight and dawn. Unlike her
own brown hair, which would offer no contrast. Yes, blond
would do. The lighter the better.

A woman who came no higher than his shoulder would
also do well by him. She liked the way he angled his head
downward just a little when he spoke to someone who

wasn't as tall as he. And then he would smile, such a warm, inviting smile—

"Lord Sachse is most charming, isn't he?" This from the Duchess of Kimburton.

"Yes, Your Grace, he most certainly is," Camilla conceded.

"I daresay that he is in need of a wife. A pity I don't have a daughter."

"Indeed it is, Your Grace."

The duchess studied her for a moment before saying, "And you are need of a husband."

"One who is not in need of an heir," Camilla reminded her, although she was fairly certain the woman needed no reminding that Camilla had committed the unpardonable sin of being unable to give her husband an heir. Not once had his seed taken root, and as that had not been the case with his first wife, no doubt existed as to who was responsible for the failure with his second.

"Quite so. A pity that. It reduces your choices."

"How is your son, Your Grace?" Camilla asked, in order to change the subject to one the duchess generally got long-winded about.

"Still sniffing around American ladies. I don't understand this fascination our lords have with them. Nothing wrong with a good English girl, I say."

Except, like Camilla, most were without money, while American ladies were surrounded by it. Primogeniture certainly provided for irrevocable superiority for England's firstborn aristocratic sons, but at what price to its daughters?

The duchess patted Camilla's hand. "Never fear. You are not so old as to be completely without hope."

Camilla hardly knew how to respond to so glowing an assessment, but as the duchess was already walking away, she could only assume that a response had not been expected. Just as well. She might have released her sarcasm on the duchess, and that would never do.

She turned her attention back to Archie. The ladies had scattered, and the Duke of Harrington had joined him. They were talking quietly, apparently about the portrait since their gazes were transfixed upon it. Two more different men she'd never known. Still, the earl and the duke had become friends.

"Lord Sachse seems to be rather fond of that painting."

Camilla cast a sideways glance at the woman who'd approached. Lydia, the Duchess of Harrington. One of the little Americans the Duchess of Kimburton wasn't happy about. Knowing the woman's husband as she did, Camilla was surprised to see them here. Since they'd been married less than a week, she'd fully expected Rhys to keep his wife beneath the covers—not parading her about London.

"Indeed, he does, Your Grace," she responded. "I can't understand why. This is our third trip to the Gallery. Lord Sachse claims that each time he looks at a painting, he sees something different. I find that notion preposterous. A piece of artwork cannot change; therefore, it looks precisely the same each time you view it."

"Perhaps the difference comes not from the painting itself but from the perception of the person doing the viewing."

"You speak in riddles, and I grow frightfully bored by riddles."

The duchess laughed, as though nothing Camilla ever said would truly bother her. The one thing she'd never been was intimidated by Camilla's coolness toward her, which in the end had earned her Camilla's respect. She rather liked the girl, although she certainly had no plans to admit it.

"The person changed, not the art," the duchess explained. "In this case, Lord Sachse has changed. I imagine he notices subtle differences in himself every day. He was not born expecting to inherit a title, so the schoolteacher he once was must give way to the man who is now responsible for the titles and all the estates that holding them entails."

She wasn't quite certain what to make of this explanation, but Camilla felt a need to defend Archie. "Lord Sachse is perfectly capable of handling the responsibilities and duties of his titles."

"I don't doubt that, Countess, but still his life is very different from what he expected it to be only a few months ago. Like me, you married into the aristocracy. No matter how prepared you are for the elevation in status, it is still rather frightening. I find it is not as comfortable a fit as I thought it would be when I dreamed of marrying an English lord."

Camilla wondered if ever in her life she'd been as youthful or filled with as much innocence as this young blond woman. "One would not know you were insecure by looking at you. That is the mark of a true lady."

She turned her attention back to Archie. He certainly didn't give the appearance of being uncomfortable with his titles. Indeed, she thought he wore them rather well, much better than his predecessor. He had an innate ability to appear noble. It was there in the way he tilted his head when he spoke, the manner in which he gave deference to those of higher rank but never lorded himself over those beneath him.

As though suddenly aware that he'd become the object of her musings, he looked over his shoulder, his dark eyes homing in on her with unwavering precision. The intensity of his gaze heated her to the core. At moments such as this, his innocence became lost to her. She couldn't pretend that he was harmless. She couldn't overlook the fact that he was a man, with a man's desires and a man's passions and a man's hungers.

She turned to the duchess. "This facility does not allow for a proper breeze. I'm going to step outside for some cooler air."

"What caused her to run off like that?" the Duke of Harrington asked. "I've never known Camilla to retreat."

"I don't understand it either," Arch admitted. He gave his attention back to the masterful painting. "She will look everyone in the eye except me. Do my eyes remind her of her husband's, do you suppose? Our being related and all."

"I suppose that might be it, but I suspect his eyes contained cruelty. I never met the fellow, but he and my brother Quentin were quite close, and as Quentin was the devil's spawn, I suspect Sachse might have been as well."

"Why would she marry a man such as that?" he asked.

"You might as well ask me why my mother adored Quentin." He shook his head. "I think what makes the evil truly evil is that they possess the ability not to appear evil."

Arch grinned, even though the subject wasn't humorous. "A lot of evil there."

"Indeed."

"If you will excuse me, Your Grace, I should go find the countess. I could spend all day here, but she grows bored rather quickly, and as she is presently striving to find me a wife, I should probably stay in sight of her."

"I daresay she'll serve you well in that regard. She is well thought of among the Marlborough House Set. She knows a good deal about most of these people."

"So I'm discovering." He wondered how much they knew about her, though. Surely it was not only with him that she hid herself. Arch and the duke walked over to the duchess.

She smiled warmly, her violet eyes sparkling. "The countess excused herself to get a bit of cooler air. Seems she was growing warm in here."

"I should have no trouble finding her," Arch said, as he took her gloved hand and pressed a kiss against her knuckles. "We shall be leaving for the country soon. If I do not see you for a while, I want you to know that I've enjoyed immensely every moment spent in your company."

"Thank you, my lord. I enjoyed it as well."

After bidding them farewell, he walked through the

museum, his footsteps echoing around him. He did so enjoy all the new sights that London allowed him to experience: modern marvels and preserved history in many cases side by side. He could see how far civilization had come and imagine how much further it had to go.

But of all the sights that London held, he thought none delighted him more than Camilla. She snagged his attention the moment he stepped into the sunshine. She sat on a nearby bench. Beside her stood a scruffy boy who appeared to be no more than eight, holding her parasol and giving Camilla the appearance of being a queen awaiting her coronation.

Arch hurried down the steps to join her. She glanced over and smiled, a completely unaffected smile, unlike the practiced ones she usually gave him. Caught off guard by the rarity of the moment, he nearly lost his footing.

When he reached her, she came to her feet, the all-too-familiar smile that didn't quite touch her eyes back in place.

"Lord Sachse, have you a sovereign for the lad?" she asked, as she took her parasol from the boy and snapped it closed.

He removed the gold coin from his pocket and handed it to her. She, in turn, gave it to the boy.

"Bless you, m'lady." The lad darted off into the crowds.

"Camilla, why did you hire him to hold your parasol?" Archie asked.

Studying the filthy handle of her white parasol, she said, "Because I grew weary holding it myself."

He withdrew a handkerchief from his pocket, took her parasol, and proceeded to wipe the smudges left by the lad from the handle. When he was finished, she took it from him and smiled. "You are most kind, my lord."

"Not as kind as you."

Obviously startled by his words, she looked up at him and released a tiny laugh. "I am hardly kind."

"Generous then."

She opened her mouth—

"Protest all you want," he said, cutting her off before she began. "But you are generous to a fault, and don't think that I don't see it, because I do. A sovereign for holding a parasol? Had it been me, I would have given him a ha'penny."

"What a ludicrous notion. An earl with a parasol. You'd have tongues wagging that you were eccentric and make my task of finding you a suitable wife much more difficult."

He grinned. "You're turning the conversation away from my point."

"Only because I find it tedious. It's a lovely day. Shall we walk for a bit?"

"If you like."

She reopened her parasol and positioned it just so before slipping her arm around his. Had he complimented her on any aspect of her person that could be noted by a stranger, she would have welcomed his words. The pleasing lines of her face. The way the pink of her dress complemented her pale skin.

But whenever he spoke of anything that could only be detected by astute observation, she shied away from his words. Shallow compliments she could accept. Anything more she brushed aside like so much rubbish.

"When we return to my residence this afternoon, I was hoping you might read to me," she said.

"I was hoping you might read to *me*—from your new French book."

"That is for my own private enjoyment."

"A pity. I so enjoy the flow of French words."

She perked up at that. "Do you read French fluently then?"

"I've had lessons."

"I'll gladly lend you the book when I've finished reading it."

He shook his head. "No need. I've no interest in reading animal husbandry—French or otherwise."

Her mouth opened slightly, and she seemed completely at a loss for words. Then she said, "But you would have me read it to you."

He stopped walking, forcing her to do the same. "You don't read French, Camilla. Why pretend that you do?"

"You don't know what you're talking about."

She started to walk off in a huff. He grabbed her hand, to stop her escape. She turned and glared at him.

"Don't run from me, dammit," he growled. "Do you think that I can't see that you keep secrets? That you refuse to let me see who you truly are? Weary of holding a parasol? No. You gave a lad a chance to earn a sovereign and have a bit of pride doing it. Why do you continually hide this part of you away as though it is of no consequence, when it is the better part of you?"

"It's a part of me that can't survive in this world, Archie." She tugged her arm free. "I shall share a secret with you." She took a deep breath. "I don't read French. But I liked the way the book looked, and so I bought it. Because it pleasured me to do so. And that's the reason I gave the lad a sovereign—because it *pleasured me* to do so."

"I believe the world would be a kinder place if everyone took pleasure in a similar manner. The lad seemed a bit young to be making his way around London."

"Only in years. I could tell that in many ways he is older than you and I."

"Because he was dirty?"

"Because of what I saw in his eyes. Children on the street do not stay children for long."

"I would not have thought a countess would be aware of the sufferings of the impoverished."

"I wasn't always a countess, Archie."

He'd known that, of course, but something in the way

she said it alerted him to the possibility that for once she might be willing to reveal a bit of her past. "What were you before, Camilla?"

"Companion to the old Sachse's wife. She took me in when I was but fourteen. I had spent a good many years in the children's home, because no one looked at me and wanted me. I was very much like that ugly duckling in the story you read to me recently." She slid her gaze over to him and smiled triumphantly. "I believe I have become a very lovely swan."

"Indeed you have. But at what cost?"

"At a cost I was willing to pay."

Her voice was not tinged with regret or sorrow, but simply acceptance. She'd made something of herself, a companion turned countess. He thought she was a woman with the ability and determination to become whatever she wanted.

Chapter 6

Camilla was finishing her morning toilette when a knock
sounded at her bedroom door. Frannie hastened to
open it, while Camilla gave a final perusal to her reflection
in the looking glass. She liked the way the dark and light
shades of grayish blue in her dress accented each other and
her coloring. The color of fabric was so important. Honestly, she'd seen the loveliest of gowns ruin the loveliest of
ladies' faces because they'd chosen the color based on what
they liked rather than on what complemented them.

Frannie returned to her side. "Lillian says your packages have arrived."

"Splendid."

She hurried to the parlor, where her servants were bringing in the last of the parcels and setting them on the floor
beside the settee before leaving. Lillian stood nearby with
her paper, preparing to make sure that everything they'd
ordered had arrived.

"Where would you like to begin, my lady?" Lillian
asked.

"Here." Camilla pointed toward a large box.

Lillian took a pair of scissors to the string holding the box closed and removed the lid.

Whenever the expected boxes arrived, Camilla always felt as though she was experiencing Christmas morning, Christmas mornings that she'd never had as a child. Although she knew what she'd find inside, she still experienced a thrill of anticipation as she reached into the box and pulled out the first dress. Just as Lord Sachse had commented at dinner the other night, it was rather plain.

"What do you think, Lillian?" she asked as she held it up.

"It's ever so plain, my lady."

"So it is. I have no use for it. I suppose there is nothing to be done except to give these clothes to the poor."

"I don't know why you continue to use this seamstress," Lillian said, her smile broad.

It was a game they played every month when Camilla's special orders arrived, pretending that what they'd received wasn't exactly as they'd ordered. It was a pretense they'd begun when her husband was alive. They'd had to be much more clever then and much more careful.

"Where are the cloaks?" Camilla asked.

"I believe they'll be in this box," Lillian said, opening a box and removing a heavy cloak. "Oh, it's very nice."

Camilla ran her hands over it. "Yes, it is. It'll keep someone extremely warm. We probably should have ordered more. Where are the dolls?"

Lillian turned to another box. "In here, I think."

She handed Camilla a doll made of cloth, with an embroidered face and yarn for her hair, something a little girl could hold tight at night and feel safe with.

"The skates for the boys are at the bottom of the box," Lillian said, as she dug through the dolls and brought out a length of thick leather with wheels at either end. "They simply strap these around their shoes."

"On second thought, it wasn't a very practical purchase was it?"

"The boys can sell them, I suppose, if they don't want them."

But a child should receive something of value to keep. She crossed her arms over her chest. "I know so little about boys. As a child, all I wanted was a doll to snuggle with when I went to sleep."

"Perhaps you could ask Lord Sachse. He might know what a boy would prefer to have to play with."

"That's a splendid idea. He'll no doubt recommend books, but still I'll ask." Reaching out, she clutched Lillian's arm. "I forgot to tell you. Lord Sachse is going to begin paying me a sum of a hundred pounds each month."

Lillian furrowed her brow. "An allowance?"

"No, no, a salary. A very nice salary to help him find a wife."

"So you're to become a matchmaker?"

"In a way, I suppose, yes." She'd never actually looked at it that way, but with all her connections, she could find a match—not only for Lord Sachse, but for any man. It was rather reassuring to realize that if she didn't become a duchess, she could always have a way to earn money. Though only as a last resort, if she were desperate. For a woman in her station, working would be rather degrading. She needed to let Archie know that he mustn't let on to anyone that he was paying her. It needed to remain their little secret. She knew Lillian wouldn't tell anyone, and Lillian was perhaps the closest thing she had to a friend.

"Here's what I was thinking," she continued. "We could use part of the money to hire ladies to make these clothes rather than the seamstress I'm presently using. I thought it would serve two purposes. Provide employment for those who don't have it, and provide clothing for those who don't have the means to purchase them."

"Where would you have them work? In the basement?"

"No, no. I don't want them to feel as though I'm ashamed of them. Still I can't have them traipsing up to the front door either, can I? But I thought they could use the servants' entrance, then come to the parlor. Light is good in here." She remembered the many nights as a child when she'd stood shivering beneath the streetlights her mother had used to cast light on the sacks she was sewing so she wouldn't have to use costly candles in their home. Slop work it was called.

It was there the men would sometimes approach her. "Would you be interested in sowing a few wild oats rather than a bit of cloth?" they'd ask, then cackle like idiots at what they perceived to be a witty proposal.

"Lady Sachse?"

She snapped out of her horrid reverie to find Lillian's eyes wide-open. "Are you all right, my lady? You're pinching my arm."

Immediately, she released her hold on her secretary. "I'm sorry. I was thinking of the possibilities. We'll discuss them all later. For now, have the servants put these items in a carriage and deliver them to the Salvation Army." Camilla supported Catherine and William Booth's recent efforts to provide shelter and aid to London's poor and socially outcast.

"Will you at least let us tell them who the items are from this time?"

She shook her head. "No. No one need know."

She turned to leave and released a tiny shriek at the sight of the unexpected man standing in the doorway. "Lord Sachse!"

"Countess."

"How long have you been standing there?"

A devastatingly handsome smile slowly spread across his face. "Long enough."

She was livid. Arch was entranced. He'd known she was harboring secrets, but why was she fearful of her generosity being discovered? Because others might see her as tenderhearted and take advantage of her goodness? Was it as she'd said during their walk from the art museum—that a generous woman would be unable to survive?

She held her tongue until Lillian left to retrieve the required servants, but the whole while he could see Camilla seething, see the tiny tremors going through her.

"How dare you!" she spit, once they were alone. "How dare you spy upon me!"

"I did not mean to spy."

"Did you not? Then why did you not announce your arrival?"

"I'd planned to. I told your butler that I would see to it, but then I decided that I shouldn't interrupt." He hadn't *wanted* to interrupt.

"You had no right."

"No right? No right to learn that my suspicions were founded? You lied to me about the purchases—without shame or remorse."

"Oh, there was remorse."

He was glad to hear it, but not to see her suddenly appearing downtrodden and defeated. She'd not taken pleasure in lying to him. He took a measure of satisfaction from that, but still it bothered him that she had yet to trust him completely. He'd done nothing to earn her distrust except be related to the man she'd married. He supposed she was of the opinion that the apple didn't fall far from the tree, but his branch of the tree was quite a distance from the one her husband had fallen from.

"What did you think I would do? Force you to return the items if I discovered they weren't for you?"

"The old Sachse would have. He was a good deal like that character in the story you read to me a couple of weeks ago. Scrooge. The entire time you were reading it to me, I wondered if perhaps Dickens had met the old Sachse and was truly writing about him."

"He may well have been, but you'll not turn me away

from the subject at hand. I don't understand why you insist on keeping your good works a secret?" Not only from him, but apparently from everyone else as well, based upon what he'd overheard.

"Because it's a private part of me, a bit that I own. The last remaining remnant of who I thought I would be." She sighed. "Makes me sound as though I belong in a mental asylum . . . as though I am a looking glass that has been shattered, and various shards reveal different sides to the same thing."

He thought her description was probably more exact than she realized. And he wondered if once shattered, a looking glass could ever again be as it was before or would it forever carry the marks that revealed it had once been handled without care.

He'd championed her before Spellman, he'd kissed her, he'd struck a bargain with her that would provide her with a modest income, but he'd failed truly to reach her, to earn her unfettered trust. He eased farther into the room, reached into the box of children's items, and pulled out a skate.

"What are you doing?" she asked.

Searching for the woman in the tower. Smiling, he turned to her. "Have you ever gone rinking?"

She looked positively horrified. "Of course not."

He considered her attire. Her dress accentuated her narrow waist and slender hips. He wondered if her smallness was at all responsible for her being unable to give his predecessor an heir.

"Go change into something that doesn't fit quite as snugly."

"Are you mad?"

He laughed. "Probably." He took a step toward her, she took a step back. He strove not to take offense. He'd caught glimpses of a woman who intrigued him, like looking through a kaleidoscope, where each turn revealed another facet to the piece. He wanted to know every aspect to her. "When was the last time you laughed?"

"I frequently laugh."

"With joy?"

She furrowed her brow. "Is there any other kind of laughter?"

"Cruel laughter. Sarcastic, harsh. The saddest of all is when people laugh to hold back their tears."

"Why must you always qualify things?"

"So you can't remember the last time you laughed with pure joy." He stated it as fact, not inquiry as he was beginning to learn that she found a way to redirect questions when she didn't particularly like the impression of her that the answer would provide.

"Of course I remember."

"Share the moment with me."

She held his gaze as though daring him to accept the moment she was going to reveal. "I laughed when I discovered the old Sachse was dead."

He imagined that she expected him to exhibit shock at her revelation. Or perhaps pity. The words were delivered in her usual icy manner. And he wondered if she'd mourned her own passing of innocence with laughter. He smiled because he knew it would unsettle her. "Just as I suspected. It's been years since you've laughed with joy. So come on. Change your clothes so we can head to the park."

"Archie, we're too old to skate."

"Nonsense, it'll be great fun."

"Shopping is fun."

"We'll do a bit of that afterward if you like, but for now hurry along."

"Arch—"

"Go along now."

She gave him one final glare before flouncing out of the room as though she wasn't at all happy with his demands, but he suspected before the morning was finished, he'd have her glad that she'd joined him.

Lillian returned with several footmen in her wake. She directed the servants to carry the packages to the waiting carriage, then gave the set of skates he held in his hands a pointed look as though she expected them to leap back into the box from which they'd come.

"I'm keeping these for the time being," Arch said.

"Yes, my lord."

She was leaving with the footmen when Arch called to her, "Lillian, can you spare a moment?"

She hesitated before returning to the room. "Yes, my lord?"

"How often does she do this?"

She gave an exasperated look that seemed to want to say that she had no idea what he was referring to, then perhaps thinking better of it because when it came right down to it, he was the one who paid her salary each month, she offered, "A good servant doesn't gossip about her mistress or reveal her mistress's business."

"A commendable trait, which I admire. I'm not seeking gossip, but answers. I'm trying to understand why she felt that she needed to keep these good works from me."

Lillian licked her lips, swallowed.

"You'll find a bonus with your salary at the end of the month," he said.

"No payment would force me to betray her."

Betrayal? Good God. What all had happened in this household before it had come into his hands?

"Lillian, it's a simple question. All I'm asking is how often."

"Every month. She thinks that if she spreads the purchases out over the year, they won't be noticed." Tears welled in her eyes. "Please don't tell her that I told you, and please don't punish her for it."

"Punish her for it? Why ever would I punish her—"

"The old Sachse did. I'm sure of it. She'd never admit it, though. He was so very tight with his money. One Christmas she purchased dolls and cloaks for little girls. When he found out what she'd done . . . I don't know what he did, and she never said, but I do know that she moved most gingerly for almost a week."

It seemed once her mouth began working, Lillian didn't know how to stop it.

He slid his eyes closed, well imaging what the bastard had done. He'd beat her. He opened his eyes. "Thank you for the confidence, Lillian. I'll keep this between us."

She raised her chin a notch, rebellion in her eyes. "She still did it, though, bought the cloaks anyway, so the children would be warm, but she did it by putting aside the small amount of money that he gave her for different items. And when she could convince him that she needed a new cloak, she would have it made with several linings, claiming that she always got so cold. When it arrived, she'd remove them all and we'd sew smaller capes for children and piece the scraps together for blankets. It wasn't much, but it was something, and it always made us feel good at Christmas." Suddenly she looked immensely embarrassed. "I've revealed far more than you asked and more than I should have. She wouldn't want you to know all that."

"I know," he said quietly. "And I shan't let on that I do know."

"Thank you, my lord. May I go now?"

"Yes."

After she left, Arch walked to a window and looked out on the garden. He thought of the way she'd stiffened beside him when Spellman had questioned her purchases. Had she thought Arch would react as her husband had—or had she simply responded based on past experience?

Was it any wonder that she'd built a wall around herself?

* * *

She was familiar with skating, of course, having observed it on several occasions. Young people enjoyed the sport because it allowed them easily to rid themselves of the chaperones who were seldom able to keep up with the nimble youths. No one frowned upon the antics of the daring couples, because they were usually in sight of other skaters, although Camilla had heard of a few people being caught in fervent kisses. As she sat on the park bench moving her feet back and forth, testing the movement of the wheels beneath her shoes, she wasn't certain how anyone could engage in a kiss while wearing skates without falling flat on their bottoms.

"Ready?" Archie asked from his place on the bench beside her.

"You go first."

"I thought we would go together, arm in arm, providing each other with support."

"If you stumble along and go down, then so shall I."

"I shan't go down."

He sounded so cocky, so sure of himself—but without conceit. Had she made the same claim, she would have come across as arrogant, because she knew no other way to protect herself except to live behind her shield of snobbery. How did he manage to say what she would but without the chill? Perhaps it was because his smile was warm, his eyes inviting.

"I'm afraid that you will have to prove to me that you have the skill to remain upright."

He held out his hand, palm up. "Trust me, Camilla."

She dipped her gaze to his outstretched gloved palm. If only she could place her hand in his. She lifted her eyes to his, imploring him to understand that she was talking about more than the skating and fully cognizant of the fact that he was as well. "I can't."

"If he weren't already dead, I believe I'd kill him."

Before she could wrap her mind around the implication

of his words and to whom he was referring, he shoved himself off the bench and rolled away from her. He faced her, and as though he'd accomplished some great miracle, he extended his arms. "There, you see? It's not so hard."

It did seem simple enough and had the possibility of being a bit of fun. She lifted herself off the bench, her feet rolled away, and she plopped back down. Not so easy.

"Have your feet tucked farther back behind the bench to give you better leverage as you're getting up," he suggested.

She shook her head. "I don't believe I can do this."

"That doesn't sound like the countess I know." He returned to her side as easy as he pleased and held out both hands. "Come on."

"Give me a demonstration of your skill."

"If we dally much longer, we won't be the only ones on the path. You need only find your balance, and the sport is quite simple."

"I need to see you traverse more than you have in order to have any confidence in your ability," she insisted.

"Very well."

He skated away from her, his hands clasped behind his back, his strides long and sure. Beautiful really. Elegant. But nothing like the beauty and elegance of a woman. He possessed a strength and power that radiated from his body, and she thought he did indeed have the ability to keep her upright.

He disappeared around the corner, hidden from her by hedges. Anxious to keep sight of him, she was halfway to her feet before the traitorous skates tried to take them in opposite directions, and she found herself plopping back on the bench, fairly rattling her teeth in the process. Then she heard the whir of the wheels, and Archie was headed back toward her, confidence in every stride, his smile beaming.

"It's fun, Camilla. You really must—eh, there! Watch out!"

She shrieked as a squirrel scampered across the path. Archie tried to avoid it. He lost his balance and took a tumble onto the side of the path.

"Oh, Archie!"

She was almost to him before she remembered wheels were beneath her soles rather than solid ground. As panic took hold, she began windmilling her arms. Her legs went this way and that, as though each were controlled by separate minds. Before she realized it or could do anything to prevent it, she landed on top of him, his arms around her, holding her in place, cushioning her fall with his body.

And it was such a young, virile body. Not soft from overeating as her husband's had been. Not smelly from too much drink and tobacco.

He grinned up at her. "You see? It was jolly good fun."

"How can you smile?"

"How can you not?"

Then he did the most remarkable thing. He laughed. Deep and long. She felt the rumble of his chest against hers.

"You looked incredibly funny," he said.

"Me? You should have seen yourself. I thought your eyes were going to pop right out of your head." Then in spite of her best intentions not to do so, she remembered how he had looked, striving to find his balance. A bubble of laughter escaped her throat.

It was met by another bark of laughter from him. Squeezing her eyes shut, she saw him again, the comical expression of horror on his face, and the laughter rolled out of her, mingling with his. She'd never seen anything so humorous in all of her life.

Abruptly he went silent. She opened her eyes, saw the intensity with which he watched her, and her chuckles died away beneath the onslaught of his raw and exposed desire.

"You have such a lovely laugh," he said.

"Don't be—"

"No!" he growled, cradling her face between his hands.

"Don't go away. The woman you are now, let her remain."

"She is a silly woman; she wouldn't be taken seriously."

He trailed his finger around her face. "Everything about you changed in that moment when you laughed. So young, so carefree. I believe I could love a woman such as that."

"She would break your heart and hers as well. She cannot give you a son, and you cannot give her a dukedom."

"I could give her a kiss."

He lifted his head, and even though she knew she should pull back, she didn't. She remained as she was, sprawled over him, closing her eyes as his lips touched hers. So tenderly, so sweetly. How could he not understand that it was because she cared for him so much that she couldn't allow him past her barricades?

He drew back from the kiss and held her gaze. "That wasn't so bad now was it?"

She pressed her fingers against his lips. "You break my heart."

She offered him no chance to react, but shoved herself off him and reassembled her barriers. "How do you propose we get up?"

He rolled into a sitting position, his chest against her back, his breath wafting along the nape of her neck. "Stay with me a while longer, the woman you are now, until the end of the path."

"Promise you won't kiss me."

He pressed his warm mouth against her neck. "Promise."

The movement of his lips over her skin almost had her turning around and begging him to break that promise. Then he was gone, and she was aware of the sound of movements as he worked to get himself to his feet. She glanced over her shoulder and thought that she might never again view him as she had before this moment. He seemed to require no effort at all to push himself to a standing position.

He reached his hands down to her, and she looked up

into his face. His hair had fallen over his brow, and he was in need of straightening, but she couldn't seem to find any impatience for his disheveled appearance.

"I'll make you fall again," she said.

"No, you won't. I'm stronger than I look, I'm braced and balanced."

She placed her hands in his and allowed him to pull her to her feet. He grinned. "You see? It's easier to stand when you allow another to help."

"I've grown accustomed to doing everything on my own."

"I know you have," he said. He slipped her arm around his. "I don't mind your leaning on me."

She couldn't remember a time when she'd leaned on anyone. She'd certainly never dared to look to her husband for support. She wasn't afraid of all men. She knew some men were kind and gentle. But she also realized that receiving that gentleness required a vulnerability that she wasn't willing to show, a step away from isolation that she wasn't willing to relinquish. She positioned herself so her shoulder was against his. "My stride is not as long as yours."

"Then I shall adjust my stride. I'm an accommodating fellow."

"I don't believe this is your first time to skate as you'd have me believe."

"No, it's not. I was amazed you rushed to my rescue. You were quite shocked to realize you were suddenly skating."

"Shocked? I was terrified."

"You hid it well."

"I always do, Archie."

"You needn't with me. I'd never ridicule you."

"I can't fathom why you give me so much attention. You're young, handsome, gentle, and kind. You could have any woman you wanted."

"Apparently I can't."

She felt the heat suffuse her face. Did he mean what she thought he did?

"I am yours until the end of the path," she told him, not certain why she felt compelled to do so.

"Perhaps we'll discover the path has no end."

She refrained from commenting as he guided her along the path, their strides in tandem. But she knew the truth. All good things came to an end, and usually much sooner than one wanted.

Chapter 7

She had the most beautiful laugh. Arch couldn't get it out of his mind as he danced during the final ball of the Season. Camilla had instructed him to pay attention to each of his partners, but it was difficult when memories of her laughter overshadowed the music being played.

The laughter had filled her eyes, colored her cheeks in crimson, and shaped her mouth to perfection for kissing. He shouldn't have taken advantage, but he'd been unable to stop himself.

Despite her years of marriage, her kisses weren't that of an experienced woman. Rather they were tentative, unsure, as though she didn't quite understand what was happening between them. Perhaps it was only that she'd never known such tenderness. He suspected her husband was the first man to possess her body, and based upon what he'd gathered of her feelings toward the man, he didn't think she hurried to another's bed after the earl drew his last breath.

He wanted very much to introduce her to the glory that could exist between a man and a woman. But could there be true passion with no love? Could there be love with no future?

"As you can well imagine, Mama is quite put out with him," his dance partner said, bringing him back to the task at hand. As he'd not been paying attention, he had no idea with whom her mother was put out.

"He is all of two-and-thirty," she continued. "She believes it is high time he took a wife."

Her brother possibly? He was dancing with the lovely Lady Anne Stanbury, sister to the Duke of Weddington, a man Arch was coming to envy because he'd had the good sense not to make an appearance.

"Do you not agree?" he asked.

"I believe one should marry for love, not because of one's age."

He smiled, finding it quite refreshing to meet a young lady who seemed to have an opinion that was in the minority.

"I understand that this is your first Season as well," she said, smiling brightly.

"Indeed it is."

"And what are your thoughts?"

"I've hardly had a chance to catch my breath since arriving."

She giggled. "Isn't it marvelous? I've rather enjoyed it."

"It has certainly been a Season I shan't soon forget."

The final strains of the tune lingered and faded as he escorted Lady Anne back to her mother.

"Duchess, thank you for allowing me the opportunity to dance with your lovely daughter."

The duchess smiled kindly. "I thought you made a handsome couple."

Lady Anne rolled her eyes. "Oh, Mama, I want to be more than a nice set of matching bookends."

"Dear girl, your first Season is at an end, and you have yet to find a suitor."

"And I'm not worried about it in the least."

"Good for you, Lady Anne," he said. "Now if you'll excuse me, I believe I have a full dance card this evening."

He began making his way through the crowd, searching for Camilla. He was on dance number six . . . or was it seven? He wasn't certain. Panic was beginning to set in. Not only couldn't he remember which dance was to be called next, but he couldn't remember with whom he was supposed to dance.

He felt a delicate hand come to rest on his upper arm. He turned and felt relief swamp him at the sight of Camilla's smiling face. "I can't remember who's next," he admitted.

Her smile grew. "I am."

"Thank God! I don't know how you keep up with it."

She held up her wrist, her dance card dangling along her glove.

"I don't suppose you could get one of those for me?"

"You don't need one. I was standing beside you when you signed every card. I know which dance belongs with which lady."

"You wrote it on the back of your card?"

"No, I simply have a very good memory." The strains of a waltz began. "Would you rather take a walk in the garden?" she asked.

He would, but he feared if he did that, he might be tempted to sneak a kiss. The last ball of the Season, and he'd spotted a lot of kissing going on when couples could elude their chaperones. Many of the ladies were already spoken for, although none on his list were. Camilla had made certain that he wasn't wasting his time, as though he'd consider moments spent with any lovely lady a waste.

After their rinking session, she'd returned to her proper self, determined to find him a wife. Sometimes he felt as though that morning had never happened. And other times, he drifted off to sleep with the memory of her laughter surrounding him.

"No, we'd best stick to the task at hand," he said. He'd promised never again to overstep his bounds, but he was finding it to be an extremely difficult promise to keep, especially when the evening required that she remain near.

He escorted her onto the dance floor, and when he took her into the circle of his arms, he wished he could chase off the feeling that overcame him: that she was exactly where she belonged.

She was dressed in a gown of the palest pink, edged in blue, her bosom modestly revealed. Pink roses adorned her upswept hair. The jewels at her throat glittered almost as much as her eyes.

"You're enjoying yourself," he said.

Her smile blossomed as the flowers in her hair had done before being set in place. "Immensely. I love balls: the dancing, the music, the beautiful clothes, the elaborate decorations. I always feel so alive."

"You're quite popular."

"My dance card could have been filled, but I wanted an opportunity to observe you with several ladies. The next dance, however, I shan't pass up. It's to be with a duke, and you shall dance with his daughter."

"I thought I just danced with the daughter of a duke."

"You did. Lady Anne's father was a duke, but he died some years back. Her brother is not in attendance."

"Is he available?" he asked, fairly certain that the duke wasn't, based on the conversation he'd had with the man's sister. Arch kept his voice lighthearted as he learned the rules of the game that she played so adroitly.

"Not to me. He has yet to obtain an heir."

She kept her gaze on his, making him feel as though no one in the room were more important. And he realized that was probably part of the game as well.

"Were you taken with Lady Anne?" she asked.

"Lady Anne?"

"The woman with whom you just danced."

"Ah, yes, Lady Anne, who believes a person should marry for love."

"It sounds as though you two are of a like mind, so she is a possibility?"

"I think not. She was very nice, but hardly half my age."

"You are going to find very few ladies here who are near your age and marriageable."

"There is you."

She gave him a look of impatience. "I am close to your age, but not marriageable *to you*, as you well know."

"Quite right. I forget myself when you look so lovely."

She blushed, and he wondered if that, too, was part of the game. If she could call her blood to the surface on command. He despised that he questioned every aspect of her behavior this evening. Above all else, he wanted honesty between them. He understood that there couldn't be love, but there could be affection, honesty, friendship.

"What's wrong?" she asked quietly.

He shook his head, then decided he couldn't expect her to be honest if he wasn't the same. "I would rather you not play games with me. Play them with your duke, but not with me."

"I've forgotten how not to play them."

"Then perhaps I shall educate you as you educate me."

The music drifted into silence, and he released a weary sigh, wishing the night would come to a hasty end. "Who is next?"

"Lady Alice."

"I danced with Lady Alice before I danced with you."

"No, you danced with Lady Anne."

Her memory astounded him. "I assume you'll see that I make it to Lady Alice's side without tripping over my own feet."

"Of course."

She guided him through the crowd, smiling at people she passed, offering a whisper here, a touch on the arm there. She was truly in her element, the gracious hostess at a ball for which she wasn't hostess. How in the world could she not see that she'd already garnered the respect that she thought she lacked? And damn it all if her smiles didn't seem genuinely offered to everyone except him.

She loved the attention, blossomed in it, and was so good at giving it back. And to his immense surprise, she seemed to give to everyone. Oh, he noticed an extra pat on the arm to a gentleman whose clothing seemed to be made of finer cloth than most, but she didn't seem to distinguish between persons based on appearance.

She stopped, touching a gentleman on the shoulder. Arch didn't much like the way the man looked down at Camilla, as though he could envision running his finger along her décolletage.

"Lord Winburrow," she said quietly, "Lady Jane Myerson has yet to take to the floor, and Lord Sachse is not on her dance card until the eighth dance. As you are such a highly regarded gentleman, I thought I should make you aware of her circumstance so you might take it upon yourself to spare her the embarrassment of sitting in the corner for so long without a dance partner."

"It is kind of you to bring her sad state to my attention, but I believe I shall sit this one out."

"As your mistress will be dancing with her husband, I believe it would do you well to be occupied with another lady before others notice on whom your attention seems to linger."

Lord Winburrow blushed scarlet and looked as though his cravat had suddenly transformed into a hangman's noose.

"I appreciate your counsel. I shall seek out Lady Jane immediately."

Arch watched the man scamper away. "You approve of his affair?" he asked quietly.

"It is not my place to judge. You will find that some women are very open about their lovers, even having them as escorts rather than their husbands. His mistress is not to that point."

He shook his head. "I don't understand the aristocracy. I suppose I should add to my requirements a woman who will not take a lover."

She peered up at him, smiling softly. "I believe you will keep any woman from straying."

"You surprised me by offering a kindness to Lady Jane Myerson after her scandalous lack of gloves."

She lifted a delicate shoulder. "Just because she isn't right for you doesn't mean she isn't perfect for someone else." Her smile blossomed into one of genuine joy. "And here is Lady Alice."

Arch remembered her now, being introduced to her as he'd signed her dance card. She was indeed pretty. Her blond hair was so pale as almost to match the shade of the pearls dotting her white gown, which made the deep green of her eyes more noticeable. Her features were flawless, her smile genuine and one of warmth.

"Lord Sachse."

Her voice was that of a nightingale.

"Lady Alice."

"I must admit I've been looking forward to our dance. The countess speaks so highly of you."

"She can speak no more highly of me than I do of her." He thought he was presenting himself as an absolute buffoon. He'd attended several balls and never crossed paths with the elegant and poised lady before him.

"I daresay that this is fortunate timing indeed, as I was about to go searching for my next dance partner."

The voice was gruff but kind, and when Arch looked at the man whom he was certain was the Duke of Kingsbridge, he knew he shouldn't have taken an immediate dislike to him, because there was nothing about him deserving of that attitude. But he couldn't seem to help himself. He disliked everything about him.

He had thick side whiskers and a heavy mustache, both white to such an extent that Arch couldn't determine what the original color might have been. Not that it was important. His eyes matched his daughter's, as did his smile and his warmth. Perhaps what Arch didn't like was that the duke seemed unaware that anyone other than he and Camilla was in the room, and when he extended his arm and Camilla placed her hand on it, it seemed she was of the same opinion.

"My lord?"

He snapped his attention to Lady Alice, who was waiting expectantly for him to give attention to her. He offered her his arm. "Shall we?"

As he escorted her to the dance area, he realized that she was extremely comfortable with her surroundings, at ease. Her smile as he took her into his arms encompassed her entire face. She seemed forthright, and he thought she'd never have secrets, would never be a mystery to unravel. She provided the openness and honesty he sought, and he wondered why he didn't find the notion more alluring.

As they twirled around the dance floor, she was as feathery as a cloud on a summer day, her eyes sparkling, her smile sublime. He thought that of all the ladies he'd danced with this evening, save one, she held the most promise.

"I'm rather pleased to see my father take such an interest in Lady Sachse," she said. "He's been widowed for nearly two years now, and he does get lonely."

"I understand he has an heir."

She laughed lightly. "Three as a matter of fact. My brothers are off on amazing adventures, while I'm left here to search for a husband. It seems rather unfair to me, as I should like very much to be on an adventure."

"Where would you like to go?" he asked.

"I'm not sure. Africa perhaps. Or Egypt. Or America. But my father is old-fashioned and believes that a woman shouldn't be interested in much beyond hearth and home."

"I suppose then that will be his attitude toward his next wife."

"If he does indeed take a wife. I certainly shan't push him toward that resolution, although a companion would be nice. And I rather like Lady Sachse."

"It seems a good many people do."

"She can be most discreet if a lady finds herself in trouble. I value that sort of loyalty."

Well, now, wasn't that interesting? "I didn't realize ladies confided in her."

"On all manner of things I'm sure."

He wanted to ask if she'd feel the same way if Camilla became her stepmother. Out of the corner of his eye, he caught sight of Camilla dancing with the duke. She looked stunningly beautiful.

"She's very lovely."

He jerked his gaze back to Lady Alice. "My apologies. I'm a bit distracted this evening. I'm under the impression that tonight is my last opportunity to assess the available ladies."

"A good many are already spoken for."

"So I've been told. If I may be so bold as to say, I'm surprised that you're not."

She wrinkled her nose. "I've not been looking seriously. My father is quite put out with me."

"He didn't give that impression."

"He hasn't much of a temper, but he is threatening to cut back my allowance if I don't take the husband hunt seriously next Season. But I'd rather hunt in Africa."

"For a husband?"

She laughed. "No, for a lion. Although I must confess

that I find a good many of these gentlemen to be most stuffy. Perhaps I *should* look for a husband in Africa."

The music stopped, and for only the second time this evening, he was sorry to see it happen.

"Thank you, my lord. I enjoyed the dance very much."

"I believe I'm to escort you back to your father."

Her smile seemed one of sorrow mixed with pity. "To my aunt. While you weren't looking, my father and his dance partner slipped out through the side doors."

He felt as though a fist had been driven into his gut. How in God's name did these people always manage to give the impression that nothing mattered? He feared his face revealed every emotion swarming through him.

"To your aunt then."

And since he couldn't remember with whom he was to dance next, he would have to go in search of Camilla.

The Duke of Kingsbridge had lived for half a century, was considerably younger than her husband had been, in attitude more than years.

"I miss the old girl," he said, as they walked through the garden, he with his hands behind his back, Camilla with her hands folded in front of her.

"She wouldn't want you to mourn forever, Your Grace," she responded kindly.

As it had turned out the tune had been his wife's favorite, and he'd become melancholy after a bit. Camilla could hardly blame him. His wife had been an exceedingly kind woman.

"I had no intention of falling in love with her when I married her," he said gruffly. "Give me an heir and a spare, and we'll both go on our way." He chuckled low. "Best-laid plans and all that."

Gas lighting throughout the garden cast a glow around them and a few other couples who'd come out for some air—and a bit more. She tried to overlook the stolen kisses that she caught sight of here and there. Most were chaste, a quick brushing of the lips, nothing at all like the kisses that Archie had bestowed upon her. The mere thought of them still had the power to ignite a fire low in her belly.

"So what of you and this new Earl of Sachse?" Kingsbridge asked.

Her stomach tightened, and she feared she'd been unable to mask her thoughts. "What of us?"

"Come, come, girl, you've had an old husband. You should have a young one."

"Sachse needs an heir, Your Grace."

"Bit of a nuisance that."

"I thought he and Lady Alice made a very nice-looking couple."

"My Alice cares more for adventure than marriage."

"She is almost twenty, Your Grace. Time for her to find a husband."

"I'll not force her to marry." He came to a stop at the end of the path and faced her. "What is it that you want, Lady Sachse?"

"I want him to be happy. I want him to have in his marriage what you had in yours."

"And you think Alice is the one?"

"I think it quite possible."

"But here we are at the end of the Season. I'll not rush her into a decision, nor will I seek to influence it. If the man wishes to take her hand in marriage, he'll have to do all the convincing himself. And I'll warn you now, she's not easily convinced of anything. Takes after her mother in that regard."

"It seems the only solution is to allow the earl and your daughter to have more time together. Perhaps you'll consider joining us at Sachse Hall for a while."

He angled his head thoughtfully. "I will consider it. But tell me true. Is he the only one you seek to make a match for?"

She gave him her warmest smile. "Not entirely, no."

His deep laugher rumbled through the garden. "It has been too long since I've played these flirtatious games. I've nearly forgotten how."

"Excuse me."

Alarm fissured through her as she recognized Archie's voice. She quickly turned, trying to mask her impatience. He couldn't have timed his arrival any worse if his watch were broken. And why in the world wasn't he flirting with Lady Alice?

"Sachse," Kingsbridge said, "come to make sure I'm not taking advantage of the lovely widow?"

"Actually, Camilla was helping me to keep track of my dance partners. I can't remember who is next."

"Then I'll leave you two to figure it out." He took her hand, winked, and placed a kiss on her gloved fingertips. "I shall keep your plans in mind."

He walked away, and she waited until he was out of earshot to hiss, "I was making great progress."

"That was quite evident to everyone."

"Whatever do you mean by that?"

"You looked absolutely *besotted* while you were dancing."

"I did not."

"You did so."

"I like him, Archie. I like him very much. He's much kinder than Lucien was, and his wife adored him."

"I didn't think there was love among the aristocracy."

"There is some." She released a deep sigh at this absurd conversation. "Lady Sylvia Giles, Lady Emily Cooper-Smythe, Lady Priscilla Norwood."

"Pardon?"

"Your next three dance partners. You might wish to memorize the names."

"I've probably missed my opportunity to dance with

Lady Sylvia. I shall send her flowers and an apology tomorrow."

He sounded so beaten that her heart went out to him. "It's not that important. It's only a dance."

"I thought everything at these functions was important."

"In a way they are, but it's your first Season, you'll be forgiven. I'll see to it."

"You have an amazing amount of influence."

"Not as much as I'd like." Reaching up, she straightened his cravat and patted his lapels. "Now, we'd best get back before the duke thinks we're up to no good and decides you wouldn't be a good match for his daughter."

"Is that what you were discussing? His daughter and me?"

"I invited them to come to Sachse Hall." She lifted her gaze to his. "We'll discuss it all later. You mustn't keep Lady Emily Cooper-Smythe waiting."

She tried to make light of it when the truth was that she didn't care if he kept them all waiting. How could she find him a suitable wife when her heart wasn't truly in the task?

She began walking, and he fell into step beside her.

"I've not noticed the Duke and Duchess of Harrington here," he said.

"Yesterday, they left on their wedding trip. To Italy. I informed Rhys that I'd heard warmer climes aid with fertility."

"Where in the world did you hear that?" he asked, clearly astounded.

"I made inquiries," she admitted. She'd asked midwives and doctors and anyone she could think of if there was anything she could do to get herself with child. "I was quite desperate. I spent time with ladies who were with child because I'd been told that would increase my chances of finding myself with child." She glanced over at him, wondering why she was willing to admit to him what she'd never told another soul. "I even kept a pearl beneath my pillow."

"Why?"

She shrugged. "An old wives' tale that promised to increase fertility."

"I don't understand how a pearl—"

"You have to understand that I desperately wanted a child. I was willing to do anything. I would have hanged myself upside down if someone had told me it would make a difference."

"Yet nothing worked."

"Not for me." She glanced over at him. "But others seemed to have success."

"Perhaps you worried about getting with child overly much."

"I don't see that it would make any difference how much I worried."

"When I was a student, and I was preparing to take an examination, it seemed that the more I worried over it, no matter how much I studied, I did miserably on the examination. But when I wasn't so keen on doing well, I somehow managed to do exactly that. I did well. It was as though when I worried I fought against myself and caused the very thing I feared would happen."

"I fail to see that your situation was anything like mine. The mind cannot control the body, for goodness' sakes. If you have a cut on your hand and worry over it healing, it doesn't *not* heal."

"I suppose not."

"I have reconciled myself to the fact that I shan't have children." She smiled over at him. "But I may be on my way to having a duke."

To her surprise, he reached over, took her hand, and carried it to his lips. She wondered why she could feel the heat of his mouth seeping through her glove to touch her skin when she'd not been able to feel the duke's.

"I want you to be happy, Camilla."

"I wish the same for you."

"Then we are of a like mind." He grinned. "I believe Lady Emily Cooper-Smythe is next on my list of dance partners."

"Indeed she is. You remembered."

His smile diminished, his gaze darkened. "I also remember that my last dance is with you. I'll not give it up, not tonight. So don't consider offering it to your duke. I'll not step aside."

He released her hand and walked into the ballroom, and all she could think was that for tonight, she didn't want him to give it up.

Chapter 8

As a general rule she loved the glitter and glamour of balls. She loved dancing, she loved steering gossip away from those she liked, yet never turned it toward those she didn't. Enemies were not something that a woman in her position could afford to have.

But tonight she was having a devil of a time not becoming melancholy. And she had no one other than herself to blame. She'd danced only a few of the dances, preferring to watch the revelers from a distance, to observe Archie with the various ladies so she might determine who seemed to complement him the best.

It had been pure torture. To watch various smiles play across his face, and to realize that after a Season of escorting him about London she'd unwittingly come to know the language of his smiles. Each one was true, not a single one false, and yet each managed to convey something a little different.

The smallest smile was kindly given, almost tolerant, a bit of interest in his dance partner, but she wasn't one who excited him. The smiles grew from there. Only with her now, during the final dance, did he smile with everything within him, as though at night's end, he found himself with the one woman with whom he truly wished to dance.

For the space of a heartbeat, where dreams soared, she considered the possibility that she might be the woman he should marry—if she could give him a child. After all she was dreaming, and in dreams all was possible . . .

And just as quickly she dismissed the entire notion. Without rank she was nothing. A pauper's daughter who couldn't even read. If those who surrounded her now ever found out, she would be snubbed, issued a cut direct. She would fall out of favor with the Marlborough House Set. She would be worthless.

So she would follow her original plan. Find him a wife. Who made him smile. Who held his interest. Who looked the best in his arms.

Then, of course, there were all the little qualifications that were of importance to him. Her voice, her intelligence, her kindness. He'd set her an impossible task.

Which made her all the more determined to prove that she could indeed select a good and proper wife for him. Because she did want him to be happy.

She cared about him and for all the characteristics he sought in a mate, she had a list of her own, which he might not agree with, but she would use as well. She had to take her station in life seriously, had to know how to dress in a way that showed her best features, had to be poised, had to know etiquette thoroughly, have an understanding of *Debrett's*. So many factors she was certain Arch wouldn't think to consider. He was extremely fortunate that she was willing to take on the task of finding him a wife.

As they moved about the floor, he seemed to be sagging as much as she was. It was close to two in the morning. Many couples had already departed, but many had stayed. Some were separating into smaller groups, where they would meet up at another house for a meal.

"You look as tired as I feel," she said, welcoming the support of his arms around her.

"I believe I've worn away the soles of my shoes."

"You cut an incredibly dashing figure this evening. Many a lady kept her eye on you, and I believe some who are already spoken for were wishing they'd not been quite so hasty."

"I've been here for a good part of the Season. What made tonight so different?"

"Tonight I believe you gave the impression of a man on the hunt."

And he had. He had danced, he had charmed, while she'd whispered about that he had indeed decided it was time to take a wife.

"I don't want to discuss the *hunt*," he said quietly, his gaze holding hers captive. "This is our last dance of the evening, of the Season, perhaps forever. I don't want anyone dancing with us. Not Lady Alice, Anne, or Emily. And certainly no dukes. For this dance, dance as though you were mine."

Oh, he asked so much, too much. Yet she couldn't ignore the plea in his eyes. They had no future, no present. They couldn't risk losing sight of their goals, and yet where was the harm in pretending for only a few moments that no secrets separated them, that she didn't fear the intensity with which he observed the world.

No one here would look at her the same way if they discovered she couldn't read. Illiterate, ignorant, stupid. She would lose their respect . . . but for a few moments . . .

She would risk it.

She tightened her hold on him and gave him a smile such as she'd given to no other man that evening—not even the Duke of Kingsbridge. Without a mirror to glance into, she had no way of knowing if her expression truly conveyed what she was feeling: that she was grateful to be with him, sharing this dance, having him near.

His skin was darker than most, and she envisioned him spending a lot of time walking through parks, riding horseback along country roads, although while he'd been in London, he seemed to prefer museums and bookshops. She knew so little about him, but it was safer that way, not to look below the surface.

And it was easily accomplished when the surface was so pleasing to look at. His features might have been hewn from rock, but they'd been polished with a gentle hand that had shaped to perfection the strength of his jaw, the bridge of his nose. Even though she knew how supple his lips could be, there was nothing soft about them as they offered the barest hint of a smile. It was his eyes that she loved most, because they were more honest than any she'd ever seen. Everything he felt swirled through them: disappointment, enjoyment, sadness, anger, happiness, joy.

His range of emotions always startled her, his willingness to reveal them always took her by surprise. He played no games. He hid behind no walls. He was as he appeared, and the fact that he offered no falseness made him an incredibly appealing man.

She'd never truly been in love. Her reasons for marrying the old earl had been apparent to them both: security, rank, and power. She'd never taken a lover, had never sought out the company of a man simply to be with him.

But being with this man offered her a glimpse of what she might have missed. And she sometimes wondered if she might save herself heartache by simply closing her eyes and pretending not to see.

Yet tonight for this last dance, she kept her eyes wide open, enjoying the company of a dangerous man who stirred to life doubts that plagued her. A man who spoke passionately about things she would never experience.

She'd become so lost in his eyes, that she'd hardly noticed that he'd closed the distance between them. They were dancing closer than was proper, but she suddenly didn't care. His thighs brushed against hers, and she felt the sparks ignite like the flame of a match held to kindling. Her heart wanted to expand, her knees wanted to melt.

But he held her upright, just as he had in the park when they'd both worn the silly skates. Something had happened that morning, something that went far beyond wheels carrying her over the ground. He'd challenged her to trust him—and she had.

She was almost as frightened now as she'd been then. She could see from the heat in his eyes and the gentleness of his smile that he wanted more than a dance. He'd not given this look to any other lady tonight, had apparently reserved it for her.

But this was how he should look at the woman he was to marry, as though there were no one more important, as though he were her prince, and she his queen.

Exactly as he'd told her it would be for him.

She didn't know how she would survive it when she finally did find a woman for him upon whom he would gaze as he now looked at her. It would hurt—unbearably. And she thought a piece of her might die.

She thought if she lived to be a thousand, she'd never again have a moment with such promise—or such regret—as this one.

Something had happened during their final waltz.

As the coach rattled over the streets, Arch wasn't certain what had happened, only that it remained, shimmering between them like the stillness following thunder that caused the ground to rumble.

It had been as though she'd lowered the drawbridge to the castle surrounding her and walked halfway, fearful to continue to solid ground while the moat churned beneath her. He'd been able to tell from staring into her eyes that she'd been giving a lot of thought to some idea, measuring, considering, dismissing . . .

Yet the entire time her attention had been totally on him. He didn't think she'd been mentally listing the attributes of each lady with whom he'd danced. That would come later.

For now the silence eased between them as they sat opposite each other in the coach. It was a comfortable silence, relaxed, and yet something told him that it shouldn't have been, that it should have been fraught with tension.

Something had shifted and changed during the dance, a realization, a recognition had taken place . . . and they both seemed equally ready to ignore it.

"I want to go home," he finally said into the quiet of the coach, of the night.

She turned her attention away from the window. "Why, yes, of course, as soon as you've taken me to my residence you're free to go on your way."

"No, I mean I wish to go to Heatherton."

"Heatherton?"

"The village where I grew up. I want to let my family see that I survived my first Season in London."

"A letter would accomplish the same thing, would it not?"

He detected a prick of panic in her voice, and he thought if he were correct, his next statement might send her through the roof of the coach.

"No, it wouldn't. My mother will want to see for herself how I've fared. I'd like you to come with me."

"To Heatherton?"

"Yes."

She looked back out the window, not that facing him would have given him much hint as to what she was thinking. The shadows inside offered her protection, and no doubt solace. He couldn't penetrate them, couldn't discern what she was feeling. He was about to tell her that he'd go alone, when she spoke softly.

"I'd like to go with you. Very much."

He'd hoped for that answer, but he'd never truly dared to expect it.

"I shall have to take my secretary," she said softly. "And my lady's maid."

"Of course. Whomever you wish. Whatever you wish."

"We can discuss your choices for a wife while we're there."

"No."

The word came out more forcefully than he intended. She turned her head toward him, no doubt taken aback by his succinctly delivered sentiment.

"All of this"—he moved his hand in a circle that she probably couldn't see clearly—"has no place there."

"Your rank is not something that you can simply take off like a coat come spring. It is a part of you always. No matter where you are, no matter what you are doing."

"I realize that, but I want our time in Heatherton to be as our last dance was—no mention of the wife *hunt*. I want to leave it behind for a spell, while we're in Heatherton. We can pick it back up when we get to Sachse Hall."

"All right."

Now it was he who looked out the window, a sense of relief washing through him, even as he wondered if taking her would be a mistake.

Chapter 9

◦◦◦◦◦

Camilla did not recall being this nervous when she'd been presented to the queen. She couldn't explain the fluttering in her stomach that grew in intensity as they neared Archie's home. She was grateful for the gloves, which absorbed the dampness on her palms.

I'm being silly, really, she thought for the thousandth time. She would meet Archie's family. Common stock. Except that they did have some aristocratic blood flowing through them. Diluted through the years, of course, but, still, she couldn't claim a single drop.

As the coach had driven through the village of Heatherton, Archie had seemed to become as uncomfortable as she felt. He'd pressed back into the shadows of the conveyance as though he had no wish for anyone to catch sight of him. She found his behavior rather odd. He'd left here a teacher to return as an earl. Every person within the village would give deference to him now.

They'd traveled north of the village until the driver had finally turned onto a narrower lane.

"I've missed the peace of the countryside," he said quietly, from where he sat across from her.

"Sachse Hall is nothing at all like your London home. I'm sure you'll be comfortable there, although you will, of course, have much greater responsibilities."

He gave her a slight smile. "I can think of no responsibility that is greater than shaping the mind of a child."

"You miss teaching, then?" she asked.

"Very much. My father was headmaster. I thought to step into his shoes someday. In a way, I suppose I have, but not as I expected."

"Archie, how am I to address your family? Did the Crown favor them with courtesy titles?"

"No, and my mother asked that I not seek a warrant for the privilege. They preferred to remain simple people."

"I can't quite fathom the notion of not wanting to be titled."

"Perhaps you'll have a better understanding of things— and me—after you spend some time here."

And she wondered if perhaps the desire for her to understand him had been what had prompted his invitation in the first place.

The carriage began to slow. Camilla gazed out the window and saw the small house. Well, she had to admit that it wasn't quite so small by simple country standards, but in no way was it as grand as the estates that had come to Archie through the death of her husband. She couldn't understand why he didn't seem to embrace his good fortune. To live in the house now visible to them or a manor with seventy-four rooms. The preferred choice was glaringly obvious.

The coach rolled to a stop. The footman opened the door and helped Camilla climb out, just in time for her to see a small white-haired woman rush out of the house. Camilla had hardly been aware of Archie coming out of the coach before he was standing in front of her, wrapping his arms around the woman, lifting her off the ground and twirling her around.

The woman's loud, joyful laughter echoed around her.

Camilla had never heard any sound that resonated with such soul-deep gladness.

"Oh, Arch, put me down!" She patted his shoulders as though she knew she had no need to cling to him. His hold on her was firm enough, strong enough, secure enough that he wouldn't drop her.

"I've missed you, Mum!" With a laugh, he spun her around one final time before setting her on the ground.

Taking a step back, she placed her hands on her hips. "Let me have a good look at you, now."

Camilla saw the love and pride reflected in his mother's eyes and felt tears sting her own. Her own mother had looked at her like that once. It hurt the heart to see such motherly devotion.

"You've lost weight, lad," his mother said.

Smiling brightly, Archie nodded. "A little, although I suspect it is the well-tailored clothing that makes me appear so trim. Camilla insists I wear only the best. Speaking of . . ." He turned to Camilla. His smile warmed, as did his eyes. He held his gloved hand toward her.

As she placed her hand within Archie's, she couldn't miss the speculation in his mother's expression. Archie drew her near.

"Lady Sachse, allow me to introduce my mother."

"Oh!" His mother released two tiny squeaks as she pressed a hand to her chest. "Oh my goodness. You got married!"

"No, no, Mum. Lady Sachse is the previous earl's widow."

His mother's eyes widened. "Oh, then you are the countess! Should I curtsy? Of course I should." And she did just that.

Camilla had always welcomed the fawning and acquiescence that others showed toward her as a result of the rank she'd acquired when she married the old earl, but here, surrounded by the lush countryside, standing before the modest home, and knowing how much this woman obviously loved her son, she felt false and unworthy. "Mrs. Warner, please, you need not curtsy before me. You are the mother of an earl, after all."

Mrs. Warner popped upright. "So I am. And a more handsome one I have never seen. And showing off your wealth, I see. Traveling with two coaches. Whatever will my neighbors think?"

"We had no choice. Lady Sachse travels with her lady's maid and secretary. Then, of course, there is my valet." He shook his head as though he thought it all seemed incredibly pretentious, and she found herself halfway wishing she'd not insisted on bringing their servants.

"I didn't think the extra guests would be a problem," he finally told his mother.

"Oh, no, of course not. They can share accommodations with my servants." She leaned toward Camilla. "I only have two indoors: the cook and the housemaid. I have a gardener and a stableman. Your men may stay with them while your lady servants sleep inside the house, top floor, a bit crowded, but better than the hayloft. Now, come inside, and I'll show you to your rooms."

"I know where my room is, Mum," Archie said.

His mother laughed. "Of course you do, but Lady Sachse doesn't. We'll need to give her the grand tour. I've instructed everyone to be here at seven for dinner."

"Everyone?" Camilla asked.

"My brother and sister," Arch said, as he placed her hand on his arm and led her toward the house.

"I didn't realize—"

"Because you never ask anything about me."

His voice seemed to echo a sadness she couldn't explain.

"Don't be ridiculous. We talk all the time."

He sliced his gaze over to her. "We talk about the cut of my jacket, Lady Jane Myerson's absence of gloves, and who is best suited for whom. You avoid answering any intimate questions I pose regarding you, and you never ask any of me."

"I respect your privacy."

"Well, don't. Because while we're here, I don't intend to respect yours."

Images of him watching her bathe flashed through her mind. "Whatever do you mean by that? Are you a voyeur?"

"Of course not. I simply meant that I want us to have an opportunity to truly get to know each other while we're here."

She glanced toward the house where his mother was waiting.

"I like your mother," she offered.

He grinned. "I believe you'll like the whole family."

Camilla was appalled and yet strangely fascinated watching Archie's family during dinner. It was rather like coming across an overturned hansom cab and knowing that one's sensibilities would be tested when the injured parties were freed of the conveyance, yet still unable to look away.

Archie's sister Nancy was lovely and pleasant enough; but her husband, Owen, was the homeliest of men. All Camilla had been able to think when introduced to them and their two young daughters was that the Lord was indeed merciful because their children had taken after their mother and been spared the uncomely features of their father.

Archie's brother, Winston, was five years Archie's junior and lacked Archie's polish. Like Archie, he had a mouth that was quick to smile. She had the impression it was equally quick to kiss. He'd winked at her half a dozen times since sitting down to the table—in between shoveling food into his mouth.

He wore neither jacket, vest, nor cravat. His loosely flowing shirt was unbuttoned at his throat, and she could see sprigs of dark hair peeking through and found herself wondering if Archie's chest also sprouted hair. She'd often thought the old Sachse should have been sheared twice a year. Yet she found herself imagining something quite different with Archie's hair. Running her fingers through it . . .

She gulped her wine to wet her suddenly dry mouth. Barbaric thoughts brought upon by the barbaric company. Dinner here was nothing like that to which she was accustomed. Once the food had been placed on the table, the cook had disappeared, and everyone had taken to serving themselves—eating, talking, and laughing with hardly a breath in between. Although dear Archie, bless him, had placed servings on her platter before placing them on his own.

While Archie sat at the head of the table, she sat to his right, with his brother across from her, his sister beside her. Even the daughters sat at the table, one on a stack of books beside her mother because she was so young and small, while the other sat across from her mother and beside her father. Archie's mother was at the foot of the table, looking on with such pride that Camilla could only think that love was truly blind because she seemed totally unaware that the gusto with which everyone ate and talked was hardly appropriate at the dinner table.

Camilla would have to find a strong wife for Archie. One who understood that children did not eat at the table with adults, that one did not serve oneself, and that conversation shouldn't include references to barnyard animals.

"Do you think you'll have some time to look over the livestock?" Winston asked, planting his elbow on the table, his chin on his hand, as he leaned toward Archie.

This statement followed his earlier assessment on one of the cows having difficulty breeding.

"I'll make time," Archie said, as he pressed his hand against Winston's elbow and shoved it off the table.

Winston opened his mouth as though to protest. Archie

tilted his head toward Camilla, and said softly, but with authority, "Mind your manners."

Winston had the good graces to look sheepish. "Don't suppose the peerage puts their elbows on the table."

"And neither should you, Win," Nancy said. "It sets a poor example for my girls."

"You'll have to forgive me, sis. Me and Mum aren't accustomed to formal dinners."

Good Lord, Camilla thought. If he considered this formal, she'd hate to be around for an informal affair.

"Mum and I," Arch said.

Winston grinned and winked. "You can take the lord out of the schoolroom, but you can't take the teacher out of the lord, eh?"

"Something like that."

"You were always a wonderful teacher. Do you miss it, Arch?" Nancy asked.

"I haven't had time to miss much of anything, except for the family."

"Do you have family, Lady Sachse?" Nancy asked.

"No," Camilla answered.

"Then please know that you're always welcome in my home," Mrs. Warner said.

"You are all too kind," Camilla said. The words were true, and she did mean them, but she realized that they didn't sound very heartfelt. "Truly," she added. "You're most kind. Lord Sachse is a very fortunate man."

"I don't know that he considers himself such," Winston said with another wink.

"Win," Arch said, with a low voice and a slight shake of his head.

"She don't know that you'd rather be here?" Winston asked.

"*Doesn't* not *don't*. And stop talking as though you've no education."

Winston grinned broadly. "I only do it to irritate you."

"Keep it up, and you and I will have a session out in the barn when we're done here."

Winston angled his head cockily. "Looks to me like you've grown soft since you left. I could beat you now."

"Don't bet on it."

Camilla stared at Archie. Surely they weren't talking about taking fists to each other.

"There will be no fisticuffs while Archie is visiting," their mother said, a firmness in her voice.

"Ah, Mum—" Winston began.

"Don't *Mum* me. I won't stand for fighting. Your brother is a man of position now. You must respect that."

"He's the one who always said a man has to earn his respect."

"Do you not respect your brother, Mr. Warner?" Camilla asked, feeling a need to stand up for Archie.

He winked at her. "There's not a man in all of England whom I respect more."

"You have an odd way of showing it."

"It's only brotherly banter, Lady Sachse. But then if you've got no family, you wouldn't know about that, would you?"

"That's enough, Win," Arch said before she could respond. "The aristocracy plays by different rules."

"So it appears. I've never been much for rules myself." He placed his elbow back on the table.

Archie shoved it off. "Which is the very reason that you and I *shall* spend some time in the barn following dinner."

"You're not going to fight, are you?" Camilla asked, although she was quite surprised to find herself exhilarated by the notion. It was almost as though Archie were defending her.

He smiled. "Of course not, but I will use harsher language than is appropriate at a dinner table."

"I daresay Winston could use a good talking to," Nancy

said. "They offered him a position at the school, and he refused it."

"I've got no wish to spend my day with a bunch of brats."

"Do you not like children?" Camilla asked.

"Can't stand the little buggers. My nieces being the exception, of course."

She dearly wanted to kick the man. He would no doubt end his life with a houseful of children while she had none.

Archie leaned toward her. "Bank the fires of anger, Countess. He's not serious. Once he determines someone's Achilles' heel, he begins shooting arrows at it."

"He's not very nice."

"I agree with Lady Sachse's assessment of your behavior. You're not being very nice this evening, Win," Nancy said. "And you've had more than enough of the attention. Archie, tell us everything about London."

"It's grand, Nancy. I think you'd like it. You, Owen, and the girls should come to visit next year."

"Oh, that would be lovely. Don't you think, Owen?"

He looked up from his plate and smiled at his wife, and with that simple gesture, Camilla almost forget that he wasn't pleasant to look at.

"If you like," he said quietly.

"I think I would."

He nodded and returned to eating.

"Would you like to come, Mum?" Nancy asked.

Mrs. Warner shook her head. "Your father and I went to London once, when we were young. I didn't much like it. Far too many people, bustling about, knocking into each other, picking a man's pocket while they're doing it."

"I find London exciting," Camilla said. "There is so much to do, so much to see."

"Perhaps you'd give me a private tour," Win suggested, with another wink.

"Have you something in your eye?" Camilla asked.

He sat up a bit straighter. "Pardon?"

"Your eye. I've noticed it twitching ever since we sat down to dinner. I thought perhaps you had something in it. I, for one, wouldn't be at all offended if you were to excuse yourself so you could remove whatever was causing the problem."

Winston slapped a hand over his eye. "My apologies if my affliction offended you. I've visited the best doctors in the area, but they can't figure out why it twitches like that."

"For God's sake, Win—" Archie began.

"No," Camilla said, cutting him off. "It is I who must apologize. I didn't realize . . . I thought you were flirting. They have no idea what causes your eye to twitch?"

Winston lowered his hand, shook his head, and winked again. "They have no idea. It's been doing it for years. Happens every time I see a pretty girl." This time his wink was accompanied by a dashing grin.

"Win!" Nancy said.

Camilla glanced over at Archie and could see that he was having a difficult time holding back his smile as he shook his head. He cleared his throat. "I apologize for my brother's behavior. He's accustomed to flirting with serving girls at the tavern."

"Oh, come on, no need to apologize. I was only having a bit of fun. When did you stop being able to take a—ow!" Winston glared at his sister. "Hey, Nancy, what did you do that for?"

"What? I didn't do anything."

He turned his attention to Camilla, and a devilish look came into his eyes. "Did you kick me?"

"I would apologize except that I suffer from an unexplainable affliction. My foot has a tendency to connect with the shin of unpleasant young men."

"Oh, my word! Jolly good for you, Lady Sachse," Nancy exclaimed, just before bursting into a fit of giggles.

Winston winked at Camilla. "I deserved that."

"Would you like another?" Camilla asked.

"No, thank you. One was quite enough."

Camilla felt a hand wrap tightly around hers where it sat on her lap beneath the tablecloth. She glanced over at Archie, and he gave her a warm smile.

"Well done."

"Was this some sort of test?"

"No, we simply aren't as formal as those in London. You can well imagine that I find dinner parties rather boring."

"You hide it well."

"I fear that a time will come when I'll hide everything."

The words remained unspoken, but she heard them loudly enough—a time when he would become as well hidden as she.

"I was thinking—"

"That's a first for the evening, Win," Arch said, as he removed his jacket and draped it over the stall door in the barn. "Whatever were you about, teasing the countess like that?"

"She teased right back. I hadn't expected that."

Neither had Arch. Her reaction had been a pleasant surprise. There were times when he wished he could figure her out, and others when he enjoyed each new discovery and was glad that she was a constant source of unexpected moments.

"I should probably have you come to London next Season," Arch said.

"Whatever for?" Win asked.

"Because if I die without issue, you're next in line, and an incredible number of rules and behaviors need to be learned and followed. After your exhibition during dinner, I think you'll require an inordinate amount of tutoring."

"If you die without issue, I'll simply beg Lady Sachse to take me under her wing. Why did you lie to her about us fighting?"

"Because the idea seemed to bother her, and Mother had already forbidden us to do so." Arch unbuttoned his shirt, pulled it over his head, and carefully placed it on top of his jacket, cravat, and vest. He rolled his shoulders and rocked his head from side to side. It felt marvelous to be unburdened.

"She's a beauty but a bit standoffish," Win added.

"She got the better of you tonight." Arch began bouncing on the balls of his feet. "Why were you being so difficult during dinner?"

"Trying to get a bit of attention. She hardly takes her eyes off you."

Arch stilled and stared at his brother.

"Don't tell me you hadn't noticed," Win said.

He hadn't. On occasion he'd thought he'd caught her watching him, but whenever he looked at her, her gaze seemed to be elsewhere. He shrugged. "She has little interest in me other than helping me learn my duties."

Win jerked his own shirt over his head and dropped it to the ground. A time existed when Arch's clothing would have been there as well instead of neatly folded and put away. "So you've asked her then?"

"I asked her to marry me, but she won't because she's barren."

"Barren? What a stroke of luck. Make her your mistress and you won't have to worry about any by-blows—"

The impact of Arch's fist connecting with his brother's jaw traveled all the way up to his shoulder.

Win staggered backward and dropped to the ground like a sack of seed tossed off a tall man's shoulder. Groaning, he rubbed his jaw. "What did you do that for? I wasn't ready."

"I thought the lesson on respect needed to begin straightaway."

Win pushed himself to his feet. "You didn't like what I was saying."

"Not particularly, no. Camilla is a lady of the highest regard—"

"Camilla? That's a bit intimate isn't it? Is she already your mistress—"

Win ducked the fist that came at his jaw, but apparently wasn't expecting the one that met his midsection. He doubled over and fell to his knees. Breathing heavily, he peered up at Arch. "Was that a yes?"

With his boot to his brother's shoulder, Arch shoved him onto his back. Easy. Much too easy.

"No, of course she's not my mistress." Not that he hadn't entertained the idea. "You're the one who seems to have grown soft here," he said, hoping to distract his brother from comments regarding Camilla.

Win came up and flew at him, tackling him to the ground. They rolled, punched, rolled. Arch was delivering the sturdier, harder blows, while he hardly felt Win's cuffs. It occurred to him that not once since his brother had arrived home from the fields had he addressed Arch by name. His entire family was glad to see him, he had no doubt about that. But there was a subtle difference in the way they spoke to him, as though they weren't quite sure of him. And now he was seeing a difference in the way his brother fought.

"Damm it, Win, fight!" he commanded.

"And risk the wrath of the Crown for harming one of its own?"

"Better the Crown's wrath than mine."

They continued to roll, grunt, and deliver ineffectual blows. Arch felt his anger and frustration growing because everything had changed when the title had passed to him. A time existed when Win would have taken satisfaction in giving his older brother a good pummeling. And now he was treating Arch as he might someone he feared.

Arch had come home because he wanted to feel like his old self, wanted to walk in his old shoes, wanted to pretend for a while that he was no longer the Earl of Sachse. He wanted to find the contentment he'd had in life when he'd known exactly who he was and what his responsibilities entailed. He despised—

The cold water lashed against his head and shoulders. Thank God, some things remained constant. Dear Nancy had always been the one to break him and Win apart. Courageous girl, because she knew how Arch would retaliate.

He shoved off Win and lunged toward her. Her screech echoed through the barn as she fell beneath him. It wasn't until he flung his wet hair out of his eyes that he realized he'd made a grave error. He didn't have Nancy pinned to the ground. No, indeed.

He was straddling Lady Sachse.

Chapter 10

"If you'll excuse me, I believe I hear Mum yelling for me."

Camilla was vaguely aware of Winston skittering out of the barn like the vermin he apparently was and intensely cognizant of Archie lying on top of her. He was raised on his elbows. Still, each rapid, deep breath she drew in caused her breasts to brush against his chest. His bare chest. His magnificent bare chest.

He did have hair, but it was only a light sprinkling, and she longed to touch it, wanted to glide her hands along his chest and shoulders. She'd never felt such incredible yearning with any other man as she felt with him. Desire. Hot and burning.

When the men hadn't returned, Nancy had told Camilla that they probably *were* going at each other and as she was busy tending to her younger daughter, she'd asked Camilla to check on the men. She'd explained that Camilla would find a bucket of water outside the barn door and was to use it to stop them from fighting. Camilla had considered announcing that a woman of her rank did not stop fights, but she'd been intrigued by the notion that Archie was actually embroiled in such an undignified activity.

She'd stood in the barn doorway and watched them rolling about on the straw-littered floor, listened to the horrible sounds of flesh hitting flesh while their grunts and groans had echoed around them.

When Archie had commanded his brother to fight harder, she'd had no choice except to put an end to the madness. She'd been shivering and shaking as she'd hauled the bucket closer and splashed its contents over them.

But nothing like she was quivering now. Rivulets of water rolled down Archie's face. His hair was wet, his shoulders damp, his breathing labored as though he was still fighting.

Her breathing was no better. The air had grown so incredibly hot that she'd begun to perspire, could feel dew pooling between her breasts.

"How is it that we seem to end up on the ground together when we least expect it?" he asked.

"Let me up," she rasped. Her voice sounded as though it came from far away, belonged to someone else, someone who didn't truly want to be released.

"Hold still," he ordered, his eyes darkening. "You've straw in your hair."

It hardly seemed a reason not to move, and yet she didn't. He shifted his weight until he was no longer straddling her, but had come to rest between her legs, his chest close enough now to flatten her breasts, the heat of his flesh seeping through her clothing. His breath wafted along her cheek as his gaze wandered from hers and seemed riveted to the spot where he was plucking away bits of straw.

She watched as the muscles of his throat—coated with dew—worked while he swallowed. She studied the grand sweep of his shoulders. He was firm and sturdy, muscle and flesh and brawn. She could see his strength with each slight movement he made, the muscles quivering, rippling, his arms bunched as they strained to support his weight so he didn't squash her completely.

She smelled the musty scent of his sweat and wondered why she experienced no revulsion. She had the uncharacteristic desire to lift her mouth to his throat and gather the drops with her tongue. Taste him. Experience the intimacy of his touch.

But she couldn't risk the intimacy. An educator who no doubt had the means to discover her embarrassing inability to read. She knew Archie well enough to know that if she opened up even a bit, he would insist she unfurl fully, reveal the tainted and impure blossoms of her true self. Then he would loathe her and find even her presence unworthy of one such as he.

She felt the weight of her hair falling away. She slid her gaze to the side, watched as he brought up his hand, filled with a mass of golden brown strands, and buried his face within the abundant tresses. Closing his eyes, he inhaled deeply, and she thought he appeared to be captured in rapture.

"You cannot begin to imagine how I have longed to see your hair unbound, flowing around you." Smiling with triumph, he held his hand out and down as though to visually measure the length of her hair. "It would dip well below the small of your back, I'll wager."

The strands flowed out of his overturned hand. He cradled her cheek, his touch warm, his eyes fevered. "You torment me," he growled. "With your haughtiness, and your do-not-touch attitude. I want nothing more than to melt the ice countess."

Then his mouth covered hers, accomplishing exactly what he'd claimed to want, melting her resolve. A distant part of her mind screamed that she needed to put a halt to this nonsense, but another part urged, "Not yet. Just a minute more. Allow one more sweep of his tongue, enjoy another taste of him, relish his nearness before you send him away as you know you must."

Yes, she needed to stop this madness before it went too far. Before his hands were skimming over her bare shoulders as hers were now trailing over his. She'd never experienced the joy of true desire . . . and it *was* a joy. To want and be wanted. To need and be needed.

She heard moans. Not certain if they came from her or him. Growls. He rained kisses over her face, her throat, before once again pouring himself into a kiss that threatened to chip away the last vestiges of ice around her heart.

But the ice countess knew what it was to be vulnerable, to be stripped bare. One could be naked even when fully clothed. She would die before she saw pity in his eyes.

She tore her mouth from his, their harsh breathing echoing between them. She pressed the heels of her hands against his shoulders. "Get off!"

She hated the desperation she heard in her voice, the fear. "Camilla—"

"Get off!" Forcing herself quickly to reassemble her armor, she turned what she knew would be a pointed, hardened glare on him, and said with deliberate, succinctly delivered words, "Get off me now, *my lord*."

She thought she would forever remember the pain that filled his eyes before he bowed his head and shoved himself to his feet. He held his hand down to her. She placed her hand in his and allowed him to help her rise, ever conscious of her hair tumbling around her, the longing mirrored on his face as he watched.

She wanted to wrap her arms around him, hold him close, and never let go. But there was no future for them. He needed a wife who could give him an heir, and she needed to safeguard her secret.

"I trust that was a momentary lapse in judgment brought on by these uncivilized surroundings."

He snapped his gaze up to hers, fury replacing the yearning. She could deal with his anger much easier.

"See that it doesn't happen again," she commanded, before spinning on her heel and marching from the barn.

She'd long ago learned how to force herself to do things that she had no wish to do, but nothing had ever been as hard as leaving him there to nurse his own wounds at her rejection.

The Wild Boar had been one of Arch's favorite haunts in his younger days. It was a man's paradise, with loud laughter, ribald jokes tossed about, and plenty of ale to go around. Men complained about the weather, the crops, their businesses, their wives. They played darts in a room off to the side, wagered, and drank more ale. They shared their troubles and their successes.

When Camilla had walked out of the barn, he'd retrieved his clothes, put them on, and strolled to the pub without alerting anyone at home as to his plans. He'd needed the solitude of the journey to sort out his thoughts, but he'd expected at journey's end he'd find the camaraderie he'd always found there in his youth. What he discovered instead was that he was no longer one of the locals.

Instead of hearty slaps on the shoulder that would have welcomed him before, he'd been met by silence, before Jim the proprietor had hurried out from behind the bar.

"Your lordship, good to have you stop by. Let me set you up over here."

Arch had received a few nods of recognition, the men quickly looking away as though it pained them to see him. Several men had doffed their hats with a mumbled, "My lord," as he passed.

So now he sat at a corner table, in the shadows, alone once again. He didn't view himself as being so very different from when he'd left only a few months before, but apparently now that he wore a title, he was seen as being different by others.

So he sat, drank, brooded, and wondered why life that had been so pleasant was suddenly a never-ending series of tests—which he seemed doomed to fail. He would have sworn he'd seen desire in Camilla's eyes. So how was it that he was left to feel that his actions had been thoroughly unwanted?

She'd returned the kiss—with fervor. Her moans had echoed around him, her tongue had waltzed with his, her fingers had danced over his shoulders. How could he have misread her interest when it had been so clearly written in her actions?

He jerked his gaze up to find Win grinning at him and holding two tankards. "Ready for another?" his brother asked.

"Without a doubt."

Win placed the tankard on the table, dropped into a chair beside Arch, and leaned back until the front legs came up and his back hit the wall. He lifted his tankard and winked. "Cheers."

Arch returned the salute and proceeded to down a good portion of the ale. Getting drunk was exactly what he needed in order to forget his troubles. How could a man in his position of wealth and power complain of troubles to a group of men who labored as hard as these did and barely survived?

"How'd you know I'd be here?" Arch asked.

"Mum. She sent me after you. Said I'd find you here when you didn't come in from the barn after the disheveled countess did. Your countess looked none too happy coming through the door."

"She didn't like having my attentions forced on her."

"You forced?"

With a sigh, he joined his brother in leaning back against the wall. "Of course not. Courting a countess is very different from courting a village girl. Do you know how many girls I kissed in the hayloft and never had a one complain?"

"She complained?"

"Thought I was uncivilized."

"Were you?"

"I wanted to be. Instead I went slowly"—albeit hungrily. "I have the impression that my predecessor wasn't a kind man, and I didn't wish to frighten her."

"She doesn't strike me as being easily frightened."

"She is more vulnerable than she appears. I want to strip away the facade she shows to the world and discover the woman underneath. I catch glimpses of her from time to time, enough to hold me spellbound."

"Sounds like too much effort to me. You're an earl now. You can probably find yourself any number of beautiful women with no effort at all."

"I dislike being an earl. You cannot imagine how lonely it is. I was not raised among the aristocracy, and while Lady Sachse can ensure that I am accepted into their ranks, she cannot make them accept me into their hearts. I came to the pub because I wanted to be accepted for *who* I am, not *what* I am. But that is lost to me—even here." He slid his gaze over toward his brother. "Even you do not view me the same. I carry no bruises from your punches. You hit like a little girl."

Win grinned. "You didn't. I won't be able to move in the morning. Is that why you wanted to fight? So you could feel normal?"

"I want to be who I was before the solicitor brought his papers and his explanation of lineages."

"Father used to say that once a man gained knowledge, he would never be what he was before he had the knowledge. In your case, what you gained . . . well, it gave knowledge to all of us, because we know you're no longer simply Archibald Warner. You're the Earl of Sachse. Sounds frightening to a simple man. These are all simple men."

"You're not simple, Win."

"No, but neither am I titled. But I have to respect that you are. You're still my brother, and I love you as such. But you're also a blasted earl."

"Which you could very well be if I die without legitimate issue."

"Then get busy doing what you need to do, because I don't particularly fancy walking in your shoes."

"Well, if Camilla has her way, I'll be married by the end of the next Season to a suitable lady who can give me an heir."

"I like her thinking."

Arch grimaced. He didn't particularly like it, especially since it involved finding herself a duke to marry. Although he had to admit that Win's earlier comment in the barn about making her his mistress continued to echo through his mind. Camilla was no innocent lass with a maidenhead to keep intact. If she were indeed barren, getting her with child wouldn't be a worry. They could share a physical relationship with no risk—except the risk to his heart.

And perhaps hers. Was that the reason she shied away from him? Because she could feel something for him beyond fondness?

And if that were the case, what did he do about it? He'd promised not to hurt her, but how could he not?

Lying in her bed, Camilla watched the shadows dance across the ceiling. She wished Archie hadn't kissed her, wished he hadn't stopped. She wasn't a young girl to be enamored of a handsome face or strong shoulders, but she had to admit that he did have a fine physique. She'd never known true pleasure at a man's touch, but she had a feeling that Archie could deliver and deliver well.

He certainly had a mastery of the kiss that exceeded all expectations. He'd kissed her three times, and each time he brought a richness that lured her in and caused her good sense momentarily to flee.

She heard what she could only describe as caterwauling coming through the slightly open window. She eased out of bed, crossed the room, drew back the fluttering curtain, and peered out. In the distance, with the help of the moonlight, she could see the outline of two men weaving back and forth across the path as though they couldn't agree where they should walk. She would recognize the one—Archie—anywhere.

Hurrying toward the door, she grabbed her shawl from the foot of the bed in passing. She rushed down the stairs, through the house, and into the kitchen, just as Archie and his brother stumbled inside. A lamp had been left on the table as though their mother had expected just such a late arrival.

Archie's cravat was gone, his shirt unbuttoned to the middle of his chest, his jacket disheveled. "Lord Sachse!" she snapped.

He jerked his head back, then moved it forward, squinting as though he were having a difficult time focusing. His eyes lit up, and his mouth spread into what she could describe only as an idiotic grin.

"Cammie! You waited up for me. How delightful!"

"Cammie?"

He held up a finger. "Camilla is too formal, and I'm so wretched tired of the formality."

His words were slurred, running together.

"You're foxed," she said.

He shook his head, nodded, then grinned again. "Yes, indeed, I believe I am. We need to talk. Win had a brilliant idea."

Horrified at what she was seeing, she looked at Winston, who seemed in danger of losing his balance at any moment. He also wore a stupid grin. "If you'll excuse me, I believe I hear Mum calling."

He smashed into the table, tottered across the room, and slammed into the wall. He promptly spun around to face her, his grin still in place, and slumped to the floor.

She was tempted to give him another kick. She turned to Archie. "I should get your valet."

He shook his head. "No, no." He gingerly walked around the table, using the chairs for support. "I didn't drink as much as Win."

He staggered over to her and slung his arm around her shoulders. She very nearly collapsed beneath his weight. She placed one arm around him and one hand against his side as much for her own balance as his. "Can you make it up the stairs?"

"Of course," he said.

It was an ungainly ascent, and several times she doubted his ability to make it to the top. But they persevered, his weight becoming heavier as he leaned more fully against her, his feet barely lifting as he moved them from step to step as though, like his brother, he wished to succumb to the full effects of the spirits and simply lie on the stairs.

They finally reached the landing, and she led him down the hallway to the room where she'd seen his bags taken earlier. There too a lamp had been left burning, and she wondered if his mother was accustomed to this sort of behavior from her sons.

They managed to make it to the bed, where his ability to remain upright deserted him. Holding her close, he tumbled them onto the bed. She shoved against his shoulders, and ordered, "Archie, let me up."

"Shhhhhhhh," he whispered in a long, drawn-out voice. "I want to tell you Win's brilliant idea."

"In the morning."

"Now."

"At least let me get you properly into bed."

His grin was wicked, yet playful. "But it is you that I want to get into bed . . . and improperly at that."

She shoved harder against him. "Archie—"

"Let me explain, then I shall let you go and put myself to bed properly."

She heaved a weary sigh. "Very well, then explain this brilliant idea, which I've no doubt is absurd if it came to Winston this night after all you've drunk."

"We should be lovers."

Her heart slammed against her ribs; her stomach tightened into a hard knot. "I think not."

"Hear me out," he pleaded, placing his finger against her lips. "It's brilliant. I promise. You see, you said you wouldn't marry me because you are barren, and I need an heir. But what if the old Sachse were the barren one, not you?"

"Impossible. As I've told you before—his wife before me had a son."

"Are you sure?"

"Quite."

Although he was lying down, he managed to angle his head so he appeared to be thinking matters over. "Perhaps his seed simply grew too tired to take root." He shook his head. "Doesn't matter."

He placed his hand against her cheek. "We would become lovers, and we would go at it like a pair of rabbits. If you get with child, I will marry you. If not, then I will marry the woman of your choosing."

Oh, what an unfair proposal. Did he not think that she might come to care for him more during their tryst? After knowing her intimately, could he cast her aside for another so easily? Could she turn away from him?

"You are not a duke," she reminded him. "I wish to be a duchess."

"As we've discussed, I can help you there. And if you are indeed barren, as we both know, you will marry an old

duke who is not in need of an heir, but you and I could remain lovers. It's perfect, Cammie."

Unless she got with child, in which case, she would
marry an earl—this earl. But even that had an appeal, to be
his, to have his child.

"What do you think, Cammie?"

She thought that when he called her that, she had a difficult time keeping her armor in place.

He closed his eyes and began to rub her cheek absently
with his thumb. "We would make love every night. I
would warm you with kisses . . . heat you . . . with my
touch. I want to be . . . inside you."

Everything within her stilled. She'd never had a man
speak to her so intimately or so specifically—reveal exactly
what he wanted to do with his body and hers. She grew
warm as images bombarded her of him doing exactly as
he'd indicated. His wants mingling with hers, their bodies
joining.

He stopped stroking her with his thumb, and his
breathing became long and even.

"Archie?" she whispered.

When he didn't move, she reached up and touched his
hair, his temple, his cheek, until she cradled his chin and
pressed her thumb to his lips. "You deserve much better
than me, Archie, even as only a lover. You have no idea how
difficult it is to turn you aside. But I must. You frighten me,
my handsome earl."

She worked her way out of his hold and got off the bed.
She removed his shoes. She didn't have the strength to get
him beneath the covers, so she folded the top blanket on
which he rested over him. If he rolled over, the covering
would slide off, but for a while it would offer a little protection from the night.

Gingerly she sat on the edge of the bed so she could
once again comb her fingers through his hair. In sleep, he

seemed so harmless. Who would think by looking at him that he possessed the power to destroy her?

"Don't be afraid," he suddenly said, nearly causing her heart to burst through her chest.

She came up off the bed and took a step back, all the while staring at him. He neither moved nor opened his eyes. When her heart calmed, she turned down the flame in the lamp and allowed the shadows to surround her.

How different things were here. How different he was. She'd never seen him inebriated. Her husband had been a mean drunk, but Archie had no unkindness in him at all. Not even when he'd been drinking.

She eased closer to the bed and knelt on the floor. She brushed her fingers through his hair. "Win's idea is indeed brilliant," she whispered, "but in the end, I believe it would break our hearts."

Standing, she bent down, kissed his brow, and fought to ignore the fact that her heart was already breaking.

Chapter 11

They were enjoying high tea. Arch was almost certain of it as he stood at the window and gazed out on his mother's garden. His nieces were seated in tiny chairs at a tiny table that Owen had built for them. A little teapot and tiny cups and saucers were set before them.

Camilla, the Countess of Sachse, sat with them and was pouring imaginary tea. Arch was completely and utterly charmed by her lack of guile, by the pleasure on her face as she played with the girls. Fate was indeed cruel to deny her the opportunity to have daughters of her own.

"Here, drink this," his mother said, shoving a cup of black coffee beneath his nose.

The aroma almost caused his stomach to revolt. His head was pounding, his body sluggish. Still, he sipped on the brew because he knew his mother wouldn't leave him alone until he did. He could be an old man, and she'd still be his mother, expecting him to obey without question. And he imagined he'd continue to do exactly that.

"I like your countess," she said quietly, out of deference for his aching head he was certain.

"She's not my countess." He took another sip, feeling

the warmth of the liquid traveling through him until it touched his head. She'd put something in the drink, he was certain of it. She had all sorts of home remedies that worked miracles.

"She can't have children," he said with a low voice, as though to impart a sad secret. He lifted his cup. "You don't have a cure for that, do you?"

Camilla having children wouldn't remove her desire to marry a duke, but he thought it would guarantee her a good deal more happiness.

His mother shook her head and looked through the window. "A shame that. She has patience with the girls."

"And with me usually. She's taught me a good deal since I arrived in London."

"Have you told her you love her?"

He silently swore. His mother had always known everything, been omniscient. Sometimes her uncanny ability to ferret out the truth had been almost frightening. She always knew if he and Win had fought—even when they took great pains not to hit about the face, not to leave any evidence. She'd known the one time he'd cheated on an examination. She'd said nothing, just looked at him, but he'd known that she knew.

She'd known when he'd kissed his first girl, and when he'd taken his first young lady in the hayloft. He didn't know how she always knew. Only that she did.

"Telling her wouldn't make a difference," he finally admitted. "Although quite honestly, I'm not certain that I do love her. I care about her to be sure, but beyond that"—he shook his head—"I don't know."

"You've never brought a gal home before."

"I couldn't very well leave her at Sachse Hall."

"I don't see why not."

He closed his eyes, his headache suddenly intensifying. "She guards her past. She has no curiosity where mine is concerned. But I was shaped by all that happened to me before we ever met. She was as well. I thought if I shared with her, she'd share with me. I don't even know why I care."

She patted his arm consolingly. "I think you do."

"She would never settle for me."

"You deserve better than a woman who would *settle*, anyway."

"You only feel that way because you're my mother." He downed the remainder of the coffee before handing her the empty cup. "I'm going to take her to see the school."

Leaving his mother there, he walked to a side door and stepped through it into the garden. He could hear the laughter more clearly, Camilla's and the girls'. They were having a grand tea party. A part of him was loath to interrupt, but he wanted some time with Camilla. Besides, he thought he owed her an apology. He had vague memories from the night before, and his mother's coffee hadn't helped to clear his mind.

As though suddenly aware of his approach, Camilla glanced up and smiled, and the warmth of it nearly stopped him in his tracks. She belonged here, and even as he thought it, he knew it couldn't be true. She wanted rank and privilege and to be embraced by the Marlborough House Set. None of that existed in this small corner of northern England.

"My lord, did you wish to join us?" she asked.

He was disappointed to realize that her smile was no doubt part of the game she was playing with his nieces.

"Actually, my lady, I thought to take you to see the school where I once taught."

"I'd like that," she said, her smile seeming to take on a bit of solemnity as though she were moving away from the world of make-believe into the one of reality, and she wasn't completely pleased with the journey.

He offered her his hand. While she wore gloves, he didn't, and he had no plans to put them on. Not here, not in

Heatherton, where his clothes had once been plain and his manners simple. He drew her to her feet. "If you don't mind, we'll walk," he said.

She nodded, glanced at his hands again, puckered her mouth as though she might comment on his not being put together exactly right, must have thought better of it, and simply placed her gloved hand on his arm. "Lead the way."

He looked down on his nieces. "Go see your grand-mother."

They scrambled away, and he knew they'd do as they were told. It was simply an aspect of life here within his family. Children obeyed their elders.

It wasn't a long trek to the other side of the village, and yet it seemed so because people greeted him as many had last night—a lord rather than their friend. He noticed the tension beginning to mount because he felt as though he were trapped between two worlds, the one into which he'd been born and the one destiny had chosen for him.

He led Camilla up the dirt road that ended in a circle before three buildings: the church, the school, and the dor-mitory.

"Is it a boarding school?" she asked, finally breaking the uncomfortable silence that seemed to have worked its way between them.

Joy shot through him because she was expressing an in-terest. "For the most part yes. Parents from the nearby larger towns send their boys here. They board in that build-ing there." He pointed to the distant wooden building with three levels of windows. "The boys from the village simply come for the day once they've done their chores." Archie had treated them all the same, because he believed that ed-ucation was a great equalizer.

"Do you not find it odd that attendance is compulsory but parents must pay a fee for their children to be taught?" she asked.

Attendance had become compulsory in 1876, but Arch

knew that people found ways to bypass the law. Poorer families preferred for their children to work.

"Many fees are based upon a family's income, and there are charitable schools," he offered.

She glanced at him, her lips pursed. "And you think they offer the same level of education as this school here?"

He sighed. "I'll admit that it's an imperfect system. What would you suggest?"

"More government involvement, more regulation. A means to provide quality education for everyone, regardless of income."

"It sounds as though you've given this a good deal of thought."

"It weighs on my mind from time to time. You cannot imagine how difficult it is for the uneducated to better themselves."

"You say that as though you speak from experience."

"Not personally." She turned her face away from him, as though suddenly taking a keen interest in the trees lining the path. "But I have seen others struggle."

"So not only do you take interest in the plight of the poor but in the uneducated as well."

"I have a good many interests."

"So I am learning."

He wished he could determine how to convince her to extend her interests more fully to him.

"This was my classroom."

Arch watched as Camilla looked the room over. The desks lined up in even rows. The blackboard where he'd made notes for his students. The shelves that housed the books he'd used. He'd left everything here when he'd gone to London. The teacher who'd taken his place had not yet settled in enough to erase Arch's presence. He was glad of it because he'd wanted Camilla to get a sense of who he'd been before he became the earl.

She walked to the window and looked out on the tree-shaded lawn. In the distance was the path that parents used to bring their children to the school for the first time.

"I should think your students would become quite distracted with all the comings and goings that would be visible through these windows," Camilla said.

"No more so than I. On days when the weather was particularly lovely, we'd take our lessons out beneath the trees."

"How unconventional."

He picked up a piece of chalk, tossed it, caught it. He enjoyed the weight of it in his palm. He wrote on the blackboard, "So great a love leads to so great a passion."

He tapped the board. She flicked a cool glance over the words before returning her gaze to the landscape beyond the window—obviously unimpressed with the sentiment he'd written. Erasing the board, he wondered what he might do in order to return to her good graces.

"Last night, I dreamed that you were alone in my room with me," he finally said, deciding that while not blunt, at least it was direct.

She glanced over her shoulder, pinning him with one of her familiar pointed stares. "Last night, you were foxed."

"So you were real and not a phantom."

"Someone had to tuck you into bed, and as your brother continually hears his mother calling for him, the task was left to me. I think you might want to have a physician look him over. It's entirely possible that he's quite mad, because I never hear her calling."

He sensed that she might be teasing, that she knew full well Win's words were merely an excuse to make himself scarce.

"Win and I have always had an uncanny ability to hear our mother when others can't." And an understanding from their youth that they would use the excuse whenever sensing that the other wanted time alone with a pretty girl.

"Do you also share his winking affliction?" she asked tartly.

"No, mine is a smiling affliction. I merely smile when I see a pretty lady."

"You'd not struck me as a man who'd drink to excess."

He thought he detected actual disappointment in her voice, not that he could blame her, but he also thought it unfair that she would find fault with him when she didn't allow his better qualities to ensnare her. "People escape in different ways. Some turn to drink, other simply turn away."

She gave him a sad smile. "Or turn to ice."

"You needn't. At least not with me."

"What are you trying to escape from, Archie?"

The concern mirrored in her voice surprised and delighted him. He crossed the room to where she stood, pressed his shoulder to the wall, and looked out the window, careful to keep her visible out of the corner of his eye. "I miss the *truth* of a simple life."

She shook her head. "The truth?"

"You pretend to be an ice countess, but you're not. When we attended balls, I've never seen so many people with the ability to look down their noses on others, and cannot fathom why they would want to. What is gained? A false sense of superiority?

"I value hard work, Camilla. I value mastering one's ability to reason and think. I value great works of literature. I value man and all he has accomplished. I find balls tedious, dinner party conversations lacking in passion, and I say jolly good for Lady Jane Myerson for daring not to wear gloves in public." He slid his gaze over to her so she was all that appeared in his vision. "I know I am unworthy of the title—"

"No, I know no man more worthy." With a gloved hand, she reached up and cradled his cheek, the first time she'd ever initiated contact, and he desperately wished that she'd followed Lady Jane Myerson's example and removed the damned glove first. "I've never known anyone who believes so adamantly in the things in which he believes as you do. And I've never known anyone who believes passion exists outside of carnal activities."

"Passion exists everywhere. In the artist, in the writer, in the architect, in the builder, in every person who cares deeply about what he is doing. Passion doesn't always take place between the sheets . . ." His voice trailed off as he realized what he might have implied, and she averted her gaze. "It never took place between the sheets for you, did it?"

She moved her hand away from his cheek. "No."

"I could give you that passion."

"I hear no doubt in your voice, and I can't decide if you are truly skilled or only arrogant."

He tucked his hand beneath her chin and turned her face to his. "I promise, with me, you would know passion."

"I have secrets, Archie. They are mine to keep, and they will always prevent me from coming to your bed."

"Perhaps they won't keep me from coming to yours."

She laughed lightly, a warm sound that touched him deeply.

"You do tempt me, Lord Sachse, but I fear you would be deeply disappointed in what you would discover within my bed."

"I don't see how I could be."

"It comes back to your desire for honesty and your discontentment with seeing only the surface of a person. You want more than I am able to give."

"I could settle for less," he said, surprised by the almost desperate plea in his voice.

"But you shouldn't have to, and I won't allow you to."

She was reerecting her icy wall, and he was tired of trying to scale it. So be it. There could be no passion without interest. And he knew plenty of women who would take an interest.

*   *   *

"Oh, m'lord, I can't believe you chose me."

As Arch removed his clothes, he was having a difficult time believing he'd chosen Bessie as well. Her voice was breathless, her enthusiasm palpable, but her excitement had nothing at all to do with him—the man—but seemed entirely to rest upon the fact that he was now a damned earl!

"I've never taken an earl to my bed before."

She'd told him that repeatedly as they'd walked over from the Wild Boar. When he'd arrived at the pub earlier, he'd let the proprietor know that he was interested in more than beer for the evening. It hadn't been long before a couple of the serving girls were giving him their undivided attention. He probably could have chosen both of them if he was in the mood for an orgy—but all he really wanted was a release of the tension that seemed to be mounting daily as his frustrations with Camilla grew.

"I would have cleaned the bedding had I known—"

"The bedding is fine." She'd never worried about it before. He knew because it wasn't the first time she'd invited him to her cottage or that he'd accepted the invitation.

"You only have to tell me what you want," she said. "I'll do anything. I want to please his lordship."

"You can start by no longer calling me his lordship." He tumbled her onto the bed and began to nibble on her throat.

"I haven't removed all my clothes."

Obviously. He wasn't blind, after all. "I'll remove them." He tugged on a lacing.

"But you shouldn't have to do any of the work. You're an earl."

He released a frustrated sigh. "I don't consider it work. I enjoy taking off a woman's clothing. It prolongs the moment and the pleasure."

"If that's the way you want it."

"It is." Although quite honestly he would prefer a bit of

spontaneity and evidence of desire on her part. He began working on the lacings again.

"How do you want me to touch you?" she asked.

"However you like."

"Do you want me to use my mouth or my hands?"

He ground his teeth together. "Whatever pleases you."

"But you're the important one here. You're the one who needs to be pleased."

And he would be if she'd stop worrying about it. With a low growl, he came off the bed and began to pace, his bare feet traveling over rugs made of rags and planked flooring that wasn't polished to a high sheen so it reflected the surroundings. A good thing, as the surroundings were terribly drab, and even as the thought passed through him, he cursed it. He didn't want to find fault with that which he'd once been part of.

"I'm so sorry, m'lord. I didn't mean to displease you."

He faced her. She'd sat up and wrapped her arms around her drawn up legs.

"You haven't displeased me."

"You look displeased."

He glanced down at himself. Yes, indeed, he did appear to be rather unhappy. Not dancing a jig down there, that was for certain. He raked his hands through his hair, unable to recall having a worse idea than finding a tavern girl on whom to slake his lust. Always before, his taking a woman to bed had come about because of a mutual attraction, a natural progression toward lovemaking because of common desires.

It had never been as one-sided as this present fiasco. Him wanting, but her wanting to please only him.

"I'm sorry, Bessie, I made a mistake."

"No, no, you didn't." She climbed onto her knees. "Give me another chance. I'll please you. I promise."

He sat on the edge of the bed, cradled her cheek, threading his fingers into her dark hair. "It's not about pleasing me. The mistake was mine in thinking that I could find what I was searching for so easily, not in selecting you. You are a lovely woman with good intentions at heart." He leaned forward and pressed a kiss to her brow. "I'm not disappointed in you, rather I'm disappointed in myself."

"But if you'd tell me what you want, I could make you not disappointed."

She was missing the point entirely. He didn't want to have to tell her what he wanted . . . he wanted to become lost in a passion that required no explanations.

Chucking her under the chin, he winked at her. "Why don't we simply forget that I came here tonight?"

"If that's what you want."

Again, whatever he wanted, his lordship could have. He supposed that he should have been grateful. He would have to adjust his thinking. He wasn't comfortable with this cloak of earldom.

"That's what I want." He got off the bed, snatched his trousers off the nearby chair, and stilled as he heard a distant clanging.

"That's the fire bell," Bessie announced.

Unlike London's fire brigade, Heatherton didn't have a steam engine to pump the water. They were dependent on one manual fire engine, buckets, and lots of strong hands. Arch drew on his trousers and quickly buttoned them. Bundling up the rest of his clothing, he raced out the door.

It was madness and mayhem and terror.

Camilla had been lying in bed, thinking of Archie. Did he truly desire her? It was a frightening notion. Her husband had certainly not desired her. He'd desired how he could hurt her, but what she saw in Archie's eyes was unlike anything she'd ever had directed her way. No one could want the woman she presented to the world—not really. She knew that.

Which meant if he wanted her, he was looking beneath

the outer shell, and that idea terrified her more, prevented her from sleeping. So she was wide awake when the bells sounded.

She rushed into the hallway and was nearly knocked over as Winston rushed past.

"It's the school!" he yelled.

"Where's Archie?" she asked.

"He's probably already there."

Then Winston was gone, and she ran outside after him without thought to the fact that she wasn't properly dressed. Archie had gone to town earlier, and if he'd not returned, then Winston was probably right. Archie would be at the fire, trying to save his beloved school—and knowing how utterly and foolishly unselfish he was, she feared he'd put himself in harm's way.

The thought of his dying in a fire nearly doubled her over. She stumbled on the road, straightened herself, and hurried on. She caught sight of Winston charging past on a horse. Damnation! Why hadn't she thought to find him first? Why had she assumed he would *run* to the fire?

She glanced back at the barn, discarded the idea of trying to get a horse, and continued running, halfway wishing she had a pair of skates. She didn't think she'd run since she was a small girl.

She heard a rumble, a galloping of hooves.

"Lady Sachse!"

She stopped and turned, just as a wagon drew to a halt. She found herself unceremoniously pulled into the back with the servants. Before she could catch her breath or speak, the driver was urging the horses on again. She saw Archie's mother sitting on the bench beside the driver—the stableman no doubt.

The wagon barreled along through town and up the path toward the school. She could see flames licking at the night sky as though the fire sought to eat the stars as well as the building. Cold terror pierced her heart.

It wasn't the school. It was the building where the students slept.

She didn't remember the wagon stopping, didn't remember leaping out of it. She only knew that she was wending her way through the throng of people. Thank goodness they had a pump. She saw men pumping while another held a hose, directing it so the water hit high on the building. Others had formed a bucket brigade, splashing water on the lower portions of the building.

But the children, where were the children?

Then she spotted four huddled together. Younger boys, dirt-smudged faces, eyes large with fear. She dropped to the ground and gathered the two closest into her arms, reaching out to offer a comforting touch to those on the outskirts. "Are you all right?"

They bobbed their heads.

"Lord Sachse went to get Tim," one said. "He should have been out by now."

"Should have been out? You mean he went into the building?"

The boy nodded. "He brought us out first, but we couldn't find Tim."

"Oh, dear God." She somehow managed to gather all four into her arms, needing comfort as much as she needed to give it. She looked to the building. Black smoke billowed out, flames darted in and out. Archie couldn't be in there. He'd come out, and the boys had simply missed seeing him.

But what if he hadn't come out?

"Stay here," she commanded.

She got to her feet and ran toward the building. She wasn't certain what she'd do. Go inside and find him, or at least yell from the doorway to provide a means for him to find his way out.

She was almost there when an arm snaked around her waist and she found herself being lifted into the air and brought back.

"Hold on there, Countess. Where do you think you're going?"

She looked up to see Win's dirty face.

"Archie's in there."

"I know." His voice rang with resignation.

"Well, do something to get him out."

"There's nothing to be done," and it sounded as though he'd pushed the words up from the soles of his feet.

No, no, she knew what it was to be powerless, and she'd sworn she'd never again feel that way. "Let me go."

"No."

She began hitting his head and shoulders. "Let me go. I have to help him!"

"If you go in, when he comes out, it just means he'll have to go in to find you."

She began kicking, scratching, and biting. "Let me go!"

Momentarily she gained her freedom, took two steps, only to be tackled by Winston.

"This isn't helping anyone!" he yelled.

She began hitting him again. "You can't let him die! You can't!"

She was desperate to escape, desperate to do something. She couldn't bear the thought of Archie lost in the fire—

She could barely see through the tears as she looked toward the building. And then she spotted him, hunched over, running from the building, holding something in his arms. She heard a crash. *Boom!*

Winston loosened his hold on her. "There he is."

"I can see that," she said, as she got to her feet.

People were yelling, a wall was collapsing. Archie ducked down farther and raced away from the crumbling structure. Rushed to where she was waiting. Coughing and sputtering, he staggered to the ground beside her. He wore nothing except trousers.

"You're burned," she said.

"I'm all right. Can you take care of the boy?"

"You can't go back in!"

He shook his head. "I won't. He was the last. But I need to help with the pump."

"The building can't be saved."

"No, but that doesn't mean the fire will defeat us."

He kissed her so hard and quickly that he was gone before she realized what he'd done.

She turned her attention to the boy he'd brought out. Tim, someone had called him. He had such large eyes. All the children had such large eyes, and they shouldn't have to see this destruction. Damn it all. Archie was right, they wouldn't be defeated.

Chapter 12

It took hours to burn. Camilla had been right. The building where the boys had slept couldn't be saved. So they'd poured their efforts into saving the school, and in dousing the lawn and trees and hedges that stood between the two buildings. They'd watered down the school as well. And when nothing more could be done, they still stayed until the final embers died.

Arch found Camilla off to the side, standing alone, a bucket in her hand. He'd seen her working alongside the townsfolk—once the children had been taken away to be tucked into beds. Those whose families didn't live close by were taken in by their schoolmates' parents. Tomorrow, Arch would help the headmaster convert one of the classrooms into a temporary sleeping room until another dormitory could be built.

But at that particular moment, he wasn't thinking about all the work that would need to be done in the next few days. He was concentrating on moving his weary body across the trampled lawn to where Camilla stood.

"How did it happen?" she asked quietly after he reached her.

"One of the older boys confessed to using a candle beneath his bed to read. Seems he fell asleep with the candle still lit. He has some burns, but he'll be all right."

He pried the bucket from her stiff fingers. "Come along, we need to get you home."

She turned on him, a savagery on her face such as he'd never seen. She hit his shoulder, his chest. "You went into the fire!"

He grabbed her wrists. "I was one of the first ones here."

"You could have died!"

She seemed to crumble just as the building had, from the inside out, and he was amazed that she remained standing. Tears began streaming down her face. "Winston wouldn't let me go in. I was so afraid. What if you couldn't find your way out? You're so scattered sometimes, always lost in your silly books, as though you don't realize the realities of the world."

"I know the reality of fire."

"I wouldn't have been able to save you."

"Ah, Camilla, my brave, brave girl." He lifted her into his arms, felt her tear-strained cheek press against his bare shoulder, a salve to the burns he'd received. "Let's get you home."

"I can walk."

"So can I."

"You're an earl. You should find a servant to carry me."

"It is no hardship to walk with you in my arms. I rather fancy it."

"I'm so tired, Archie."

"I know you are. I'll have your maid prepare a bath, then we'll put you to bed."

Everyone was still stirring about when they got home. He knew they'd all been at the fire, but they'd not stayed as long as he had. He had Win haul the tub to Camilla's room while Arch sat her on her bed. He didn't know if she was stunned or simply exhausted. He ordered her maid to help her bathe, promising to return with some salve when Camilla was finished with the bath.

While he waited he decided to give himself a good washing. He was in the kitchen when Win walked in.

"Your little countess was a tigress tonight."

"She told me that she tried to go into the building."

"She did. I almost didn't have any luck holding her back. She's not someone you want to anger, is she?"

Arch dried himself. "No, she's not."

"Don't recall you going to fires with half your clothes missing."

Heatherton was a small community, but particular men were designated to fight the fires so they'd always know who was in charge and who could be counted on to be there. Arch had simply fallen into old habits when he'd heard the bells clanging.

"You've nothing to say?" Win asked.

"I was occupied."

Win grinned. "I know. Bessie brought your shoes by. Seems you snatched up your clothing but forgot them. She's always been an accommodating lass."

"Let's keep her visit between brothers, shall we?"

"Of course. As well as your visit to her cottage."

Arch was bone-weary and not in any mood to deal with Win's irritating humor. He took the jar of salve out of the cabinet where his mother kept it and headed out of the room.

"She was really quite amazing, your countess. I wouldn't have thought she'd have gone to help."

He glanced over his shoulder at his brother. "She has a good heart, Win. But she keeps it to herself, as though she fears no one else will take care with it."

"Just watch your own heart, brother."

He didn't think his own heart was in much danger. He walked through the house and up the stairs to the room that had once been Nancy's and was now being used by

Camilla. He rapped lightly on the door and heard quiet footsteps. The door opened, and Frannie peered out.

"Is Lady Sachse finished with her bath?" Arch asked.

"Yes, my lord. I was about to braid her hair."

"I'll see to that." He stepped back and jerked his head to the side.

Frannie opened her mouth, closed it. She knew better than to question an earl and understood the value of keeping private matters private. He had no fears that his late-night, early-morning visit would go beyond these walls.

Following a quick curtsy, she hurried down the hallway. Arch stepped into the room, hesitated, then closed the door.

The room smelled of Camilla. Her rose scent. He thought that if he breathed deeply enough and often enough, he might be able to erase the odor of smoke and charred remains.

She sat at the vanity, staring into the looking glass, but he thought she was watching his reflection as he neared rather than her own. She was neither timid nor shy, so he knew she would have voiced her objections to his closing of the door if she had any.

She wore a clean nightgown. Her hair hung loose, a curtain of golden brown strands dipping just below the settee on which she sat. He met her gaze in the mirror. Her eyes had a lost look about them as though she'd not yet recovered from the ordeal of the night, and as badly as he wanted her, he knew he wouldn't take her there beneath the roof of his mother's house.

But he needed whatever they could have, and if it were no more than her presence, it would be enough.

He crossed the room, knelt before her, and held up the jar. "When I lived here, I was a volunteer on the fire brigade. I wasn't always as careful as I should be, and now and then I would get a burn. My mother makes this salve. I have no idea what's in it, but it always soothes."

"I didn't get burned," she said softly.

"No." He took her hand and turned it over. "But you're not in the habit of carrying buckets either."

The sight of her torn and raw flesh caused his heart to tighten. He'd feared that she'd have blisters, but she'd worked too hard and worn away bits of skin. He opened the jar and dipped out a bit of salve. Gingerly, tenderly, he spread it across her palm.

"Frannie could have done this."

He lifted his gaze to hers. "Would you rather have Frannie here?"

Slowly, she shook her head.

He smiled at her. "I'm glad."

He took her other hand and began to apply salve to the tortured skin. "Does that feel good?"

"Yes."

When he was finished, he leaned back and lifted her foot. It was tiny, delicate. He hated that it was scraped, cut, and bruised. "Ah, Camilla, look at your poor feet."

"I'd rather not, thank you."

"What were you thinking to run out of the house without shoes?"

"You weren't wearing shoes."

"When I was growing up, I seldom did except in winter. My feet are much tougher than yours."

Gently he rubbed the salve over her sole. She had such tiny toes. He wondered how she'd react if he took one of those toes into his mouth or pressed a kiss to her lovely arch.

"Weren't you afraid, Archie?"

Stilling his ministrations and his musings, he raised his gaze to hers. "I hardly thought about the dangers. I knew only that if I didn't find the boy quickly and get out, that I'd never see you again, and I wasn't quite willing to make that sacrifice."

Tears began to well in her eyes. Reaching out, she brushed his hair from his brow. "You're unlike anyone I've ever known. You're not arrogant or sophisticated or impatient. You're unselfish. You're so terribly kind. I hardly know what to make of you."

"Stop comparing me to others and accept me as myself."

"Had you died tonight, I would have hurt so badly. I don't want to hurt."

"If you never hurt, then you can never know great joy. Without risk, you can have no reward. Everything would be equal, and life would be dreadfully dull."

"You want me to risk my heart, and I have none to risk."

"Yes, you do. But you've locked it away. Give it a chance. Unlock it."

"You ask too much."

"Then I shall work to unlock it for you." He lowered his head and kissed her foot, felt her fingers gliding through his hair.

He didn't blame her for being afraid, but he also knew how glorious love could be. He'd seen it with his parents. He saw it with Nancy.

Unfolding his body, he stood and lifted Camilla into his arms. She felt so right there, with her head nestled into the nook of his shoulder. He carried her to the bed and set her down, drawing the blankets over her.

"I'm still so frightened," she said quietly. "Will you hold me? Just hold me?"

"I will do anything you ask."

He stretched out on the bed and drew her up against his side.

"My husband never held me."

"I would hold you every night, all night, just for the simple pleasure of feeling the warmth of your body against mine, having your scent surrounding me, hearing your breathing, knowing you were mine."

He shifted his body so he was no longer on his back, but could gaze on her. He kissed her, knowing they would go no further than the touch of lips. She had the sweetest mouth. He was tempted to plunder, to take, to possess . . .

but the moment wasn't right. He wouldn't take advantage of her fears or her gratitude that he'd survived.

He felt that tonight she'd at least inserted the key into the lock that guarded her heart. His reward would come from turning it slowly, leaving her with no regrets. He shouldn't pursue at all, because he did indeed need an heir.

But as he deepened the kiss, he decided he would worry about his responsibilities to the title later. For what remained of the night, he would be content with where he was, holding her close, tasting her, feeling the weight of her body next to his.

Drawing back, he looked down on her. How badly he wanted to move the blankets aside, lift her nightgown, and fill himself with the sight of her nakedness sprawled over this bed. Instead, he kissed her again, before whispering, "Go to sleep."

Then he held her, with his body aching not from the battering it had taken tonight but from the desperately needed surcease he'd denied it.

They would leave for Sachse Hall in a few days, then he could begin his true campaign to turn the lock to her heart and lure her into his bed.

"Archie?"

"Mmm?" Idly he stroked her back.

"I did weep when Lucien died. I can't imagine why because I despised him."

"Relief perhaps."

"No, I laughed with relief. I think because when all was said and done, he lived a very sad life. I worry that the same will be said of me."

He rolled over again to face her. "It shan't be. Just as you plan to tout my good virtues to the single ladies of London, so shall I tout yours to all I meet."

"I have so few."

"On the contrary, Countess, you have far more than you realize."

"Where were you earlier?" she asked. "Before the fire."

He slid his eyes closed, contemplated telling a lie, but decided that he wanted honesty with her in all things. He opened his eyes and held her gaze in the shadows. "I was with a young lady who wanted to be with an earl. I don't know how the aristocracy does it. I found it to be most unpleasant to be with someone who refused to look beyond my title."

"You grow accustomed to it in time."

"I don't think I ever shall."

"Was she pretty?"

"Not as pretty as you. And just so you'll know, nothing intimate passed between us. We simply talked."

"Will you see her again?"

"No. I discovered she wasn't what I wanted, nor was I what she envisioned."

"Archie, I was afraid you'd die tonight."

"I know."

"I was afraid that you'd die without knowing that I care for you a great deal."

She'd given him a spark of hope, but for what? They could care for each other, they could love each other; but in the end, they would only hurt each other.

Chapter 13

She was a widow who'd never slept with a man through the night. Her husband's visits had been brief, to the point. Except on those occasions when he'd been drunk and in the mood to torture her, then it had seemed his time with her was never-ending.

Because her feet were sore from the scratches and bruises she'd acquired the night before, Camilla leaned on Archie's arm and gingerly walked around the rubble that had once housed the students. She imagined her feet would have been much worse if he hadn't applied salve to them before putting her in bed, although she thought her heart might be less bruised.

She'd never known such comfort or trust, for surely it was trust that allowed her to fall asleep so easily. She couldn't get over how marvelous it had felt to awaken and find him still beside her, his arm around her, his cheek pressed to the top of her head.

She'd never meant to tell him or anyone that she'd actually cried when Lucien had died. But, snuggled within the bed, he had seduced the secret from her. She'd almost told him everything, except that she'd not wanted to ruin the tranquillity of the moment with the truth. How could she explain to a man who gave no thought to scrawling letters over a blackboard, a man who placed such value on education, that she wasn't educated?

She glanced over at Nancy and Owen, who were also inspecting the damage. She wondered if Nancy cuddled against her unattractive husband and shared secrets with him. In the dark, his homeliness wouldn't be visible, and perhaps whatever comforts or reassurances he gave her more than made up for having to look at his unsightly countenance.

Owen said something to his wife. She peered up at him and smiled. Tucking her against his side, he grinned at her, and it was as though some magical transformation had taken place. He appeared the same, and yet looked so different, as though all the good and charitable aspects to his character were shining through for the entire world to see. Was that the power of love? That it could make even the unsightly beautiful?

And what of those carved from ice? Could it make them warm?

"They're interesting to watch, aren't they?"

She snapped her attention to Archie. "Pardon?"

He tipped his head slightly in the direction of the other couple. "My sister and her unattractive husband."

"I wouldn't expect you to be so unkind in describing the man who married your sister."

"But you agree, do you not, that he isn't a handsome fellow?"

"I can't help but agree when the truth is so apparent."

"But if you watch them long enough, you begin to see in him what she sees."

She nodded. "I was only just noticing. It's rather amazing. I thought perhaps it was a trick of the sunlight."

"No, it is love. She is his queen, and he her prince."

"Why not her king?"

"Because a king would have to place his importance above that of the queen, and Owen loves Nancy far more than he does himself."

"She is a fortunate lady, your sister."

"She is indeed. Will you find a wife for me who looks upon me as Nancy does Owen?"

"I will certainly strive to do just that. You deserve to be regarded with such lofty affection." And she found herself desperately wishing she could be that woman. Before melancholy could take hold, she turned her attention back to the ruined building. "I think you should provide the school with the funds to rebuild this structure—but of brick this time, so it is less likely to burn."

"Mr. Spellman would consider that a frivolous use of my funds."

"Who cares what he thinks? The whole point in being wealthy is so you can do with your money as you wish."

"I thought the whole point in having money was so that you never did without."

"Well, certainly that is one advantage. Another is to use it to make yourself happy."

"And providing the school with funds to rebuild would make you happy?"

She scowled at him. "No, it would make you happy. It is, after all, your school."

His laughter echoed around them. She did so love his laughter.

"Making me happy makes you happy, so you won't object to my allocation of funds."

"It is not my place to object to how you spend your funds, my lord. You may spend it all, and it will make no difference to me, for I shan't marry an impoverished duke."

Nor did she suspect that she would marry one whom she loved, because she feared that her heart had already begun to inch toward the man walking beside her.

*   *   *

Arch stood in the front yard, staring at the village in the distance. The servants were loading the last of his and Camilla's belongings onto the coaches.

"I've packed you a lovely lunch. You and Lady Sachse should stop somewhere along the way and have a picnic."

He glanced down at his mother. "Perhaps we will. I'd like for you, for all the family, to come to Sachse Hall for Christmas."

Wrapping an arm around one of his, she sidled up against him. He didn't remember her seeming so frail.

"We might do just that," she said softly.

He swallowed hard. "I won't be coming back, Mum."

"I know."

"I was hoping to find what I had before, but it's gone."

"You've changed, lad. You've experienced things most of these folks never will. It's made you different."

"It's more than that." But he didn't know exactly how to explain it. "What do you think of Lady Sachse?"

"That you care for her more than she cares for you. But then you always did have a soft spot for wounded creatures."

Surprised by her astute observation, he glanced down to find her studying him as much as he wished to scrutinize her. "So you agree that she's been wounded?"

"I can see it in her eyes, but even if I couldn't, I'd met her husband—when your father and I went to London. He wanted to spend a little time with his distant cousin. A little was about all I could stand. His wife at the time was sweet enough, but Lord Sachse caused my skin to crawl. If I'd been married to him, I think I would have given my son to Gypsies before I'd have let the boy grow up under his father's influence."

"Bit harsh, isn't it?"

"I didn't like him, Arch. Didn't like him at all. Your countess would have done well to stay away from him."

"She was sixteen, Mum. Too young not to be lured by the potential of his power. She's looking for a duke now."

"Well, I've always believed it was good for a woman to have goals."

Hearing Win's laughter, he turned and saw his brother standing near Camilla. "They must be comparing *afflictions*," he mumbled dryly.

"I did think she was very clever to respond to his teasing as she did."

"Yes, she's a very clever lady." He hugged his mother closely. "We need to be going, but I look forward to seeing you at Christmas."

"Take care with her heart, Arch, and with yours."

It was difficult to take care with something he didn't have the power to possess.

With Archie beside her, Camilla walked along the edge of the babbling brook. They'd only driven for a short time before he'd ordered the driver to stop so they might have a picnic. She'd feared he'd use the opportunity to woo her, but he seemed to have other matters on his mind.

They'd not spoken at all while they ate the simple meal. She'd found comfort in the silence.

"How are your feet?" he asked. He'd shortened his stride to accommodate her.

"Healing." She glanced over at him. "I used your mother's salve again last night."

"You should have called me. I would have gladly applied it."

She'd almost done exactly that.

"I like your family," she admitted, changing the subject.

"They like you."

"I shall have to keep them in mind as I'm helping you to find a wife. She should be pleasing to them as well, because I think you'd find fault with any woman who wasn't."

"They mean a great deal to me."

"You're very fortunate to have them. Although I must confess that I'm most surprised that they don't live with you."

"My father is buried in Heatherton. My mother won't leave him. Besides, she's settled in her ways and rather enjoys the life she has there."

"But your brother is next in line."

"Yes, he is. We spoke of the possibility of him coming to live with me next year. These first few months I expected to stumble quite a bit, and I wanted some time to grow accustomed to my new position. I could hardly educate Win when I had so much to learn."

"I could have taught you both at the same time."

He slid his gaze over to her. "Another reason not to have him around just yet. I prefer not to share you."

She considered mentioning that he'd not known her when he made his decision to come to London alone, but something in his serious expression told her that he'd adeptly moved on to another subject and that suddenly they were no longer discussing the reasons his family wasn't living with him.

He stopped walking, faced the water, planted his feet apart, and put his hands on his hips. He looked very much the way she imagined a sea captain might, standing tall on the deck of a ship, before issuing orders to his crew.

"You said you had secrets."

Her heart leapt into her throat, and she felt as though she couldn't find any air to breathe. He didn't look at her, just stood there as though lost in the journey of the stream.

"Secrets that would keep you from coming to my bed."

Her heart slowly slid back into place, and air somehow managed to find its way into her lungs. "That's correct."

"How many?"

"How many what?"

"How many secrets?"

"This is ludicrous—"

He spun around, and she stepped quickly back, almost tripping over the hem of her dress.

His mouth was open and whatever he'd been about to say must have slipped from his mind, because he did nothing except shake his head. She'd never seen him look so beaten, not even after battling a fire that had destroyed a building.

"Two," she blurted. "Two secrets."

"And the consequences of my uncovering them?"

"Shame, mortification . . ." She shook her head. "You'd never again look at me as you sometimes do, as though I were special to you."

"You are special, Camilla. I don't know why you fail to see that."

"Because I know myself better than anyone."

"I want you, I can't deny that. But I want all of you or none of you."

"Then you shall have none of me."

"We shall see, Countess, we shall see."

He walked away from her, the challenge she'd seen in his eyes as unsettling as his words. He was a man who knew how to fight fire, but what did he know of battling ice?

Apparently a good deal. She didn't know which terrified her more: that he might discover her secrets or that he'd unleash the desire she'd seen smoldering in his gaze.

Chapter 14

Sachse Hall was a large, cold, cavernous structure. And so terribly quiet.

Arch couldn't say that he didn't like it, but when he walked through it—as he was presently doing—he felt as though he wore a cloak that didn't quite fit. The servants moved about like silent wraiths, ever conscious not to disturb the master of the house.

And he'd always enjoyed the clanging of pots and the pounding of bread dough, the smell of flour and cinnamon, and the cook's joyful voice lifted in song. None of that activity was apparent here, although he was certain that it was taking place because delicious meals were spread before him on the large dining room table each evening.

Gilded framed portraits adorned the walls. Marble statuettes, many of them questionable in taste, sat in alcoves. Armor had been fitted together so that it seemed knights stood guard at several portals. He fully expected one to give him a salute at any moment.

And the place contained far too many rooms for one man to walk through. He could hardly see the point. He supposed if he'd grown up with all this, he might have had a better appreciation for it. As it was, he thought it a waste of materials and objects. Seventy-four rooms. Why would any man need seventy-four rooms?

He found the whole place ostentatious. Camilla, on the other hand, seemed quite at home here. As always, she was a fountain of knowledge, knowing the history behind each artifact. He'd suggested she compile it all so it could be passed on to those who came after him. Enthusiastic with his suggestion, she'd indicated that she would begin dictating to her secretary as soon as possible. After all, that much information would surely leave her fingers black with ink.

He'd only smiled. The things she worried over.

He, himself, found satisfaction in applying ink to paper, and his hands remained unmarked. When he'd commented on that fact, she'd given him one of her indulgent smiles and assured him that her caution was necessary in order to impress a duke.

She still had her sights set on a man of high rank, and that knowledge rankled. He'd thought they'd shared something special while in Heatherton.

She reminded him of the moon, growing larger, more visible, only gradually to disappear again.

He turned down the hallway that led to his study. The footman acknowledged him and opened the door.

"Thank you," Arch said quietly.

The footman blushed. Apparently, Arch wasn't supposed to be thanking these people for doing their jobs. He thought that over time his muscles would become weak, and he would go to fat, because he was allowed to do nothing for himself. He didn't haul the water for his bath, couldn't help with the care of the livestock, and had a man who helped him dress. He was surprised that he didn't have a servant who sat beside him during dinner to deliver the food to his mouth.

As he walked into the room, Camilla smiled. "Good afternoon, Lord Sachse. I was writing a letter to your family to thank them for their hospitality."

He angled his head toward Lillian. "I suspect your secretary was actually doing the writing."

Camilla's smile withered. "Well, of course. But the words are mine."

"My apologies. It seems I'm in a foul mood. It's too quiet around here."

"I was thinking the same thing. I thought perhaps I would begin extending invitations to a few select people."

"Who exactly?"

"I was thinking the Duke of Kingsbridge."

"And his daughter, I suppose."

"Of course." Camilla turned to Lillian. "We'll finish later."

"Yes, my lady."

After Lillian left, Camilla rose and faced him. "It seems to be more than the quiet that has you in a foul mood."

"I've asked you to go with me on a picnic, and you've refused. I've asked you to accompany me on walks about the garden, and you've been occupied with all your silly letters."

"They're not silly. They're an important part of being a countess."

"I know that they're important, Camilla, but not more so than I. Last night, I dined alone. Since we've arrived here, I feel as though you're avoiding me."

"It's for the best, Archie. You shouldn't have expectations where I'm concerned."

Ah, but he did. He had great expectations of getting her into his bed, of turning the ice countess to fire, of melting her through and through, until she remained the warm woman he knew she could be.

"And this Kingsburrow—"

"Kingsbridge."

"Do you have expectations where he's concerned?"

Her gaze darted around the room as though she was seeking the answer or perhaps the courage to admit why this particular gentleman was to be issued an invitation. She cleared her throat before settling her gaze back on his, defiance in those brown eyes of hers.

"You met him at the last ball of the Season. I told you then that he's been a widower for some time. He has three grown sons. He's far from impoverished, so he has no need to look across the Atlantic for a wife. He has five estates valued at—"

"Camilla, I don't care about his worth."

"I do." She angled her head haughtily. "I must. There is very little of worth that I can bring to a marriage—"

"You bring yourself," he interrupted hotly, despising the fact that she constantly failed to give the proper value to people. "I don't understand why you continually fail to acknowledge your value. Strip me bare of all this"—he flung his arm around in a circle—"and I'm still valuable, a person of worth."

"Well, jolly good for you. I don't feel as though I am, and I wish you'd stop judging me by your standards!"

"I'm not judging you."

"Yes, you are. Constantly. I've repeatedly told you that I can't be what you want, and yet you persist in trying to shape me. You know things about me that I've shared with no one. You know me better—"

"I feel as though I know you not at all!" Releasing a heavy sigh, he shook his head. "I didn't seek you out to quarrel. This Queensbridge—"

"Kingsbridge."

The fire in her eyes excited him. He knew he shouldn't allow it to, but it did. And he could bring the fire to the surface so easily simply by teasing her and mucking up the man's name. Then it occurred to him that she might not be so quick to anger if she didn't care about the man. It seemed the joke was on him.

"Kingsbridge then. You'll invite his entire family?"

"Only him and his daughter. His sons are gadding about the world somewhere. Is there anyone else you'd like to invite?"

"The Duke and Duchess of Harrington, if they're back from their travels."

"They should be. Anyone else?"

"I hardly know anyone else."

"I'll give it some thought. I don't want too large an affair."

"In other words, you don't want anyone distracting Kingsburn—"

"Kingsbridge!"

"—from his pursuit of you."

"I do hope you will address him properly when he is here."

Quickly, so she had no chance to object, he tucked her beneath the chin and winked. "Of course, when he is within earshot. When he isn't, I believe I shall continue to take delight in tormenting you by bumbling his name."

He walked away from her and went to his desk. Several stacks of letters awaited him. "Don't suppose you'd help me by reading through some of my correspondence?"

"Reading strains my eyes and gives me a headache. I could call Lillian in—"

"No." He sat behind his desk and studied her. "Have you ever had a doctor examine your eyes? Perhaps you need spectacles."

"There is nothing wrong with my eyes. Now if you'll excuse me—"

"Stay."

She was two steps into her hasty retreat before his word stopped her. She glanced over her shoulder at him. "I thought you were about to become busy handling the affairs of the estate."

"I am, but I don't wish to be alone while doing it. I would suggest that you sit by the window and read a book, but as that would put a strain on your eyes as well, perhaps you could simply watch the garden, be available should any questions arise. After all, you had promised to help me learn my duties."

Her gaze darted toward the door. He could see a subtle straightening of her shoulders as though she was shoring up her resolve, and he wondered what it was she feared his discovering while in his presence.

"Of course, I'm more than pleased to be of service." She moved to the chair by the window and sat facing him, rather than the garden. "Do get on with your business."

He looked over the stacks of papers and letters and hardly knew where he wanted to begin. At the beginning, he supposed.

He went through a dozen inconsequential letters from ladies letting him know that they'd been pleased to make his acquaintance during the Season and hoped he'd call on them when he returned to London for the next Season. While he appreciated their sentiments and attention, the letters truly held no interest for him.

Finally, he came upon a letter that did, "It's from Spellman," he told Camilla. "He thinks our donation to the school is foolhardy, but he's seen to it."

"So typical of Spellman. As tightfisted as he is with your funds, you'd think he thought they belonged to him."

He set the letter on top of all the others he'd read. The next missive came from the school, and immediately he felt the loneliness that had been surrounding him since he'd arrived here lift. "Ah, Camilla, listen to this.

'My lord,

We at the Haywood School for Boys have received the funds you've so generously donated that will allow us to rebuild the dormitory lost to us.

The courage and assistance that you and Lady Sachse exhibited during the dreadful fire—'"

Arch shook his head. "They make it sound as though I'd done something special when I'd done the same thing countless times before while I lived there. Not at the school, of course, but at other buildings."

"What else do they say about my courage?" Camilla asked. She was sitting on the edge of the chair, delight mirrored in her eyes, no doubt because of the praise afforded her.

With a sigh, he continued on.

"The courage and assistance that you and Lady Sachse exhibited during the dreadful fire has earned you our undying gratitude. In your honor, we wish to name the new dormitory Sachse Hall.

We hope you will honor us by attending a ceremony to officially name the building once it is completed.

I have the honor to remain,
Your lordship's obedient servant,

Hubert Beresford, Headmaster,
Haywood School for Boys"

He tossed the letter toward the pile of read missives. "What rubbish."

Camilla rose and crossed over to the desk. "On the contrary, Archie, it's a great honor. A bit confusing for them to give it the same name as this estate, but still . . ." She picked up a letter and smiling brightly, read aloud, " 'The courage and assistance that you and Lady Sachse exhibited during the dreadful fire has earned you our undying gratitude. In your honor, we wish to name the new dormitory Sachse Hall.' I find it marvelous."

She lifted her joyful gaze from the letter and looked at him. "Whatever is wrong?"

"Apparently a great deal." He reached across his desk and picked up the letter from the school. "You took the wrong letter."

She looked momentarily flummoxed, but quickly regained her composure. "I am well aware of that fact. I was playing a prank on you. You really must advise them that they should select another name."

Slowly he came to his feet. So much was beginning to make sense. The impression he'd had that she'd not read his letter when she'd said that she had. The French book. Her never reading to him. Her keeping her secretary near to spare her fingers being coated in ink and her eyes from the strain of reading. Her confession that she had a secret that would keep him from her bed, and he'd wondered what she could possibly have done that she'd thought he'd find fault with. He was a teacher, and she . . .

"You can't read," he said quietly.

"Of course I can." She tossed the letter onto the desk, held out her hand, and snapped her fingers. "Hand me the proper letter and I shall read the entire thing to you."

"Even if I didn't read the entire missive to you?"

He felt cruel for lying to her, but he wanted, needed to know the truth. Was this the secret that held her distant? Her fear that he, as a teacher, would more easily discover what she undoubtedly considered a flaw?

"You read me the entire letter."

"Did I, Camilla?" He extended the letter. "You tell me."

"I will not play these ridiculous games. I am a countess. I have no need to prove anything about myself to you. You are a small and petty man, and I don't like you. May you rot in hell."

She spun on her heel and rushed out of the room, leaving him to stare in her wake. How in the world had she managed to convince people that she could read? How had she managed to survive without reading? She was intelligent, had incredible recall, yes. But lacked the ability to read? Her secret. Her damned secret. He'd unwittingly uncovered it at last, but at what cost?

* * *

Damn him! She'd known he was a threat, had begun to hope he wasn't. But her fears had been justified.

She'd run from the house without a shawl or cloak. It hadn't seemed that cold outside, only cool in the autumn air, but she was shivering as she sat huddled in a distant corner of the garden. Hidden away . . . just as she'd done at the children's home when the teacher there had ridiculed her because the marks were unfamiliar. Letters he'd called them. They could have been someone's idea of an odd painting for all she knew. She couldn't decipher them. No matter how long she stared at them, they made no sense. Scribble. Black and hideous.

"Camilla?"

Ah, damnation, how had he found her? She thought she'd come far enough into the gardens that he wouldn't follow.

"Go away."

"I can't."

He knelt beside her.

"Please, I'm fine. I simply grew tired of walking. I'll return to the house soon."

"You're not fine. You're trembling."

He removed his jacket and placed it around her shoulders. The warmth was luxurious, and his scent surrounded her. She'd always taken such delight in the way he smelled. But she could find no comfort in his nearness now. He wasn't stupid enough to believe any of her earlier babblings, and well she knew it.

"Camilla—"

"He called me dim-witted, ignorant."

"Who did?"

"The teacher who taught those of us at the children's home. 'Read!' he commanded. 'Read!' How could I when I'd never held a book. Because I was eight, he thought I should know how. He was the ignorant one, to think knowledge came with age, rather than experience."

"You're not ignorant, Camilla."

"I saw the look on your face, saw the disgust in your eyes—"

"Because you were being dishonest with me, not because you couldn't read." He grabbed her shoulders and jerked her around so she was forced to face him. She saw no disgust now. She saw something far worse.

"Don't you dare pity me," she hissed.

Slowly he shook his head. "Admiration is not pity."

She released a brittle laugh. "Do you think you can fool me? Do you think I don't see the truth?"

"No, I don't believe that you do." Bracketing her face with his hands, he held her steady, leveling his face with hers, holding her pinned in place with the steadfastness of his gaze. "Drop the damned barriers that you use to protect yourself and look into my eyes. Truly look into my eyes, and see what I see when I look at you.

"A woman whom I trust to advise me on matters of which I am totally ignorant. A woman who has the ear of the Prince of Wales, a man who will one day be king. A woman who is charitable in nature, but wishes for no one to know, so she receives no credit for her good works. A woman who pretends to be hard and callous, because she has the ability to care so much but has been hurt so often that she shields herself from the world . . . and from me."

"You're a teacher!"

He stroked his thumbs across her cheeks. "Then let me teach you."

Tears blurred her vision, threatened to choke her as they gathered in her throat. "So you can ridicule me? Lose all respect for me?"

"I will only lose respect for you if you pass up the opportunity that I'm offering you. I can teach you to read. You are one of the smartest women I know. And I would never ridicule anyone who attempted to learn, even if they struggled, I would respect their efforts."

"What if I can't learn to read? What if I am truly stupid?" It had always been her worst fear.

He gave her a warm, caring smile. "If I believed that for even a moment, I would have never challenged you in the study. I would have pretended that you'd picked up the right letter. I would have let you hold on to your illusion. I believe in you, Camilla, even if you don't believe in yourself. All I'm asking is that you believe in me and my abilities to teach."

She turned away because it hurt so much to look into his eyes. She'd never had such faith directed her way. What if she disappointed him or caused him to doubt himself? If she hurt him?

"Trust me, Camilla."

She looked back at him. "I do, Archie. It is myself that I don't trust. What if I let you down?"

"As long as you give me a chance to teach you, you won't."

Sniffing, she nodded. She'd never been so terrified in her entire life. "All right. I'll let you try, but I don't want anyone to know."

"Of course not. It'll be our little secret. But that means we'll have to celebrate privately once you've succeeded."

"I hear no doubt at all in your voice."

"Because I have none."

Then his mouth was on hers as though he could instill his confidence with the slow, provocative movement of his lips. He'd taken this whole discovery as though it were nothing more than an inconvenience, easily dealt with, easily fixed. But he would soon learn otherwise. What could Archie offer her that she'd not had before?

Then he deepened the kiss, and she was no longer thinking of lessons or letters or how exciting it would be to open a book and have the opportunity to read to him for a change. No, she was thinking that if he were as skilled at teaching as he was at kissing, that he might indeed succeed where others had failed.

The chill of the afternoon gave way to the warmth of passion, swirling through her as lazily as his tongue swirled through her mouth. No hurry. Never in a hurry when kissing.

She became vaguely aware of her hair tumbling around her shoulders, his feral growl as though he'd accomplished some goal. She thought she should take him to task for taking advantage of the moment, but he was going to teach her to read . . .

He was going to teach her to read.

She pulled back, aware that they were both breathing heavily.

"When do we start?" she asked.

"Immediately. I've just given you your first lesson. The letter O. The shape of a mouth just before it kisses."

She laughed. "Be serious."

"I am. I'm going to teach you as you've never been taught."

Like naughty children, they sneaked away in the afternoons to what would have been the children's wing of the manor if the heir had survived or Camilla hadn't been barren. The wing contained a room in which she was fairly certain her husband and those who'd come before him had been initially taught before they went off to elite schools.

Archie had acted as though he'd found treasure when he began looking through the books on the shelves. "These are very elementary books," he'd said.

"Elementary?" she'd asked.

"Easy reading."

For someone who knew how to read perhaps. For her they were indecipherable. Well, except for the letter O. She was able to point it out, although doing so would often distract her because she'd begin to remember the kiss Archie had given her in the garden. She was fairly certain that teachers weren't supposed to be intimate with their students.

But it was so very hard for her not to imagine that intimacy when Archie's love of learning was so apparent whenever they came to this room. She was beginning to understand why he was as curious as he was, why he asked so many questions and studied everything he saw. He simply loved learning, and more, he loved sharing what he knew.

"Today, I want you to read a sentence to me," he said, getting up from behind the desk where she assumed the tutor would have sat.

"I didn't think you'd taught me all the letters yet," she reminded him, her stomach tightening with dread that she'd fail her first test.

"I haven't." He sat beside her. "But all the letters I've taught you are in this sentence. All you have to do is make the sound of the letter, and you can read the word."

He set a piece of paper in front of her and pointed. "Here's the first word."

She studied where he was pointing. He'd taught her a few simple words, one-letter, two-letter words. How to tell when a word began and ended by the space surrounding it.

She cleared her throat. "A."

He moved his finger over to the next word. Three letters. A challenge to be sure.

"First tell me what the letters are," he ordered.

"C-A-T."

"Very good. Now sound them out."

She did so—keeping her thoughts a secret—until a word began to form that she dared to say aloud. "Cat?"

He grinned, leaned back, and crossed his arms over his chest. "Exactly right. Move on."

She placed her finger under the next word since he apparently had no plans to do so. "Had."

She moved her finger to the next one. Easy. "A."

She pressed her finger beneath the final word. Wrinkled her brow and shook her head. "I don't know."

"What do you think it is?"

She shoved the paper away. "What I think it is doesn't matter. It's obviously wrong as it makes no sense."

"Tell me what you think it is."

"You'll laugh."

"I won't."

But he would. He placed his hand over hers and squeezed. "Have I laughed once since I've begun teaching you?"

"No."

"Then why would I laugh now?"

"Because I don't know what it says."

"Tell me what you *think* it says."

She glared at him. "A cat had a hat."

He grinned broadly. "That's exactly right."

"It can't be, Archie. It makes no sense. Cats don't wear hats."

"Sometimes sentences don't make sense." He placed his elbow on the table, his chin on his palm, and studied her as though she made no more sense than the sentence she'd just read.

The sentence she'd just read.

"Oh, my word." A bubble of unexpected laughter escaped. "Did I read it correctly?"

"You tell me."

"Letters don't lie, do they, Archie?"

"Not outright, no. Sometimes they try and trick us by not sounding as they should, but we'll deal with those later. In this case, the words were as you read them."

"Oh!" She jumped up because she couldn't contain the excitement. She began pacing around the room. "I did it. I read a sentence. I actually read a sentence." Stopping, she held his gaze. "I'm not stupid, Archie."

"Of course you're not."

"Who would have thought?" She rushed to sit down and slapped her hand on the table. "Give me another sentence to read."

She was undoubtedly the most intelligent woman he'd ever known. He wanted to find every person who'd ever led her to believe she was stupid and pound them all into the ground with his fists. And now that he'd opened the door, and she'd walked through it, she was insatiable.

"Man," he said, sitting at his desk. He waited while she wrote it out at hers.

The problem he ran across was trying to stop her from going too fast, from trying to grasp what was still beyond her reach—those pesky words that didn't sound at all as they looked. Sachse being one of them. Saxee was closer to its pronunciation.

"Bake. As in, she will bake a cake," he said.

"I think I shall write out cake as well. It's very much like bake. Will you give me extra credit if I spell it correctly?" She peered up at him, such hope and enthusiasm in her eyes that he so did not want to disappoint her.

Having been so badly wounded before, she was easily bruised now, so he worked diligently to expand her scope gradually while shoring up her confidence for the times when words might not come so easily. He was astounded by her capacity for memorization.

"Relax, Archie, you gave me the word last week. I know it is spelled with two different letters that sound exactly the same. Honestly, if you don't ever challenge me, how will I move beyond the simplest of words? I want to be able to read the books in my library, not the ones here in the children's library."

"Why did you purchase books if you couldn't read?"

She shrugged. "I love the notion of books. Someone took their thoughts, applied them to paper, and shared them with the world. And some authors have such extraordinary thoughts. I'd certainly never think to build a man from discarded parts of other people. Rather macabre, yet fascinating. Don't you think?"

"I read *Frankenstein* to you, didn't I?"

A look of wistfulness came over her face. "I hope to read to you someday."

Not likely. When she was proficient enough, she'd no doubt be wed to another. She'd sent out her invitations to a host of people, and they would soon have a gathering of people whom they'd be entertaining.

"I look forward to it," he said to keep her spirits up so she'd not know the gloomy direction of his thoughts. "Now, let's continue with the test. Duke."

She applied pen to paper, and he strived not to think about the test that he would have to face in the near future, giving her up to the very word he'd instructed her to spell.

Chapter 15

He'd opened her up to a world that knew no boundaries. He'd shown her a book that contained every word ever written along with its meaning. A dictionary. Incredible. To have in one place every word that had ever existed. And there were so many.

He was finally beginning to give her more complicated words to learn, words with more syllables. She loved them all. The small words, the big ones.

To look at the letters and to know in an instant the word they'd come together to form. What she'd once thought was so frustratingly difficult, now seemed so amazingly easy. All because of Archie. Because of his patience. And he made learning so enjoyable with his little games and challenges and his sentences that made no sense but were fun to read.

Sitting in bed, reading a book she'd taken from the children's room, she thought she'd rather be reading his silly sentences than this book about a boy and his dog. She'd tried reading some book about pride but had gotten no farther than "It is a truth . . ." before she'd become stumped.

She'd skipped over the two words she didn't know, and

finished the sentence. It seemed the story was about a man searching for a wife. A romance perhaps. Archie never read those types of stories to her.

She would take it to their lesson tomorrow and they could read it together. She rather fancied a love story.

Then she began to wonder why she should wait. The clock had only just struck eleven. She wondered if Archie was still awake. What harm would come from investigating?

She set aside the book about the dog, retrieved her night wrapper from the chair, and slipped it on. Then she picked the pride book off the night table beside her bed. Perhaps it was a story about a woman with too much pride—such as she. That notion made her want to read it all the more quickly.

She hurried out of her bedchamber and down the hallway. A silly idea she'd had to put herself in one wing and Archie in the other. As though distance could keep her safe.

She stumbled with the thought. Safe, yes. She liked safety, but he'd already discovered her secret, so what did she fear now? Him and the power he could wield over her heart.

It was just a silly story. It would keep until tomorrow. That was the beauty of books. The story was always there. One had but to turn back the cover to find it.

Only she wanted to read it now, and she wanted to let Archie know that even though it had difficult words, she'd managed to get the gist of the idea. A man wanted a wife. And as she and Archie were both searching for spouses, they might enjoy reading the story together.

He'd brought her such joy, and she'd brought him so little, she felt a need to make it up to him and quickly. They would soon have guests arriving and she'd be devoting herself to the Duke of Kingsburrow—Kingsbridge!

Yes, they should begin reading tonight because they'd need to stop as soon as their guests arrived. She continued on, picking up her pace, more comfortable with her decision the farther away from her bedchamber she became.

She fairly flew down the stairs, rounded the corner, and nearly jumped out of her skin as the butler moved out of the shadows.

"Smythe, what a surprise! It's rather late for you to be up and about, isn't it?"

He looked momentarily startled as though he wasn't quite certain who'd spoken to him. She realized too late that her voice hadn't carried its usual tartness.

"I was making the final rounds," he finally said.

"And you're doing it splendidly. Do you know if his lordship is in his chambers?"

"Yes, madam, I believe he is."

"Jolly good. Back to your rounds, but don't stay up too late. You need your rest." And he certainly didn't need to see her coming back from the earl's bedchamber in the early hours of the morning. The thickness of the book led her to believe that they would be reading for quite some time.

The house was beastly large. It had never bothered her before, but Archie might as well be on the other side of the world. She was quite out of breath and ready to sit down by the time she reached his bedchamber door. She considered knocking but didn't want to wake him if he were asleep. However, if he was in the sitting area before the fireplace, then she would join him.

She opened the door a crack and was immediately greeted by light. Ah, so he wasn't asleep obviously. She swept into the room. "Archie, I was wondering—"

And froze.

He came to a halt at the same time. He'd been striding out of the dressing room and judging by the dampness of his hair, she assumed he'd only recently finished bathing.

And had yet to put on any clothing.

He was magnificent, standing there, facing her, apparently as stunned to see her as she was to see him. She'd viewed his chest before, but the rest of him . . .

My word.

She didn't think she'd spoken her thoughts aloud, but he suddenly came to life like a puppet whose strings had been yanked. He crossed over to the bed, grabbed his dressing gown, and slipped it on as though he had until dawn to do so. Not until he'd covered himself and secured the sash did he speak. "Camilla, I'd not expected to see you in here."

"I'd not expected to see you either." She sounded as though her voice came from the bottom of a well, and only then, did she realize that she'd ceased to breathe.

He angled his head. "Which begs the question, Countess. Whom did you think to find in my bedchamber?"

"You, of course. I simply meant that I'd not expected to see . . . all of you."

He crossed his arms over his chest and leaned casually against his bedpost. "Why are you here, Camilla?"

"I was reading"—she'd never thought to say that about herself—"reading, Archie."

She stepped farther into the room. "But I was having a time of it, not knowing all the words, and thought perhaps you could help me with the difficult ones."

He dipped his gaze to the book she held in her trembling hands. When had they begun to shake?

"That's not a book from the children's room."

"No. It's from the library. I want to read it."

"It will contain many words you've not yet learned. You'll find it frustrating."

"Not if you help me. I thought we might read it together."

He shoved himself away from the bed, a secretive sort of grin playing along his mouth. "I'd like that. Come and sit on the sofa before the fire."

"I'll simply step out into the hallway and return after you're dressed."

"I'm dressed *now*."

"Barely."

"Enough."

He sat on the sofa and patted the cushion beside him. "Come on."

His gaze held a challenge, but kindness as well. They were in their nightclothes, but they'd be on the sofa and nothing untoward could happen there. It was only the bed where danger lurked, and she certainly had no plans to climb into it with him.

She felt her head nod as though she had no control over it. She returned to the door, closed it, and tried not to notice how its resounding click sounded like a death knell.

Taking a deep breath, she walked across the room and sat on the sofa, as far from him as possible, her hip practically hugging the side of the sofa as though it were a lover.

"I can't help you if I can't see the words on the page," he said, and although he sounded innocent enough, she thought she detected a bit of a dare beneath the low rumble.

"I can simply pass the book over to you—"

"And then I'll have to search for where you were." Lazily, like a cat lengthening its body beneath the sun, he stretched his arm out along the back of the couch. "Move closer."

She glanced over at him. He was well and truly covered, exhibiting no evidence that he was interested in anything other than reading. She scooted over a bit, and his expression clearly said, "Not enough."

With a deep sigh, she moved nearer, straightened her nightclothes, and tried to ignore the warmth of his skin penetrating both the silk that covered his thigh and hip and the silk covering hers.

"*Pride and Prejudice*," he said, quietly.

She jerked her attention to him, her heart thudding as though he'd leaned near and whispered in her ear. Come to think of it, he was terribly close, and she thought his breath might be ruffling the fine hairs on the nape of her neck. Her braid was trapped between her back and the couch, and she felt him tugging on it.

"The title of the book," he murmured as though understanding her confusion.

"Oh, yes, I knew it was pride and *something*." She looked at the title and focused on the third word, cataloging it to memory so she'd recognize it when next she saw it.

"I understand it's a story quite favored by the ladies," he said.

She turned back to him. Was he nearer? He was holding the end of her braid, brushing the tip across his lips the way a painter might apply a light coating of paint to canvas. "Have you not read it then?"

A corner of his mouth curled upward. "I've read it."

"I envy you. You've read a good many books."

"You should never envy anyone without knowing what price they paid to acquire the very thing that you envy."

"What price did you pay?"

His smile dissolved as though it had never been. "Not nearly as high a price as you paid to be a countess. Let's read, shall we?"

Reading was certainly preferable to rehashing her desire—no her need—to gain a title, to hold on to it, and to reach a bit higher. She opened the book and began reading, quite quickly since she'd read it once before already. "It is a truth . . ."

She peered up at him. He seemed to be looking at the flames dancing on the hearth, the end of her braid held against his lips as one might hold a lover's mouth.

She cleared her throat. He shifted his attention to her and raised an eyebrow.

"I thought you were going to follow along," she said.

"I am."

"If that were the case then you would know that you are to fill in the next word."

"Perhaps you should tell me what you think it is."

"If I *thought* it were *anything*, I would have said."

"You can't memorize every word ever written. You need to learn to decipher a word based on the sounds that the letters make."

She released a wearisome sigh. "It is close to midnight. We are not having a lesson. I want to read this story and I want you to read the words that I don't know. A little like playing together on the piano."

"Universally."

"Universally *what*?" she asked, wondering what in the devil he was talking about.

"Universally acknowledged."

"What's universally acknowledged?"

He brushed the end of her braid along her cheek, and she wondered why it was a more sensual fluttering when he did it than when she did.

"The words you can't read in the book are *universally* and *acknowledged*."

"Oh! Oh, I see. I didn't realize you'd returned your attention to the story."

"I hadn't. My attention is still on you."

She was beginning to think that coming here was a frightfully bad idea, but she couldn't seem to bring herself to close the book and leave.

"Then how do you know those are the words?"

"Because I caught a glimpse of them when you first began to read, before I looked away."

"And that's all you require to be able to read them?"

"Yes."

"Will I ever be able to read like that?"

He stilled his hand, and she felt the power of his gaze as it roamed over her face. "I believe you can do anything that you set your mind to."

"I never want anyone to be able to guess that I came into reading so late in my life."

"Ah, yes, you are quite the ancient one, aren't you?"

"Don't make light of my concerns, Archie."

"I'm not. And no one will ever hear from me that you've only recently mastered reading. I will warn you now, however, that you'd best not pick up a book this thick in front of a gathering and expect to read it aloud word for word."

"I wouldn't dream of it." Although she had, on numerous occasions. Open a book and regale her audience with her mastery of reading. Share a story with them. She wanted to read to an audience the way a diva wished to raise her voice in song during an opera. She returned her gaze to the book and read a bit more haltingly than she would have liked, "It is a truth . . . universally acknowledged . . . that a . . ."

"Single."

"Single man in . . ." She hated that the really large words were so difficult.

"Possession."

She'd know that word the next time she saw it.

"Of a good . . ." she continued, then stopped.

"Fortune."

"Must be in want of a wife."

"Therefore, I must be in want of a wife."

She snapped her gaze to his. "Of course you are. You are in possession of a good fortune. And I am in want of a husband because I am not in possession of a good fortune. Is that another universal truth do you think? In regard to women?"

"Undoubtedly. But there is another truth of greater importance."

"What would that be?"

"That you are beautiful beyond measure."

He slid his hand along her shoulder until his long slender fingers came to rest against the nape of her neck, and his thumb was stroking the underside of her jaw . . . slowly, provocatively, and she had the strangest desire to dip her head slightly and run her tongue along his thumb, perhaps draw it into her mouth.

Where in the world did that notion come from?

She'd certainly never felt that way about any gentleman, certainly not Lucien, who'd come the closest to touching her in this manner—only his hand around her throat had usually meant that he wished to choke her.

"Please," she pleaded, "I can't be what you want."

She dipped her gaze to discover that his robe had parted, no longer hiding him from her view or keeping his longing out of sight. She lifted her gaze back to his. "I shouldn't have come here this late at night," she rasped.

"It wouldn't matter when you came here, my reaction would be the same."

"Not if you knew the truth."

Her words gave him pause, she could tell because surprise flitted across his face like a flame trying to remain alight, only to die out. He released a wearisome sigh. "What other secret are you hoarding?"

She'd thought he'd turn away from her when he discovered she couldn't read. But he hadn't. Oh, there had been anger in his eyes, but only because she'd kept the truth from him. Afterward, he'd done all in his power to give her the gift of reading. He'd proven she wasn't stupid or ignorant. She was smart, she could learn.

She could hide her final secret in the dark from her duke, but she didn't think Archie was a man who'd be content with the darkness. He liked too much to look at everything in the light so he could completely understand it.

She could walk out now, and they would never have more than this. There would never be complete trust between them. And after all he'd given her, she thought it cruel to judge for him rather than to allow him to judge for himself.

Very deliberately, she closed the book and set it aside. Slowly, ever so slowly, without looking at him, she released all the buttons on her nightgown, from her throat to her navel. She'd quite literally had it beaten into her that she was worthless. She'd never wanted anyone to know.

But he had a right to know. The knowledge would tamp his desire . . . forever.

Shifting on the sofa, she faced him, still not looking at him. She couldn't stop her fingers from shaking as she took hold of the parted cloth and peeled it back farther. "He took a riding crop to me when I disappointed or displeased him."

He didn't move. He made no sound.

She finally dared to lift her gaze to his and saw burning within his eyes what she'd never expected to witness from Archie . . .

Pure, unadulterated hatred.

Chapter 16

Arch stood like a man possessed. Rage burned through him, nearly blinding him, and he didn't know what to do with it, where to unleash it. He crossed over to the fireplace and with one long mighty swipe, he knocked everything off the marble mantel: the golden candlesticks, the crystal vases, the statuettes.

Then he spread his arms wide, gripped the cold mantel, and held firm because, if he didn't, he thought he'd destroy everything else in this room, everything in his house. Bowing his head, he took in great draughts of air, trying to still the fury that caused his body to tremble.

Little wonder she didn't trust, little wonder she hoarded secrets. He'd seen in her eyes what it had cost her to reveal her scars to him, tiny slashes that marred her skin. He'd seen the shame, the mortification, and been unable to offer comfort because in that instant he'd wanted to commit murder . . . and he could have done it without feeling a bit of guilt.

"I'm terribly sorry," she said softly.

"No," he growled. "Never apologize for anything that he did."

His arms aching from the tension in his shoulders, he released his hold on the mantel and faced her. She was on her feet, the movement apparently closing her gown, although she'd yet to rebutton it, so he was left to view the tiniest gap of shadowy skin.

"The wonder of it is that you have any desire to marry at all," he said.

"I know that not all men are as he was. But neither are all men as you are, wanting the whole truth or none of it, wanting to see and understand every thread that has been woven together to make me who I am.

"Most men are content with the surface, with the superficial. Few want to burrow as deeply into a woman's heart as you do. I am the sum of my secrets."

"No." He shook his head. "The secrets are only a part of you and now they are . . . gone. And what remains before my eyes is a woman who endured, but didn't lose her humanity. A woman who rushes to a fire in her bare feet and her nightclothes, a woman who gives to the needy and takes no credit, who pours imaginary tea for little girls." He took a step toward her.

"You have amazed me from the moment I met you. You accomplished more without the ability to read than most people do with it. And when the opportunity to learn was presented to you, you snatched it up . . . again amazing me with how quickly you mastered the skill."

He took her face between his hands, watched as the tears in her eyes flowed onto her cheeks. "I told you once that I *thought* I could love a woman such as you. Now I *know*. I do. I do love you."

Still holding her head, he lowered his mouth to hers with all the tenderness that he could bring forth. He wanted this to be the last time that he ever tasted her tears when he kissed her. She wrapped her hands around his forearms, holding tightly, but he didn't have the impression that she wished to shove him away but rather that she simply wanted to touch him. He couldn't imagine the burden of never sharing one's true self with anyone, of having no one to trust completely. He'd grown up in a house of honesty, where imperfections were accepted. In truth, he found perfection rather dull.

Yet he would have done anything to have spared her the suffering she'd experienced at the hands of one of his relations. God, the thought sickened him. He and the man who'd done this to her shared the same blood. It was disgusting, sickening, revolting.

He heard a quiet moan, one of rising passion, and he realized that whatever had happened between her and the old Sachse had no place in his bedchamber, in their lives. It was over with. Done.

It wasn't his place to make amends. It was his place to love her as she deserved to be loved.

He slid his mouth to her throat, slid his hands to her shoulders. He wanted the gown gone, but he needed her to understand that nothing about her person revolted him. None of her secrets revealed mattered. All that was of importance was that he loved her, adored her.

Holding her gaze, he slipped his hand beneath the silk, nudging the cloth aside until the first tiny scar—a small white mark above her breast—became visible. Dipping his head, he kissed it.

Camilla felt the rush of heat from his mouth, the stroke of his tongue over one scar and then another as he slowly traveled over her skin, seeking out the imperfections, and making them seem not quite so shameful.

He lowered himself to his knees as his lips followed the path of her scars to her stomach. She looked down on his dark hair as he gave his tender ministrations to each of the unsightly marks. How did he manage with a look, with a touch to wipe away her shame?

He'd built her confidence one letter at a time, one word after another, until she'd dared to share this final secret with him, and he was erasing its significance one loving kiss at a time.

Bending over slightly, she pressed her cheek to the top of his head. How was it possible that this man could be as giving as he was when he demanded so much?

Complete surrender. Total surrender. Secrets bared. Imperfections accepted. Nothing held back. Everything revealed, so it could be measured and understood, so its significance could be weighed, its importance determined, and in the end, it seemed all that truly mattered to him was her. All the things she'd feared him discovering allowed him to care for her more. Gave him reasons to love her, gave her the freedom to accept that love.

Love. He loved her. She who had always thought herself unworthy of such a tender emotion was now the recipient of it, and she was left to wonder why she'd ever felt the need to hide. Just as when she'd been a girl and had pretended to know how to read and the pretending had prevented her from learning to read . . . so again had she almost repeated her mistake. By pretending not to care, she'd almost lost the chance to be loved.

She tried to hold him close, but he was not yet done. As her gown and robe slipped along her skin and pooled on the floor, he found a scar on her thigh, one on her hip. So many, too many to count, and yet he ignored not a one.

When each one had received the brush of his lips, he stood, lifted her into his arms, and carried her to the bed. The notion of protesting his actions slipped into her mind and slipped out, and she realized that in his arms, in his bed was where she truly wanted to be. Those desires were what had prompted her to unbutton her nightgown to begin with. Perhaps they were what had truly sent her to his room, book in hand.

He laid her down gently as though he feared she might break, but after all the humiliations she'd experienced in her life, she wasn't going to break now. Not when gentleness and love surrounded her.

With uncharacteristic boldness—because she'd never been the aggressor when it came to what passed between a man and a woman—she tugged on the sash of his robe. He removed the covering, and she experienced a moment of panic as he stood fully revealed. Without joining her on the bed, he reached over and cradled her cheek. She lifted her gaze to his eyes, eyes which she'd long ago come to cherish.

"I won't hurt you," he said.

Honesty. He'd always claimed to want honesty between them, and this moment called for it as no other did.

"I don't think you'll have a choice. He wasn't nearly as . . ." How to explain? Obviously not all aspects of the family had been passed down from generation to generation. She finally decided on, "as magnificent. I'm fairly certain that it is quite likely that you won't . . . fit."

A corner of his mouth hitched up into a warm, yet cocky grin, filled with masculinity and pride. "Oh, I'll fit. Have no fear of that."

Have no fear? No she didn't fear this man. He'd uncovered all her secrets, accepted them all. How could one fear acceptance? And if she disappointed him in bed . . . she didn't think it possible. He was a man who expected no more of her than he did of himself. He did what no one else had ever done. He accepted her for herself. She lifted her arms, spreading them wide, opening herself and her heart to him.

He came to her like the gentleness of night. Slowly. One moment it was but a promise, the next it had arrived.

And so did he, laying himself over her.

As he took her mouth, he nestled himself between her thighs. Not inside her. Just near her. The warmth of his body radiating between her, over her.

Oh, he was so lean, so fit, it seemed he was perfection,

like the many sculptures that adorned this house. Muscles knotted, tense. But unlike the cold marble, his were hot and quivering.

His tongue waltzed with hers, his mouth greedily devoured. She did with him what she'd done with no other. She touched him. His hair, his face, his neck, his shoulders, his back. She wanted to know the varying textures of all of him. She wanted to touch every glorious inch, down to his toes. But she couldn't reach his feet and didn't want his mouth to leave hers so that she could.

She'd never known that a kiss could last so long, could shift and change, and bring forth a rising tide of passion. No, no, not only the kiss, because he was doing more than kissing her. His hands stroked and caressed. He filled a palm with her breast and teased her nipple with his thumb.

Then his hand was gliding along her skin, lower, lower, along her thigh, then up, across her hip, between her thighs. Breaking off the kiss, he lifted himself, his eyes burning with yearning such as she'd never seen.

She'd never felt this wanted, this desired. He threaded the fingers of one hand through her hair while the other cupped her intimately. She felt the first stroke of his finger, watched as he closed his eyes and moaned low as though the pleasure that speared her had also shot through him.

Was that the essence of love? That pleasure given was pleasure received?

It was a concept she'd never considered, and with his next caress everything faded away except for the sensations. His harsh breaths echoed around her. The pleasure pitched and roiled. She grabbed his shoulders, anything to keep her anchored.

"I'll fit," he growled, as though challenging them both to call him a liar.

He pushed. She tensed.

"Am I hurting you?" he asked.

The desperation voiced in his question momentarily

brought her back from the brink of pleasure along with the startling realization that the pain she'd always felt wasn't there. Oh, she certainly was aware of the pressure, but it was a pleasant sensation, not a prelude to conquering, but an overture for sharing.

"No," she whispered, answering him at last. "There's no pain."

The glorious pressure increased as he pushed deeper, stretching her, stretching her until he accomplished exactly what he'd promised. The fullness of him as he buried himself to the hilt filled her with satisfaction such as she'd never known. To have him fully, completely nestled inside her was as satisfying to her as she thought it might be to him.

She wrapped her legs around him, pressed her thighs against him. He opened his eyes, and she saw his look of triumph . . . and rejoiced in it. His power was hers. His strength hers. They were equal, yet different. Partners. Sharing. Giving. Receiving.

He dipped his head to kiss her as he began to rock against her, sliding his body over hers, in hers. Passion took hold with a fury. She thought she might come off the bed. Wanted to. Wanted to stay.

She matched his rhythm. Giving and taking.

Pleasure coiled deep within her belly, radiated outward to the farthest tips of her limbs. She pushed on him, pulled on him, tightened her thighs around him. He growled. Pumped harder, faster.

The pleasure unfurled, arching her back. She cried out, heard his guttural cry, felt his final thrust, then the quivering of his body as he buried his face in the curve of her shoulder.

She wanted to laugh. She wanted to weep. She wanted to shout, to whisper.

In the end, she simply smiled and drifted off to sleep.

* * *

He'd known, of course, that she'd never experienced full sexual satisfaction. Allowing one's body to give in to all the wondrous sensations required a good bit of trust, and trust like pleasure was something she was only just beginning to experience.

But like reading, now that she'd had a sampling of it, she wanted to experience it fully. And he was more than happy to oblige.

Every night, when it was exceedingly late and the majority of the servants were already abed, she would make an appearance in his room, dressed in her nightclothes, holding a book pressed to her chest.

"I thought we would read together."

He'd grin with knowledge of the truth and anticipation of the journey. "If you like."

"In bed."

Humoring her with the pretense, he'd pull back the covers, plump up the pillows. They seldom got beyond a sentence or two before he was nibbling on her bare shoulder, her collarbone, her breasts. He took great pains never to cause her any discomfort, was never rough, was always gentle.

He strove not to allow their *secret* to detract from their enjoyment, but he couldn't help but resent a little that she gave no indication in front of others that she favored him . . . and she had made it perfectly clear to him that he wasn't to give any indication that he favored her. He still needed a wife who could give him an heir, and she still had her goal of acquiring a duke.

Understanding her driving need to be a duchess didn't make it any more palatable. She'd considered herself nothing, unworthy of even herself. Rank was an easy fix. If that was what she wanted, he wished for her to have it.

"Why so sad?" she asked.

They were stretched out on his bed, her back against a mound of pillows, he at her feet. He gave his gaze the freedom to travel up the naked length of her until it came to rest on her eyes. It seemed these days that they spent more time with their clothes off than on. "I was simply wondering if you'd still come to see me when our guests are here."

She puckered her brow. "I don't know. We'd have to be ever so careful, so discreet. I think the servants are beginning to suspect, but I don't want the duke to think, to know . . ." She rubbed her hand up and down his calf where it rested against the side of her chest.

"You're not married to him yet," Arch pointed out, rather practically he thought when he would have preferred to growl it. "It's not as though you're being unfaithful."

"What of Lady Alice? You don't want to give her the impression your attentions are elsewhere."

He ran his tongue along the sole of her foot. Her toes curled. He didn't care what Lady Alice or Lady Anne or Lady Jane thought. Still, he understood that when the aristocracy was about games needed to be played. "I suppose it would be best if we kept our distance."

"Pretend we're just taking a holiday from each other." Her voice sounded breathless and when next his gaze traveled the length of her, it was to find her eyes closed.

"I don't much like pretense."

She opened an eye. "You seemed to like it well enough last night when you were pretending to be a stallion."

He grinned, cockily, quite full of himself. "And you humored me by being my mare." He stopped grinning, considered her for a moment, remembering the excitement and something else. "You didn't much like me coming at you from behind, though, did you?"

She lifted a shoulder. "I don't recall complaining."

He scowled. "Be honest with me, Cammie. I never want us to do anything with which you're not comfortable or don't enjoy fully."

"I enjoyed it. Of course, I did. You always make sure I do. You're so comfortable with every aspect of two people coming together for pleasure. I want to be like that, I truly do. But it's all new to me, Arch. That's all. Sometimes I don't know what to expect. I'm not quite clear as to what you have in mind, but you never disappoint."

"If you didn't like something, you'd tell me, wouldn't you?"

"Of course."

"No more secrets *between* us." He knew he had to qualify the statement because there were secrets around them, secrets they kept from the servants and others: her lessons in reading, her lessons in bed. But he didn't want her having secrets that he didn't know about.

She nodded. "I promise."

"Good." He cupped her foot between his hands and kissed her arch, swirled his tongue over her sole, between her toes.

"That seems terribly wicked," she murmured with a sigh.

"Oh, my darling, I plan to get a good deal more wicked before we're finished tonight."

He carried through on his promise in ways that Camilla had never imagined, certainly had never envisioned. And with anyone except him, she thought she might have felt exceedingly uncomfortable. He kissed his way up one leg, licked his way up the other. The heat started at her toes and shimmered up to her hair, only to rush back down to her heels.

He kissed her hip, her navel, her hip again. Then he settled his face between her thighs, kissing, licking, stroking with his tongue. She released a tiny gasp, clutching the sheets. She pressed her feet against his sides. "Arch!"

He lifted his head. "You don't like it."

She nodded. "I do. I shouldn't but I do."

"Then relax and enjoy."

Relax? How could she relax when her body was humming with sensations. Each stroke of his tongue carried her higher. She became lost in the pleasure, spiraling ever higher. Oh, no secrets between them, but they would certainly have secrets. She'd never tell a soul about this.

She released a tiny screech and as the world shattered around her, he was plunging deeply inside her, carrying her farther over the edge even as he carried himself. Together their bodies jerked and clutched, and in that moment, she realized there would never be another person in the entire world that she trusted more than she did him.

Chapter 17

They arrived on a Wednesday in every sort of conveyance available. Fifty of London's elite.

They came with their personal valets, ladies' maids,
drivers, footmen, horses, gowns, luggage, laughter, gossip,
and expectations.

Arch didn't know how Camilla managed it all, but she
did so—flawlessly. She welcomed them, introducing them
to him with little hints to help him remember them.

"My lord, you remember Lady Priscilla Norwood, the
Earl of Blythemoore's daughter . . . you danced with her at
the Duke of Kimburton's ball."

Good God! How had she remembered all that, because
he certainly didn't. Still he responded as expected, "Of
course. A delight to have you visit us."

And so it went all morning. Greeting people he couldn't
remember. Watching in amazement as Camilla made them
feel welcome, acquainted them with the servant who
would see to their needs, had them shown to their rooms,
their luggage carted up. He didn't know how she kept
track of it all.

Lillian stood nearby with lists of things she was checking off, but Camilla never referred to them, and he knew that although she'd made great progress in her reading, she wasn't yet skilled enough that she'd be able to use the lists without stumbling over something.

So she didn't use the lists. Everything was from memory. Remarkable. Absolutely remarkable.

At one point he'd asked her if he could scrawl each person's name on a scrap of paper and pin it to his or her chest. She'd laughed at that.

"Relax, Archie. It's not that difficult to remember everyone's names. Pretend they're your students."

"With my students I had a seating chart. I could cheat to figure out who was who."

Her eyes had sparkled. "Splendid idea. I'll have Lillian give you the seating arrangements for the meals that I've worked out. You can use it to cheat."

There was a moment of panic when the Duchess of Lynchbrooke wasn't pleased with her accommodations and a lady of lesser rank had to be shuffled around until the older was satisfied. Arch thought he'd have no trouble remembering who the duchess was, and he made a mental note to avoid her as much as possible.

A moment of disappointment followed when a missive arrived from the Prince of Wales indicating that he'd be unable to attend and sending his regrets.

Then the Duke and Duchess of Harrington arrived, and Arch couldn't have been more pleased.

"Familiar faces at last," he said, as he greeted them.

They were a handsome couple, he with his black hair and gray eyes, she with striking violet eyes and hair spun from moonbeams.

"It seems you're to have quite a gathering," the duke said.

Rhys Rhodes had only recently come into the titles, following his older brother's death. Arch had felt an immediate kinship with the man because, like him, he'd not expected to be titled.

"It's been utter madness," Arch confessed. "I don't know how the aristocracy does it."

The duchess smiled with pure joy. "This is my first country party. I'm overjoyed to be here."

Her voice was soft and carried a musical drawl. She'd arrived from Texas only a few months before, and, unlike him, was enamored with the etiquette and protocol. Still, she was no snob, and he enjoyed Lydia's company very much.

"I believe Camilla has a good many activities arranged." He leaned near and lowered his voice. "At least I'm hoping so as I haven't a clue how to talk with all these people. I shall no doubt bumble it all."

She squeezed his arm reassuringly. "If I can manage, you'll do fine."

"Perhaps you could lend him your books," Rhys said. Then he looked at Arch. "She has an abundance of books on etiquette. One she wrote herself. I've told her she should see about getting it published."

"I'd be the first to purchase a copy," Arch said.

"Camilla seems in her element," Rhys said, looking over to where she was greeting some other recent arrivals.

"She astounds me with all she manages," Arch confessed. "I couldn't do it."

"I have no desire to do it," Rhys said.

"I, on the other hand, plan to take notes," Lydia said, "so I'll know what to do when we entertain at Harrington."

Smiling with confidence, Camilla strolled over. "Well, I do believe everyone is here and situated. We need to change for luncheon, my dear," she said to Lydia. "Do let me know if there is anything you need advice on."

Her voice held sincerity, which Arch thought Lydia most likely appreciated. For much of the Season, the ladies had

been at odds with each other, both vying for attention from
the duke. Lydia had won out, and he thought Camilla was being a rather good sport about it now. He wasn't quite certain
why the Duke of Harrington hadn't been concerned about acquiring an heir when he'd initially become betrothed to
Camilla, but it was no longer important. What mattered was
that the duke and his wife were madly in love, and it was apparent with each gaze they gave each other.

A few more pleasantries were exchanged before Camilla
offered to help Lydia select the proper attire for her first
country luncheon. Rhys stared after them as they headed
for the stairs and once they were out of sight, he turned to
Arch. "What have you done to the countess?"

"I beg your pardon?"

Rhys angled his head thoughtfully. "Camilla has always
possessed a . . . a selfishness, a brittleness. She's never, not
as long as I've known her, been this pleasant."

Arch smiled with satisfaction. "All I can say, then, Your
Grace, is that you never really knew her."

As the first day melded into the second, Arch was fairly
certain that the same couldn't be said of the Duke of Kingsbridge. He was indeed coming to know Camilla. He
seemed to have her undying devotion. He wasn't certain
how she managed always to sit near the duke during meals.
He was certain *Debrett's* wouldn't have put them together.
They took strolls through the gardens, and when Arch
would ask a lady to go on a walk with him so he could follow closely behind, he would hear Camilla's joyful laughter
echoing around him.

Games of badminton and croquet provided entertainment in the afternoons. Luncheons and dinners were ex-
travagantly prepared meals. The guests' stay would end
with a grand ball Friday evening, with everyone departing
Saturday. It couldn't come soon enough as far as he was
concerned.

No time for a hunt this go-round, for which he was immensely grateful.

The Duke of Kingsbridge and his daughter came down for breakfast shortly after Camilla and Archie had sat at the table. Their other guests had yet to appear, which wasn't uncommon. Camilla would order that the food remain on the side table for many hours, so everyone could awaken at their leisure.

"I say, Sachse, have you a yacht?" Kingsbridge asked.

Archie cast a quick glance at Camilla before saying, "Not that I know of, no."

"A pity, a pity. They're a good deal of fun."

"But extremely expensive to keep, Papa," Lady Alice said.

Camilla didn't remember Lady Alice looking quite so young.

"Too true, my dear, too true. Still, if you go to Cowes, let me know. I'll lend you my yacht."

"That's very kind of you, Your Grace," Camilla said.

Winking at her, he lifted his glass, and she was reminded of the last time that a gentleman had winked at her across the table. She peered over at Archie and could tell from his half smile that he was remembering as well. It was a special moment, shared by only the two of them, and she thought it would be marvelous to have shared memories that were special with someone else that could be quietly remembered as this one was.

"Have you met the Prince of Wales, Sachse?" Kingsbridge asked.

"No, I haven't," Archie said.

"A shame that. He's a fine yachtsman. Has a beautiful ship."

"We always go to Cowes after the Season," Lady Alice explained. "Papa tends to go on and on about it until he gets it out of his blood."

"I've never been to the seaside," Archie said.

Lady Alice smiled sweetly. "You must go sometime. I love the seaside."

Camilla didn't like thinking that this girl might acquaint Archie with the seaside as she'd acquainted him with London. That Lady Alice would see the sparkle in his eyes as he experienced new things, discovered the wonders of the sea.

"I'm not sure how well I would fare near the sea," Archie said. "I don't swim."

"Neither do I," Lady Alice said, laughing lightly. "But it's still enjoyable to walk along the shore. Have you gone to the seaside, Lady Sachse?"

"No, I always thought the sand would be a bit of a nuisance."

"You're quite right, my girl, it could be." The duke leaned back and patted his stomach. "Marvelous food, marvelous."

He was trim for a man of fifty, but not nearly as trim as Archie. She'd always considered taking a man to her bed as something to be endured. Having experienced it now as something to be enjoyed, she wondered how she would ever *endure* it again. Although with the duke possibly there would be pleasure as well. After all, his wife had loved him.

"I thought we might go for a ride in the carriage this afternoon," Camilla offered. "It's a nice day. We could use the brougham."

"Capital idea," the duke said.

"I'd rather go riding. Have you horses?" Lady Alice asked.

Before Camilla could comment, Archie said, "Yes, we do. And I'd be more than happy to join you."

Camilla joined Archie at the stables, where he was waiting for the carriage to be readied as well as two riding horses.

"I didn't know you rode," she said.

"I was raised in the country. Of course I ride," he said, without looking at her.

"I would have preferred for us all to go in the carriage."

"So I could continue to have my shortcomings announced to the world?"

"Whatever are you talking about?"

"Let's see . . . I've never met the Prince of Wales. I've never been to the seaside. I don't own a yacht. No telling what else will be discovered during a ride in the brougham."

"The duke was only making conversation."

"No, my lady, he was trying to impress you." He shifted his gaze over to her, and she was taken off guard by the hardness in his eyes. "And he was doing a damned fine job of it."

"I was hardly impressed. I've dined with the Prince and Princess of Wales. And I mentioned that I wasn't fond of the sea."

He tugged on his gloves, and she thought he did it only to give himself something to concentrate on, because they looked fine as they were.

"I'm not comparing him to you," she said softly.

"Because there is no comparison to be made. He is a duke. I am but an earl. And rank is what you value."

She turned away so he wouldn't see the truth in her eyes. Before she'd come truly to know him, before she'd learned to read, she'd valued rank above all else . . . but now? Now she wasn't so certain . . . but it hardly mattered.

She forced herself to smile. "Here come our guests. So be charming, Archie. She is a lovely lady."

"I shall charm her until there is no more charming to be done."

He began to walk past her, and she reached out, grabbing his arm and stopping him. "Simply be yourself, Archie. That is all you need for her to fall madly in love with you."

She thought she saw pain cross his features. "This is not

the way that I would have gone about finding a wife." He leaned toward her, lowering his voice until she almost couldn't hear him. "You would have known that had you been in a position to read my letter."

He straightened and smiled. "Lady Alice, we have the horses ready. I thought we'd follow along behind the brougham, so your father need not doubt my intentions."

"That's a capital idea, Sachse," the duke said, chuckling. "You keep an eye on me, while I keep one on you."

Camilla was beginning to think that her capital idea wasn't so capital after all. She'd never had a jealous lover. She'd never had a lover at all. Never had anyone jealous. To have both was exhilarating and bothersome. She didn't want to hurt Archie's feelings, but the purpose in having guests was so they could determine possibilities.

She allowed the footman to help her into the brougham. The duke climbed in and sat opposite her. She glanced over and saw that Lady Alice was already mounted. Smiling and confident.

"Come, Lord Sachse, I'll race you to the main road." With a laugh, she set her horse galloping, Archie quickly in pursuit.

"Ah, to be young, eh?" the duke said. "Driver, let's not let them get too far ahead, shall we?"

With a lurch, the carriage started forward. Camilla stared in the distance, but the riders were already becoming mere shadows.

"What if she won't have him?" the duke asked.

Camilla jerked her attention to Kingsbridge. "Pardon?"

"What if my Alice has no interest in your earl?"

Her earl. Yes, he was her earl, but she couldn't claim him as such. "Then your daughter is a fool."

And she was beginning to wonder if perhaps she was as well.

Chapter 18

⌒◝◝◞◜◜⌒

Arch hated it. Hated the way the young available ladies were being put on show this evening following dinner.

Some played the piano. Some recited poetry with exaggerated drama.

Presently Lady Alice was singing, while her father stood behind the chair in which Camilla sat, his hands resting on her shoulders as though to stake his claim and say, *She is mine.*

Arch hated that even more.

When the song came to an end, everyone applauded. Camilla most enthusiastically. "That was marvelous, Lady Alice. You have the voice of a nightingale." Camilla looked over at Arch, an expression in her eyes that seemed to say: What do you think? Do you agree? The voice of a nightingale? Is she the one? Will she do?

Had singing been one of his requirements?

He looked away because he didn't want to provide an answer, didn't want to see the duke bending down to whisper something in Camilla's ear. But even without looking, he could hear her laughter. Every woman in this room could be laughing hysterically, and still he would be able to home in on hers. He knew its sound by heart. The way it tinkled softly, then deepened as her joy increased.

He'd enjoyed his morning ride with Lady Alice the way one enjoyed a pleasant cup of tea in the afternoon. A respite from the grind of responsibilities, but not anticipated before it was placed before him, nor missed once taken away. His assessment seemed cruel. She was a delightful woman, pleasant enough . . . but there was nothing about her that intrigued him, that made him want to dig more deeply, discover all the aspects to her.

He was aware of movements, murmurings. He turned his attention back to the gathering.

Beside him the Duke of Harrington said quietly, "People are going for a nightly stroll before bed. Kingsbridge and Camilla have already gone out to lead the way."

"I suppose I shall be expected to select a lady to accompany me."

"I will offer you my wife, if you like."

He breathed a sigh of relief. "Her company would be more than welcome."

He'd not noticed that Lydia was standing beside the duke. He extended his arm toward her, and she took her place beside him.

It wasn't until they were outside in the lit gardens that she said, "I am amazed by all that must be done to keep people entertained."

"You'll do a splendid job once you decide to have company."

"Kingsbridge seems rather taken with Lady Sachse."

"Indeed he does."

"As do you."

"But she is not for me, Duchess."

"Who is?"

"I don't know."

And that was the truth of it. No one stirred him as Camilla did. Even the lovely lady walking beside him hadn't drawn as much interest from him. And he couldn't deny that she was a delight. Although he also suspected that she didn't find him as intriguing as she found Harrington.

"Have you considered courting an American lady?" she asked.

"I need someone well versed in the ways of the aristocracy, as it is too foreign to me. I would forever be putting a step wrong without a lady beside me to keep my feet on the right path."

"Lady Sachse has always struck me as being rather ambitious."

"She has the drive and determination to be so."

"You admire her?"

"Very much so. There are aspects to her that are contradictory, and yet they somehow belong to her in a way that is refreshing." He chuckled. "I am speaking in circles that make no sense. I will be glad when our company departs." He patted her arm. "Present company excluded."

"I've not known you long, but I do think you'll make some woman very happy."

Ah, yes, he thought he could manage that. The question was: Would she do the same for him?

As Frannie guided the brush through her hair time and again, Camilla studied her reflection in the mirror and tried to determine exactly what was different about her, because surely something had to have changed on the outside for her to have gained the attention of the Duke of Kingsbridge. She thought that perhaps she looked a bit younger—no doubt from the skating she and Archie did. Her mouth didn't seem as hard, nor did her eyes.

"Is something amiss, my lady?" Frannie asked.

"Do I seem different to you?"

"You seem . . . happier."

"Happier? Yes, I suppose I am."

She had to credit Archie with a good deal of that happiness. He took her mind off her struggles, made learning fun. She enjoyed spending time with him. What a shame he wasn't a duke. What a shame she was barren.

The Duke of Kingsbridge was a nice gentleman, and she enjoyed spending time in his company. He made her smile, on occasion he'd even made her laugh a time or two. But she knew he'd never make her heart flutter or her skin tingle or her soul sing.

What a lot of romantic rubbish. She'd definitely spent too much time with Archie. He had her believing in impossibilities.

As though summoned by her thoughts of him, he was suddenly standing in her room. She'd not heard the door open, but apparently Frannie had because she'd ceased brushing and was staring at Archie as though he were a demon raised out of hell.

Considering the uncustomary way his features were arranged in harsh lines, Camilla could hardly blame Frannie for her surprise.

"Leave us," he ordered, in a voice that would brook no arguments.

Frannie hurried from the room, and Archie closed the door in her wake. Camilla rose. "Archie—"

Before she could properly chastise him for barging into her bedchamber unannounced and with a servant still present, he'd closed the distance between them, taken her into his arms, and planted his mouth against hers. He displayed none of his usual tenderness, but seemed to be a man in desperation of possessing her.

Beneath her fingers, his body was tense with need. A time existed when she would have been terrified, but now all she wanted was the fulfillment that he could provide. She'd spent the majority of her day flirting with another man while Archie had never been far from her mind. She'd seen him walking with another woman and been sorely tempted to scratch out her eyes.

It hurt, it hurt, it hurt to know that he'd so easily found interest in another. And yet here he was, his mouth hot against hers, his hands running over her body as though he'd forgotten what every dip and curve felt like and was anxious to renew the acquaintance.

She heard material rip and didn't care. Time for caring would come later. All she wanted was his flesh against hers. He lifted her into his arms, crossed the room, and unceremoniously dumped her onto the bed.

So unlike his usual behavior. And when she looked into his face, she did know a moment's hesitation, a spark of fear. She'd never seen such a feral expression on his handsome countenance. His eyes were heated, his breathing harsh, his mouth set in the firm line of a warrior. He tore off his clothes as though they were the enemy intent on strangling him.

Then he blanketed her body with his and buried himself within her with a long, sure thrust that had her crying out—not because she wasn't ready, but because she'd wanted him inside her as desperately as he'd wanted to be there. He pumped hard, fast, and furious. She kept pace, digging her fingers into his buttocks, holding him tightly as the blood roared through her as she knew it had to be roaring through him.

It was madness, insanity, and yet she was powerless not to give in to this animalistic mating that was so uncharacteristic of what she'd come to expect from him. And yet, she found it exciting, when she thought she should have found it frightening.

But this was Archie, her dear, dear Archie, who would never harm her, never think less of her no matter what secrets she shared.

The pleasure mounted more quickly and with more intensity than she'd ever experienced. They cried out in unison, arching, gasping, shuddering, clinging.

She fought back the tears as she lay beneath him with

tiny tremors cascading through her, while the weight of his body pressed down on her, his harsh breathing filled her ear, his face nestled at the curve of her neck.

"Satisfied?" she asked.

"No," he growled, and came off her as though he'd been shot from a cannon.

Drawing a blanket over her, she watched as he prowled beside the bed, repeatedly dragging his hands through his hair, his breathing still harsh, his eyes feral.

"Archie, whatever is wrong?"

He came to an abrupt halt and glared at her. "I don't like seeing you with Kingsbridge."

"So you thought you could come into my bedchamber and possess me like some barbarian?"

He flinched. "Did I hurt you?"

His voice was rough-edged, and she thought nothing he ever did would hurt her as much as she knew she would have to hurt him. Slowly she shook her head. "No."

He wrapped a hand around the bedpost and leaned against it as though he needed the support to keep himself upright. "I love you, Camilla. You cannot imagine how I feel when I see you laughing with another man, looking at him as though he could hand you the world."

"I like the Duke of Kingsbridge."

"So I could see. I felt as though a sword had been run through my heart."

Tears stung her eyes. She rose up onto her knees. "I love you, Archie."

"Then marry me."

The heartfelt plea was nearly her undoing, but she forced herself to remain steadfast and strong for both of them. "I can't give you an heir."

He sat on the edge of the bed and tenderly cradled her face with his palm. "Then I won't have an heir."

"So you'll shove the responsibility that comes with your title onto Winston?"

"I never asked for this damned title. Why must I sacrifice my happiness for something I never wanted?"

"Because it has fallen to you—whether you want it or not." She brushed his hair off his brow. "I don't believe you are a man who would turn aside from his duties."

With a deep sigh, he lay down beside her and drew her against his side, holding her in place while his hand idly stroked her arm. "I would if you would let me."

"No you wouldn't."

"What if you weren't barren?" he asked. "Would you give up your duke for an earl?"

"No," she said quietly, and felt the disappointment travel through his body. She lifted herself slightly so she could gaze into his eyes. "I would give him up for you."

With a low growl, he slammed his eyes closed and held her more tightly. "Is there any chance that you're not?"

"I don't see how there could be. The old Sachse had a son. He frequented my bed often and never got me with child."

"But he got the first countess pregnant only once. Perhaps something happened to his seed."

She hesitated but forced herself to admit, "I don't think so. Besides, as much as you and I have been together, I would think that if the possibility existed, I would be with child now."

"So all we will ever have is this? Sneaking into your room in the dead of night—"

"You hardly sneaked tonight."

"I was in torment, seeing you with Kingsbridge."

"You seem to get along well with his daughter."

"I was simply being a good host."

"She's rather pretty and nice. She would make a good wife."

"The last thing I want is to marry into the same family as you, so our paths would cross constantly. It would be pure torture."

"It would give us an opportunity to be together. I know some ladies of the aristocracy who openly travel with their lovers, while their husbands do the same. I consider them very enlightened and modern couples."

The silence eased between them, and she wondered if he was pondering the possibilities that might exist if he were married to the daughter of her husband.

"I won't be unfaithful to my wife, Camilla," he finally said quietly.

Disappointment rammed into her, even as gladness swept through her. She'd known he'd feel that way. She rose up and looked down into his eyes. "Then, yes, all we'll ever have is this time before one of us marries."

"Then we'd best make the most of it, hadn't we?"

And he proceeded to do exactly that.

Chapter 19

"**F**ather seems rather enamored of Lady Sachse." Forcing his attention away from where Camilla sat on a bench beside the Duke of Kingsbridge, who was reading from a book of poetry he'd borrowed from the library earlier, Arch smiled at Lady Alice. "I can hardly blame him."

She tapped the croquet ball lightly and looked over her shoulder at him. "Because you are equally intrigued with her?"

"Are my affections so apparent?"

She nodded. She was a lovely girl, and he couldn't for the life of him determine why he wasn't more interested in her. "I assure you that Lady Sachse has no interest in me."

"She may have no interest in marrying you, but I assure you that she has an interest in you."

"Well, that interest will cease once she is secure in another man's keeping, so you need have no fear that I would infringe upon your father's territory should his interest in spending time with Lady Sachse go beyond the reading of poetry."

"I know it's not polite to speak ill of the dead, but my father didn't much care for the old Sachse."

"I don't think many thought much of the old earl."

"Do you like being earl?"

"Not particularly. Although it does have the advantage of bringing you into my life."

He despised the words the moment they were uttered. They sounded so incredibly insincere. Lady Alice's laughter echoed around him, like tinkling bells rung at Christmas.

"You're catching on to the flirtatious ways of the aristocracy," she said, warmth in her voice and her smile.

"You'd best take care not to encourage me overmuch. I thought my sentiment sounded rather silly."

"Because you're a man. I daresay any lady would be flattered with your attentions."

"You are kind to think so."

"Perhaps it is none of my affair, but why is Lady Sachse not more interested in you?"

"Because I need an heir, and she believes herself to be barren."

Lady Alice blushed, and Arch swore beneath his breath. She was all of nineteen, hardly knowledgeable in the ways of the world. She probably thought babies were found in cabbage patches. "My apologies—"

"Oh, no." She held up a hand. "I am well aware of the importance of an heir. Father has already seen to that duty. I think it a shame that it is considered as such, but that is the way of things, is it not?"

"I seek more than that from a wife."

"Then your wife will be most fortunate."

She peered up at him, and he almost could convince himself that he saw hope within her eyes.

He held up his mallet. "I have no skill with this game. Perhaps you would find a walk through the gardens more to your liking."

Her smile blossomed. "I would indeed."

And perhaps if they walked far enough, he could forget that Camilla existed.

Camilla watched as Archie and Lady Alice walked arm in arm toward the elaborate water gardens that her husband had taken a fancy to and had his gardeners build. There were ponds stocked with large fish with golden scales that made them quite visible. At places, water cascaded over stones, imitating small waterfalls. The greenery was lush, the vegetation thick, and she could well imagine that a gentleman might manage to sneak a kiss or two without being spotted.

"You've lost interest in the poetry, my lady."

She snapped her attention back to the duke. "Oh, no, Your Grace. I was simply admiring"—she swallowed hard to force the words out—"how splendid a couple your daughter and Lord Sachse appeared to be."

"I was just noticing that myself. As they are both young, perhaps we should take a stroll ourselves."

She'd never felt as old as she did at that moment. "Lord Sachse would never take advantage of a guest."

"What young men intend and what happens are not always the same. Come." He stood and extended a hand. "Let's make sure they're not up to a bit of tomfoolery."

She could hardly refuse when the request came from a duke. At least that was the reasoning she used to convince herself that her actions weren't mitigated by a deep desire to make certain that Archie wasn't kissing the lovely Lady Alice.

She placed her hand on his arm and allowed him to escort her toward the water gardens. While she thought she'd been an exemplary hostess, giving attention to everyone, she also thought it was quite evident with whom her interests truly lay. She and the duke had managed to spend quite a bit of time together.

And she was fairly certain that when he returned to his

estate, he would be leaving behind the woman who was to become his wife.

She'd outdone herself.

Arch couldn't help but be amazed. Camilla had somehow managed to get a full orchestra there. The mirrored ballroom was filled with flowers. Chandeliers sparkled. Everyone was dressed as elaborately as though they were in London.

He wanted to dance with her, of course, and she'd reserved a place for him on her dance card near the end of the evening. It was torment to wait, torment to watch her swirl around the dance floor with partner after partner.

There was no doubt that tonight was her night to shine. Compliments were lavishly given, and he had to admit they were deserved. Every one of them.

Every guest had nothing but praise to offer, each one had enjoyed himself or herself. Every meal had been perfect, every entertainment enjoyable.

He was fairly certain that any disappointment she would have felt because he didn't believe he could embrace any woman presented to him as a potential wife would be overshadowed by her joy that she might have effectively snagged the attention of Kingsbridge.

He wanted her to be happy, he truly did. But damn it all, he wanted her happiness to be with him.

He stood off to the side, watching her dance with Harrington. She looked lovely beyond compare in a ball gown of the palest green. It shimmered beneath the chandeliers.

"Sachse."

He turned to Kingsbridge. "Duke."

"I was wondering if I might have a word with you . . . in private."

"In another few dances, I will partner with Camilla. I would so hate to miss that dance." He knew he shouldn't have said it, knew he should have pretended that none of this mattered.

"It won't take us long, and what I have to say concerns her."

"Will my library suffice?"

"Very nicely . . . if it has a liquor cabinet in it."

As a matter of fact it did, and once they were safely ensconced inside with the door closed, Arch poured them each a generous glass of bourbon. After handing Kingsbridge his glass, Arch moved to stand beside the fireplace. He knew he was being an ungracious host but had a feeling he wasn't going to welcome what it was that Kingsbridge wished to discuss.

Kingsbridge cleared his throat several times. Took a sip. Cleared it again, and Arch realized the man was nervous. He took pity on him.

"Would you care to sit, Your Grace?"

"Yes, I would." He sat in one chair near the fireplace, and Arch sat in the other.

The duke released a long sigh. "I feel too old for this. Still it must be done. You strike me as an intelligent man, Sachse, so I daresay, it's not missed your notice that my attention has been on Lady Sachse since we arrived."

"I had indeed noticed, Your Grace."

"Splendid. Then it should come as no surprise to you that I wish to marry her."

No surprise at all. Still Arch felt as though the duke had picked up a poker, stuck it in the fire until it burned red-hot, and thrust it through Arch's heart. He got up and returned to the place he'd originally taken beside the fireplace and stared at the flames rather than the duke because he was no good at the games the aristocrats played, and he knew he couldn't hide his true feelings on the matter. For Camilla's sake he didn't want the duke to know what they were.

"Have you asked her?" he asked quietly.

"Indeed I did. This afternoon in the garden. She's quite agreeable to the idea. As you are the closest thing she has to a male relation, I thought I should seek your permission as well."

He turned to face the duke because this he could say in all honesty. "If marriage to you is what she wants, then you have my permission and my blessings."

The duke came to his feet, suddenly looking much younger. "Splendid. Yes, indeed. Splendid. You'd think a man of my age and standing wouldn't be so nervous about so simple a matter."

"I appreciate that you were. It lets me know that you care for her. My predecessor left nothing to her. She was too young and naive when she married him and had no one to look after her welfare. I will insist that we come to terms on an agreeable settlement, so she'll have no reason to regret her marriage to you."

"I'll notify my solicitors in London to immediately get together with yours. I daresay, it shan't take much work as I, too, wish to see that she is provided for. I'm not as young as I once was, and I wouldn't want her left with nothing."

"Then we're in agreement that her welfare and happiness comes first."

"Indeed we are."

Arch lifted his glass in a salute. "Then I wish you the best."

Dressed only in her nightclothes, Camilla walked into the library, relief mingled with annoyance going through her at the sight of Archie sprawled in a chair before the fireplace. She didn't know when he left the ballroom, but he hadn't been there for her dance. She'd been looking forward to it so much. He'd not been around when the guests had been drifting back to their rooms.

But Kingsbridge had been. He'd danced with her over

and over, even though it wasn't proper, and he'd been in the jolliest of moods.

"There you are. I've been looking all over for you."

He lifted his gaze and squinted as though he couldn't quite make out who she was. "Have you?"

His words were slurred, a glass dangling from his hand threatening to spill the last drops of its contents onto the rug. She snatched it away and set it on a nearby table.

"You're foxed."

"Quite so. An inordinate amount of drink dulls the pain." He shook his head. "Or at least it's supposed to. It's not working. Pour me some more, will you, darling?"

Her heart squeezed at the endearment. She knelt before him. "I thought you would come see me tonight. In my bed-chamber. I've been waiting."

Reaching out, he tiptoed his fingers around her face. "Kingsbridge and I had a duke to earl talk earlier. Seems he wishes to make you his wife. He asked for my blessing."

"Did you give it?"

"How could I not when I want nothing more than to see you happy?"

Tears stung her eyes, and her chest ached as she rested her head on his knees. This moment should have been the happiest of her life, but as he threaded his fingers through her hair, she thought she'd never known such misery. What must it have cost him to bless her union with another man?

She lifted her face to his, wishing she hadn't, wishing she couldn't see the tears in his eyes. "I will be happy with him," she assured him.

He gave her a sad smile as he touched the corner of her mouth, where her own tears pooled. "He seems to be a good man. I could have chosen no better for you."

Unless it was himself, and that was impossible. When the duke had asked her in the garden if she would marry him, she'd not hesitated to give a resounding yes, not because she truly wanted to marry the duke, but because she had to take measures to ensure that she was no longer available to Archie. He had to take a wife. He had to have an heir.

They were both becoming too comfortable with the arrangement. They would forever find excuses to put off the inevitable. He continually found fault with every woman, and she was beginning to suspect it was because he held out hope that by some miracle his seed would indeed take root within her. But she knew that he'd poured enough into her that if it hadn't taken root by now, it never would.

She had no hope of ever giving him a child, much less an heir. Her womb was as barren as her heart had once been. He'd filled her heart, and his love had taken root there. For her, that was a miracle, that in spite of all her imperfections and flaws, he'd still come to love her.

"Give me one more night, Archie."

"One more," he whispered, "but not tonight. I've almost drunk myself into oblivion. I want a last night with you that I will remember."

She laid her cheek on his lap, turned her head to stare into the fire. His hand came to rest on her hair. She thought of all the stories he'd read to her. So few had happy endings . . . most were bittersweet or sad.

But at least with him, she'd had happiness. For a short while, but it was enough to carry her through the remainder of her life.

Once all their guests had taken their leave that morning, Archie had advised Camilla to dress as though they were going to a ball put on by royalty. And she'd spent most of the late afternoon doing exactly that. She based each selection on what she thought he would find most pleasing. She'd never before dedicated every aspect of her appearance to a man's pleasure, yet she found herself doing exactly that.

She selected an ivory gown with a long, flowing train trimmed with tiny red roses. The square neck revealed the barest hint of cleavage, to entice him, and she placed a drop of perfume between her breasts. Her coiffure was topped with a heron's feather aigrette and one red rose. She wore dainty earrings and a simple necklace. She considered not wearing gloves, but since she didn't know exactly what he had in mind, she couldn't dismiss the possibility that he was in fact taking her to a ball.

Still she'd hoped for a special evening that included only the two of them. A final night together, as he'd said, to remember.

Although she'd begun to wonder if she'd ever be ready. Frannie had been unusually clumsy this evening, having to start over on her hair several times until she'd finally managed to get it to stay up. Camilla had almost lost patience, but she'd bitten back unkind remarks because she'd not wanted anything to ruin the evening, and usually Frannie was so adept at getting her ready. She hoped Frannie was not about to take ill.

"You look so lovely, my lady," Frannie said, as she adjusted the train.

"Thank you, Frannie."

"The earl will be most pleased."

She couldn't very well admit that she hoped so. Whatever would her lady's maid think of her then, when word had undoubtedly already spread that she was to marry a duke. But still she did hope that the earl would be pleased.

As she left her room, she couldn't quite believe how much she was looking forward to the evening. She and Arch had done numerous things together, but it had never been with this expectation: that what they were doing was for each other, and each other alone.

She walked down the grand, marble, sweeping staircase, more pleased than she could show that he was waiting for her. Apparently, he, too, had gone to great pains to dress as though he was going to attend a royal ball. He was wearing a black, swallow-tailed coat over a dark burgundy waistcoat and white shirt. His silver-colored cravat set it all off perfectly. As he stood there smiling at her, she knew beyond any doubt that he was the most handsome she'd ever known, the most regal earl. At that moment, she thought he could pass for a king.

As she neared, he held his gloved hand out to her, and she placed hers within his.

"You're so beautiful," he said quietly. "And for tonight you will be mine."

"Where are we going?" she asked, surprised to find that she sounded so breathless. But he had that power. To steal her breath and just as quickly to return it.

He carried her hand to his lips, and even through the glove, she could feel the warmth of his kiss against her fingers as he held her gaze, and promised, "Not far."

He wrapped his arm around hers, and she felt as though she were a vine, clinging for support.

"Will it go to your head if I tell you that you're handsome?" she asked.

His grin somehow deepened, making him better-looking than she thought possible. "Then we're a matched couple."

Not so matched, she thought wildly, for tonight was only pretense. Fundamentally, they each lacked what the other needed, but she didn't want to reflect on that, not now, not this moment, not with him when he was striving so hard to give her something special because she couldn't give him forever.

He escorted her down the long length of the wide hallway. A footman standing at attention outside the ballroom opened the door.

She glanced at Archie. "The ballroom?"

"I told you to dress as though you were going to a ball." He led her inside and it was as she'd never seen it. Lit only with candles, strategically placed to throw light and shadows around the room, to create an intimacy in a place that had been designed to appear expansive. Even the mirrored walls seemed to have shrunk down to nothing.

Then suddenly music began to play, and she squinted into the shadows. "Is that an orchestra?"

"Yes, I want to dance with you tonight the way I've never been able to dance with you before: as though I adore you. I want no barriers tonight, no false appearances, no pretenses that you aren't the woman I want in my arms."

"Arch, we can't carry on blatantly in here. Whatever will the servants think?"

"They're not stupid, Camilla. I suspect they already know. Tonight is ours and ours alone."

He led her to a table. Small, round. From the garden, she suspected, although she couldn't be certain as it was covered with a white cloth. Orchid blossoms adorned the center, simply lying there without a vase, no stems, and in the middle sat a flickering candle. A footman pulled out a chair, and she sat. Then Arch sat beside her. Not across the long length of a table or even a short distance away. But right beside her, so he could hold her hand, and she wondered how in the world he expected her to eat.

As though reading her mind, he released her hand and began to tug off his gloves. "Shall we prepare to eat?"

She removed her gloves and set them on the edge of the table.

"I have an idea," he said, leaning toward her. "Let's be bold tonight and not put our gloves back on. Let's dance with bare hands."

Knowing how warm his hands could be, she found herself nodding at his scandalous notion. Who was to see? Who was to know? It would be their secret.

The food and wine were served as they'd been for the dinners they'd had when their guests were here.

"How did you arrange all this?" she asked, absolutely amazed.

"Lillian helped me. She's picked up a few of your tricks."

"I can't believe you managed to keep all of this a secret. I didn't even see the orchestra arrive."

"Frannie helped there," he said with a grin.

"Frannie? Whatever did she . . ." Her voice trailed off as she recalled all the difficulty her maid had preparing her hair. She narrowed her eyes. "How did she help you?"

"I told her to keep you occupied for three hours while I arranged things."

"She kept messing up my hair."

His grin shifted into something of promise. "Which I intend to do as well a bit later."

And she could hardly wait, but wait she would, although the anticipation was more than she could bear. It was incredible really, to have already spent so many nights in his arms and so look forward to spending another. She didn't want to remember that it would be the last, but she did want to remember it for always.

They hardly spoke as they ate, neither did they rush. They simply watched one another, sipping their wine, eating their pheasant. She remembered how he'd told her that he wanted a woman with whom he could be comfortable with silence. She hadn't realized then what he'd been referring to. But this was it, where nothing needed to be said in order for all to be understood.

When the last of the meal had been served and dishes carried away, he picked up an orchid blossom, leaned toward her, and tucked it into her bodice, between her breasts, a bit of silliness that made her laugh, made him smile. Then he stood and helped her to her feet.

"May I have the honor of this dance?" he asked.

"The honor is mine, my lord, to be asked by you."

He led her onto the shadowy floor. The orchestra had

been playing softly while they were dining, and now the tune shifted into a waltz, and she realized that he'd left nothing to chance tonight. Everything was magic. A few months ago, he'd never even been to London, and now he had the ability to orchestrate the most romantic night of her life.

Her bare hand rested in his, and she wondered why people had ever decided that gloves were needed. The warmth of his touch was intoxicating. They danced more closely than was proper—had they been in a room filled with guests. But as it was only the two of them, they danced as they wanted.

Grandly, he swept her over the ballroom without worry of bumping into anyone else. This room, this night, this waltz was theirs and theirs alone.

He didn't carry her as far with the next dance, and the one that followed found them doing little more than standing within the candlelight, gazing into each other's eyes. Then he drew her close, dipped his head, and kissed her, a kiss filled with promise, a kiss that would lead to farewell.

She didn't want it to end with good-bye, but she shoved the thought aside because they would never again have a night like this, and she didn't want it marred with sadness. It had no choice except to end as it would . . . but until it did end, she was his, and he was hers.

He slipped an arm beneath her knees and lifted her, cradling her against his chest. The music continued to play, the lonely strains following them across the ballroom as though to entice them into staying, but his kiss had effectively enticed her into wanting to leave.

The footman opened the door, and Arch carried her through. There would be no secrets in this household now, she thought, as he strode down the hallway and up the stairs that led into his wing of the house. And she no longer cared. Let the servants know. Let all of England know.

Tonight she was where she wanted to be. That she couldn't remain there was a worry for another day.

A footman opened the door to Arch's bedchamber and closed it once they'd entered. Flickering candles, the scent of orchids, and a turned-down bed greeted her. Her heart tightened as she realized he'd gone to such great lengths, down to the tiniest detail.

All for her. All for her. She'd always enjoyed being waited on, but this was too much, too much from him, and not enough from her. This was *their* last night. A night for *them both* to remember. She'd not have him looking back on it and seeing all he'd given to her and not realizing she'd given to him as well.

He set her feet on the floor, and still there was nothing said between them, nothing needed. They undressed each other, him standing naked and proud before her long before her clothes were all removed. She had more layers, more items. But eventually all the clothes were gone and there was nothing between them. And he'd done as he'd promised, released her hair until it had tumbled into a mess around her.

She came into his arms as though she alone belonged there, planted her mouth against his, and initiated the kiss before he had a chance. She heard a muffled growl, and his chest vibrated against her breasts. She scraped her fingers along his scalp, up into his hair, and his arms tightened around her.

He angled his mouth for a better fit and began walking her backward toward the bed. But the bed wasn't yet where she wanted to be. She offered resistance, and he stopped. She nipped his chin.

"What are you doing?" he asked.

"I have plans of my own for the night," she said in a sultry voice that almost didn't sound like her.

She trailed her mouth along his throat, bringing her hands down to his shoulders. He skimmed his fingers over her back.

"What plans?"

"Something I don't think you'd ever suggest for fear I'd not enjoy it." She slid down his body until she was kneeling before him. She glanced up at him, could see the need, the desire, the fire burning in his eyes.

She pressed her lips against the moistness. He spasmed and thrust his hands into her hair, his fingers pushing against her scalp.

"I love you," she whispered.

Arch heard the words pounding in his blood, watched as with the sweetest smile, she pleasured him. He dropped his head back as his body tensed, and sensations of gratification speared him. He'd planned every moment of this night, but he'd not planned for this. He didn't know if it was her words or her actions that drove him to his knees, but suddenly he was there, taking her into his arms, struggling to get to his feet, and getting her into the bed.

He slashed his mouth across hers. It was torment not to be inside her. He slid his hand between their bodies, between her thighs, only to discover that she was indeed ready for him: hot, moist, and willing. He pushed inside her and she raised her hips, allowing him to go deeper.

It was always like this. The rhythm they set required no instruction. It simply . . . *was*. Sliding, stroking, kissing. He could see her face in the candlelight, and the wonder of her expression always amazed him, as though each time, whatever sensations he brought to life surprised her. It was no different for him. He felt more with her. The pleasure was harsher, more intense, as though his nerve endings were laid bare to her touch.

She had a power over him that no lady had ever had. He reveled in it, wallowed in it, wanted it to last forever . . . but that was impossible. He couldn't scale another mountain if he never came down from the first. He thought he would never grow tired of scaling new heights with her wrapped around him, her body pulsing with his, tightening, coiling . . .

She was gasping, shrieking, calling out his name, her fingers digging into him. When the pleasure reached the ultimate pinnacle, sent him soaring over, spilling his hot seed into her, his body shuddering with the force of it, he was vaguely aware of her clinging to him, tremors cascading through her body.

Breathing heavily, he lifted himself slightly and gazed down on her. "Are you all right?"

A glorious smile spread across her face as she nodded, reached up and skimmed her fingers along his face. "I wasn't certain I'd survive."

"I almost didn't," he admitted.

She laughed, and the muscles holding him inside her tightened and pulsed around him. When her laughter quieted, he asked, "What possessed you to do what you did earlier?"

She shook her head slightly. "I don't know. I wanted you to know how special you are to me. I'll never have with anyone else what I have with you."

He kissed her forehead, her nose, her chin. "I am not so selfish as to wish that you don't have this with someone else."

But even as he spoke, he knew that, for himself, he'd never have with another woman what he had with her.

Chapter 20

As she walked through the gardens, her cloak wrapped around her, Camilla thought it had been rather silly of her and Archie to think that everything could return to the way it had been before they'd fallen in love. They'd not slept together since their last glorious night, but it haunted her that she might never again experience something as wonderful, as breathtaking. Although in truth, she thought few among the aristocracy with their arranged marriages probably did. So she couldn't have been more grateful that she had indeed experienced it.

She tried to find comfort in what had happened when Kingsbridge had left. He'd kissed her hand and assured her, "We shall be happy together, you and I."

And she'd smiled.

While inside her heart had cracked. He was a kind and gentle man. But she would never love him greatly, and therefore, the passion between them would be lukewarm at best. Damn Archie for showing her the wonder of fire when she'd been content with ice.

She looked around the gardens where she'd always found solace before. Now none existed. Winter was coming upon them, and it somehow seemed significant, as though all of Sachse Hall would be saddened by her departure. How vain could she be to think that even the plants would miss her?

But she would miss all of this, when she'd never expected to. Under Archie's care, everything was different: warm, vibrant, alive . . . and in the spring, it would be the same.

She would return to Sachse Hall for visits perhaps, and as the years progressed her visits would become fewer until they ceased altogether. Such was the price one paid for imperfection.

She was accomplishing nothing with this melancholy walk through the gardens. She had much she needed to do in order to see to it that everything was left in readiness for Archie. She doubted that she'd have time to be of much assistance once she married. Although surely the duke would understand that she couldn't leave the earl completely alone.

She needed to find him a wife and find him one quickly. If only he didn't have such high standards and insist upon love. Just as she'd always suspected, love did little more than sticky up the situation.

Still, she was glad that she'd had it if only for a short while.

She returned to her bedchamber. She would meet Archie in the library soon for an afternoon reading session. They seldom met in the children's wing anymore. She was progressing quite nicely, although the larger words and those that didn't sound as they were written still gave her a bit of trouble. She wondered how she would continue to learn after she was married.

Perhaps she'd hire a tutor—secretly, of course, as she dared not reveal to the duke that her reading skills were sorely lacking. Even as she had the thought, she dismissed it. She didn't want to begin her marriage by trying to do things without her husband's knowledge. No, she'd lived that way once before. Never again. She wanted her next marriage to be very different from her first.

She glanced at her jewelry box. She'd never read Archie's letter, and she wondered if it was best simply to leave well enough alone. What if he'd said something unkind? No, she couldn't imagine that of Archie. Still her curiosity was piqued. If she was ever going to read it, she should read it before she left Sachse Hall, so if she had any trouble with the words, Archie could help her with it.

She remembered now that he'd said something when the duke was there, something about his letter. That she would know how he'd planned to find a wife if she'd read it. Whatever had it said? And if she read it now, would it help her to find him a wife quickly?

She placed the jewelry box on her bed and went through the ritual of removing the trays, the jewelry, and finally the false bottom. There was Archie's letter, safe and sound where she'd tucked it away a lifetime ago. She removed it and pulled the letter from the envelope.

She'd loved the way his writing had looked then, she loved it now. But now she was able to appreciate it so much more. She couldn't read it as easily as she'd hoped, but she could make out a good deal of it . . . especially the part about a quiet recognition.

That was how her love for him had come upon her. Not like the boom of a bass drum or the clang of cymbals from an orchestra. It had slipped upon her during low conversations, and patient lessons, and tender gazes, and gentle touches.

She loved him. She loved him so much that it hurt. But it would hurt more not to.

She blinked back the tears that wanted to pour forth. They'd had one last, glorious night, and it would have to suffice for a lifetime. Although she thought that she might hold out hope that perhaps when they were old, and their hair had turned to silver, and their eyes were not as sharp, when he had his heirs, and his wife was gone, as was her husband, perhaps then she and Archie could come back together. Perhaps they could share their winter years. It was something to look forward to, something to give her hope, a reason to believe that all was not lost.

The entire notion saddened her. To realize that true happiness would have to be postponed until children were born and spouses died. Until great joy had been experienced, and great loss endured.

Oh, she would be content with the duke, but Archie had taught her that joy was so much better.

His children would be a joy to her. She would send gifts to them and watch them grow up into the fine young men and women that she knew they would be. His children could do no less, because they would have him as an example and a teacher.

Carefully she folded his letter. She would keep it and take it out on lonely nights to read again. Another notion that saddened her. To think that she might indeed have lonely nights.

She was about to slip his letter into place when her gaze fell on the other letter: the one that the countess had written to her as she lay dying. She removed it. She could at last see to the countess's wishes, *should* see to them before she married, while Archie was there to help her. There might be words in the letter that she couldn't decipher, but he would assist her if she needed help, and together they could do whatever it was the duchess had requested.

She closed her eyes. Was she only prolonging the inevitable? Looking for an excuse to keep Archie in her life . . . would she forever find reasons for him to help her? *Read to me, assist me with this word, do you think I've learned enough to read this book?*

She certainly couldn't ask any of these questions of her duke . . . how would she explain that some words were still beyond her grasp without revealing that she'd only recently learned to read?

No, best to see to this matter now, before she became a duchess.

Carefully, she opened the envelope, which had been sealed these many years. Nearly fifteen. She removed the letter, unfolded it, and with a contented sigh at the possibility of finally doing as she'd promised, she began to read.

The first words were simple, small, but they made no sense. They'd been written with a hand that was obviously struggling because it belonged to a woman who'd been so ill. She couldn't have been much older than Camilla was now, but she'd unexpectedly taken ill . . . and never recovered. The lines she'd scrawled were wiggly, unclear, which made the words more difficult to read.

Camilla stared at them more closely. She couldn't have read them right. She had to be missing something. The words seemed clear enough, but she had to have misread them. They couldn't possibly say what she thought they did.

My son is alive.

Chapter 21

"What does it mean?" Camilla asked.

Arch stood before the fireplace in the library, holding the letter Camilla had brought to him in a near panic, the firelight dancing over the words in a seemingly macabre fashion. He shook his head, as stunned as she'd been when she'd first come to him.

"Apparently she took her son with her when she went to America to visit a friend who had immigrated some years earlier. She then left him rather than have him raised under the influence of his father."

Camilla began pacing with agitation. "How could she do something so unheard of? He would have gone off to school—"

"But been home during holidays. She mentions that the child was becoming as hateful as his father, and that she was in danger of losing him anyway. And she'd come to despise her husband. Leaving the boy with a family she knew and trusted, then declaring that he'd taken ill and died served two purposes: it put him beyond the earl's reach while causing the earl immense anguish. It seems she wasn't quite as sweet and kind as you envisioned."

"You have no right to judge her. You never lived in the same house as he. He could cause a saint to become a devil."

Or to become an ice countess. Arch couldn't deny that he'd seen evidence of the man's legacy. He didn't think he could blame the mother for wanting to spare her son or prevent his following in his father's footsteps.

Again he looked at the letter. "She mentions that she spirited away some funds, so that the lad could be well provided for. How she managed that, I haven't a clue."

"There are ways that a desperate wife can put aside money without her husband knowing."

Arch remembered Lillian explaining how Camilla had hoarded money her husband gave her. He supposed it was possible that with planning a woman could accumulate a tidy sum.

Shaking her head, tears welling in her eyes, she sank onto a chair and lifted her gaze to his. "Whatever are we to do?"

She thought he had the answers? All he had at the moment was frustration and anger. "How could you have not shown this to someone?"

"She asked me not to. She forbade me to read it until the earl was dead. She didn't want him to see the truth revealed in my eyes. I remember now. She said something like, 'I'll not have undone all that I've done.' Or something like that. I can't remember exactly, and I never have any trouble remembering anything.

"I never once entertained the possibility that her son was alive. She was always mourning, keeping his rooms untouched as though she expected him to return any day. Telling me how much she missed him. She behaved as I'd expect any bereaved mother to act. I can't tell you how many days she wept, and I could do little more than hold her, but she was never comforted."

"But when the earl died—"

"I couldn't read, Arch! I had no idea her letter would

contain something of this magnitude. Why would she trust something this important to *me*?"

"For exactly that reason. She trusted you."

He stared into the fire, hardly able to believe this unexpected and unbelievable turn of events.

"He might still be dead," she whispered. "Her son. From things Lydia has told me, America is not completely civilized. There are dangers."

"According to the countess's letter, she left him with a family in New York. She's provided their name and address." He looked at the letter, sighed, and gazed back at the flames. "We'll have to speak with Mr. Spellman. Perhaps he knows someone we can hire who can go to New York and investigate the possibility that the rightful heir is still alive."

"If he's found, you'll lose your title."

He glared, brandishing the letter at her. "Are you suggesting we ignore this?"

Slowly she shook her head, looking terribly defeated. "No."

He crossed over and knelt before her. "They're going to want to know why you didn't bring this forward sooner."

Nodding, she licked her lips. "I know."

"We could tell them it was misplaced or forgotten about—"

She placed her fingers against his lips. "She trusted me, Arch. She trusted me to bring her son back here. If I hadn't been so proud, if I'd only said, 'Countess, I can't read,' she'd have given the task to another."

Tenderly he cradled her cheek. "But then I would have never met you, and regardless of how this turns out, I'll always be thankful that at least I had that: moments spent with you."

Spellman stared at the letter.

Arch and Camilla sat before him in his office. They'd

come to London specifically to meet with him, the journey made in silence, with neither having much to say on the matter.

"Well," Spellman said, as he leaned back in the chair and tapped the letter lying on his desk. "Isn't this interesting? Why didn't you bring it to me sooner?"

"Because I couldn't read until recently, and so I had no idea what it said," Camilla announced.

Arch reached over and squeezed her hand to offer strength and assurance. Her voice reflected no shame. Once she couldn't read, now she could, and whatever doubts she'd had about herself had disappeared with the knowledge gained.

"You couldn't read," Spellman reiterated.

"That is not the important issue here, but if you must belabor the point, I could *not* read until Lord Sachse recently taught me."

Spellman shifted his gaze to Arch. "I suppose that might be debatable: whether it truly was the *Earl* of Sachse or simply Mr. Warner who taught you to read."

"Don't be annoying, Spellman," Arch said. "We've come here because it's important to both of us that we make certain that the right man is carrying the title. If Thomas Warner is still alive, he must be found and he must return to England to claim what is rightfully his."

"This is most unusual," Spellman said, rubbing his brow. "I hardly know where to begin."

"I would think the best course of action would be to hire someone to go to New York and visit the people mentioned in the letter. Find out if the boy"—he shook his head—"he is no doubt a man now if he is indeed alive. If he is alive, we need to find him and make certain that he understands what awaits him here."

"You're quite right. We need to determine what has become of this boy . . . or man . . . or heir, I suppose. I know a gentleman who used to work for Scotland Yard. He investigates private matters now. John Buehler. I'll contact him. He won't come cheap."

"We'll pay whatever we must. Now is not the time to quibble over expenditures."

"I quite agree."

"I suspect this search might turn into a lengthy process. The countess and I will return to Sachse Hall. I would like reports assessing the progress made in finding Thomas Warner as often as possible."

"For what it is worth, *my lord*," Spellman began, "I thought you made an exemplary earl."

"Thank you, Mr. Spellman. I'll not give up the notion that I'll remain earl, but the countess made incredible sacrifices to protect her son. I hope he is found."

"I must admit that I could hardly blame her for placing him in another's keeping. She was a kind woman, but not strong. I had occasion to see the earl with his son. I believe he would have grown into a callous, bitter man, possibly cruel as well. Let us hope he has had a kinder influence."

"I must disagree with you on one matter, Mr. Spellman," Camilla said quietly. "The countess was stronger than you realized if she was able to leave her son in another country where she couldn't easily see him, to face the old Sachse and announce that the child had taken ill and died. I was more than familiar with his wrath when he was displeased, and he would have been most displeased with the news. I think she was incredibly strong to do what she did knowing she would face his fury. I'm not sure I would have had that courage."

Arch squeezed her hand again. "You would have."

She shook her head. "He didn't ask me to marry him. He *told* me I would marry him. I was a young girl who thought I had no choice. I greeted each month with a mixture of sadness and relief that I wasn't carrying his child."

"He was a powerful man who abused his power," Arch said.

Nodding, she looked at Mr. Spellman. "Find Thomas Warner, Mr. Spellman, as I would like very much to have the opportunity to tell him how very much his mother loved him."

Arch and Camilla returned to Sachse Hall, cocooning themselves in against a harsh winter, sitting before a fire and reading together aloud from the same book, cuddling beneath the covers and making love through the long nights.

Arch had planned to distance himself from her after her betrothal to Kingsbridge; but she was in need of comfort with what she considered a failing, and for reasons he couldn't understand, he sought comfort as well.

It wasn't as though he had grown attached to the earldom. Still, he'd begun to think of it is as his. He'd added books to the library, removed some of the more offensive sculptures and replaced them with ones he considered pleasing to the eye. He'd grown accustomed to the servants moving quietly about.

He realized with wonder that he'd accepted that he was the Earl of Sachse and that he would miss it if Thomas Warner were found. Reports from Spellman indicated that Buehler was having sporadic luck in locating the heir. The family with whom the boy had been left had died during an influenza epidemic almost twelve years earlier. The orphaned child had been placed on a train and sent west. Buehler was continuing his search.

It was near the end of January that he received a missive from Spellman that for some reason filled him with a sense of foreboding as he carried it to his study. Usually he and Camilla read the letters together, but he had a desire to be alone when he read this one. Perhaps because he knew Buehler was close to an answer. If the young man were dead, having died recently, Camilla might feel she was responsible for not getting the heir to England sooner. If he'd died long ago, it would make no difference. And if he were found alive . . . Arch wasn't quite certain how he would handle that yet.

He sat behind his desk and opened the letter. As always, Spellman got right to the heart of the matter.

Thomas Warner has been found. He'll arrive at the main London residence in ten days.

Arch sat back in the chair. That was it then. All he'd come to know would be lost to him. He'd not expected to miss it.

That evening during dinner, he told Camilla, "I have to go to London tomorrow."

"Did you hear something from Spellman?"

"No, I just need to take care of some matters."

"I'll go with you."

"I'd rather you stay here . . . to look after things."

"Is everything all right?"

"Everything is going to be just fine."

That night he made bittersweet love to her, knowing that in truth, he was probably saying good-bye.

Chapter 22

Arch was desperately in need of advice, and he couldn't go to the one person in all the world whom he trusted more than any other, since the advice he was seeking had to do with her. So he went to the Duke of Harrington, stopping at his country estate before going on to London.

"Let me offer you some whiskey," the duke said. "My half-brother sends it to me from Texas. It's got quite a kick to it, and you look to be a man who could use something that doesn't go down too easily."

Arch nodded to the offer of whiskey. He explained the letter that the countess had left with Camilla, how she'd only recently read it. He didn't explain why she'd waited so long, and the duke didn't ask. Arch suspected that, having once been surrounded by scandal, the duke was less likely to pry into others' affairs but tended to be satisfied with information shared and leave it at that.

Arch finished with, "They've located him. He's on his way to London, and I'm going to meet him there."

Harrington stilled, holding the bottle at an awkward angle. "Can't say that I'd be thrilled to learn that my older brother was suddenly resurrected."

Arch shook his head. "I have no quarrel with the man being given what is rightfully his."

The duke finished pouring the drinks and handed a glass to Arch. "I'd suggest taking a good healthy swallow."

Arch did and thought his throat was in danger of catching on fire. Tears filled his eyes before he could blink them back. "Good God."

"Once you get accustomed to it, it tends to hit the spot," Harrington said. "Have a seat."

Arch sat in one of the wing-backed chairs in front of the fireplace. The flames offered welcoming warmth, but he remained chilled. He was beginning to wonder if that might be the case for the remainder of his life.

The duke took the chair opposite him. He didn't press Arch to speak, but rather simply sat there quietly, watching, waiting while Arch gathered his thoughts, because certainly the duke had to realize that the discovery of the heir was not something that required his advice.

There was no hope for it except to blurt it out. "I've fallen in love with Camilla."

"That doesn't come as a surprise. I figured that out when we were at Sachse Hall."

Arch held the glass between his hands, studying the way the firelight played over the contents of the glass. The color reminded him very much of Camilla's hair. He didn't think she'd appreciate the comparison, but then almost everything reminded him of her these days.

"I'm not familiar with all the laws and rules that affect the aristocracy, but it is my understanding that if a woman is a commoner and she marries a man of rank and he dies, she retains his title. But if she then marries a commoner, she loses her title."

"Yes, that's the way of it."

He'd so hoped he'd not properly understood how it all worked.

"Camilla's reasons for not marrying me were twofold:

she could not give me an heir and she desired to be a duchess. With one she was unselfish, with the other selfish." He lifted his gaze to the duke's. "You've known her longer than I. She told me once that she'd rather die than be a commoner again. Do you think she meant it?"

The duke bestowed on him a look fraught with pity.

"Never mind," Arch said, as he came to his feet. "No need to answer aloud. We both know how much she values being part and parcel of the peerage."

He walked to the fireplace, put his hand on the mantel, and stared at the dancing flames. "I'm not certain why I came here. I knew the answer before I walked through your door. I no longer need an heir, but marrying me would require her giving up what she values so highly." He shook his head. "I can't ask that of her."

"What would it hurt to ask?" the duke inquired. "She might surprise you."

Or break my heart.

"She has spent a good deal of the past few months surprising me—rather pleasantly."

He took a gulp of the whiskey. It didn't burn nearly as much, but it still managed to warm him throughout.

"She was never really mine," he said quietly. "Even when she was mine, she wasn't mine. I'd grown so accustomed to having her in my life that I'd forgotten that she was only on loan." He finished off the whiskey and turned to face the duke. "I shan't miss your world."

He went to the main London residence, the one in which Camilla had lived. Although it had been closed up for the winter, as the servants were making it ready for a guest, he was very much aware of Camilla's presence wherever he went. He slept in her bed, which even with clean linens still smelled of her. He smiled when he spotted her French book. He found the skates sitting in a corner as though she might have plans to use them again.

He walked through the house capturing images of her, to fill in the few tiny places in his memory where she didn't yet dwell. There were so few. Eventually he realized that he was on a senseless quest, because he could never reach a point where he was completely satiated with thoughts of her. His mind would always make room, would always let in a bit more of her.

The futility of his efforts was doing nothing except prolonging the inevitable.

So, he set himself to the task of going over the books for the estates, making certain that everything was in order and could be easily handed over to the rightful earl when he arrived. A thousand times he considered returning to Sachse Hall and letting Camilla know that the heir had been found, explaining that decisions needed to be made, and offering her a choice. Him or a dukedom?

Him with his simple life in the country, his school of boys with eager, young minds, his teasing brother, and his married sister who was once again with child. He and Camilla could share his sister's children, they could look after the boys at the school. She would have children in her life, even if they didn't come from her womb.

But she would sacrifice her title. Completely and absolutely. Not only would she never be a duchess, but she would no longer be a countess. How could he ask her to give up all she valued?

He couldn't.

How could he put her in the unconscionable position of breaking his heart to his face?

He couldn't do that either.

So he buried himself in the books and drowned himself with whatever was available in the liquor cabinet. Meals were brought to him that he ignored. He had no appetite. He couldn't escape the irony of his situation.

In the spring, he would have lost her anyway—to the Duke of Kingsbridge. But he could have convinced himself that it was because she wanted Arch to have an heir that she was making herself unavailable to him and marrying the duke. Now he could hide behind no pretense. He no longer required an heir, and in all the nights since they'd discovered that there was a chance that Thomas Warner was alive, Camilla had never once said, "If they find him, and you no longer need an heir, then I am yours."

Although in truth, neither had he dared to ask her, "If they find him, and I no longer need an heir . . . what then?"

"Ah, Camilla," he mumbled, rubbing his face, roughened with a beard that had grown for too many days to count. When had he last shaved? He couldn't remember. He couldn't remember anything beyond Camilla. He lifted his glass. "To your happiness, my darling."

He brought it to his lips, only then realizing that it was empty. As empty as his life would be without her.

He released an outraged cry torn from the depths of despair and his heart. With a mighty shove, he sent the books and ledgers that represented all he'd once owned crashing to the floor. He knew a time would come when he'd draw comfort from memories of her, but tonight all he felt was the pain of incredible loss. He laid his head on the desk and wept, finding no comfort, no solace, no hope.

He'd never found fault with the sunlight, but this morning he found fault with the way it slanted through the windows and sliced across his eyes. He found equal fault with his head for aching and his mouth for containing a most disgusting taste. His neck was stiff and sore, his shoulders tight. He'd never felt this badly the morning after battling a fire; but then with a fire, the risk was only to his body, not his heart.

With a groan and a moan, he pushed himself up slightly and planted his face in one of his hands. He would have preferred using both, but one of his arms was numb. It was coming to life now, adding to his misery.

"Here, drink this," said a deep, slow drawl.

With great difficulty, he lifted his squinting eyes to the man standing before him. He was tall and wore something that greatly resembled a greatcoat, but somehow wasn't. Arch dipped his gaze to the glass in the man's hand.

"What is it?" His voice sounded as though it was scraping over rocks.

"My own version of hair of the dog. It tastes like hell, but it'll undo some of what these empty bottles say you've done to yourself."

Arch's hand shook as he reached out and took the glass. "What's in it?"

"You don't want to know. Just drink it. The best way is one long gulp without breathing, so you don't smell it and are less likely to taste it."

Arch did as instructed, downing the nauseatingly thick liquid. A chill and a shudder coursed through him. He set the glass on the desk, only then noticing that the ledgers had been neatly stacked along one side. He gave his attention back to the man. "Who are you?"

The man sat in the chair, lifted a leg, crossed his ankle over his knee, and a balanced a hat that Arch had never seen in fashionable London on his thigh.

"You tell me," the man said.

"The devil . . . come to bargain?"

The man's laughter was deep and sonorous, his dark eyes glittering. "I'd certainly bargain my way out of this if I could, but according to old Spellman, I've got no choice in the matter."

"You're the Earl of Sachse."

The man's jovial mood seemed to desert him. "That's what I've been told."

"I can see the resemblance between you and your father." And a little between the man and himself. Generations separated them, but evidence of the Warner bloodline was there.

With a heavy sigh, he sat back in the chair, surprised to discover that he was feeling a trifle better. "I'd not planned to make your acquaintance under such degrading circumstances."

Sachse shrugged. "Over the years, I've downed my share of good whiskey—and not-so-good whiskey. I apologize if it was the discovery that I wasn't dead that turned you to the bottle."

"Oh, no, not at all. I never grew truly comfortable wearing your shoes. I shan't miss it, but there are matters that concern me that I'd like to discuss with you. I'd prefer to make myself presentable first, if you don't mind."

"Don't mind at all." He rubbed his jaw. "Could use a little sprucing up myself."

"I'll have the servants show you to a bedchamber. Shall we meet back here in an hour?"

"An hour will be fine."

"Splendid."

Although Arch didn't feel exactly splendid, he wasn't certain he could blame it all on the spirits. Rather that before the day was over, he'd be rid of all this, and already he missed it.

Arch had been fully prepared not to like the man, but Thomas Warner was an incredibly likable sort.

"Are you hungry?" Arch had asked once they'd met again in the study.

"Starving."

"Let's get you something to eat then. You need but ask the servants for anything you want, desire, need. They'll see to it immediately as their job is to please you and make your life as comfortable as possible. I'll introduce you to everyone and explain their various duties."

Sachse grinned. "Some fella at the top of the stairs thought he was going to help me get dressed."

"That would be the earl's valet."

"Well, I'm perfectly capable of dressing myself. Had to aim my gun at him to make my point."

"You have a gun?" Arch asked.

"Peacemaker. I don't go anywhere without it."

"Well, I assure you. Guns aren't needed here."

"I feel naked without one strapped to my thigh."

Camilla was certainly going to have her hands full with this earl—and just as quickly, he realized that she'd soon be giving all her attention to her duke.

"No need to be getting all sad about the gun," Sachse said. "I don't usually wear it indoors."

Arch forced himself to smile. "No, I was thinking of something else. Come along. Luncheon should be ready."

They sat across from each other, one on each side of the narrow portion of the table, rather than at the distant ends, because the earl hadn't wanted to talk loudly to be heard. Arch liked the way he thought.

"What can you tell me about my father?" Sachse asked.

"Not a great deal. I never actually met him."

Sachse looked across at him. "You're his cousin, right?"

"Distant cousin, yes. So I'm your cousin as well."

"I figure he must not have been too likable for my mother to have done what she did. Either that, or she wasn't real fond of me. I can't remember her." He shook his head. "Can't remember him."

"From what I've gathered your mother was a very kind woman. Your father tended to be a bit of a bully. His widow will be able to tell you more about each of them, as she knew them well."

"Where is she?"

"Sachse Hall. One of your estates."

"One of them?"

"You have three. I'll show you all the books and explain how each works."

"I looked through a few of the books while you were sleeping."

"Are you good with figures, then?"

"Yep."

"Splendid. That'll make the transition somewhat easier." Although he feared he was being overly optimistic. Camilla would take exception to the man's clothing. His trousers were made of fabric with which Arch was unfamiliar. His shirt appeared to be white cotton and his tie was little more than braided string. He wore no jacket or waistcoat.

"So tell me more about the widow," Sachse said.

"The widow?"

"My father's widow."

"Ah, yes. Lady Sachse. Camilla. She is extremely kind, generous to a fault. Your father made no provisions for her in his will. Before we realized that you were alive, I'd offered to pay her twenty thousand pounds as an expression of my appreciation to her for helping me to learn my role as earl. I don't personally have that much money, but if you could see your way clear to still give it to her, over time I would repay you." Over the remainder of his life, if he were to be honest about it.

"Someone on the ship told me that a pound was worth about five dollars."

Arch shook his head. "I wouldn't know about that. I've had no reason to inquire about American currency."

Sachse sat back and studied him. "That's a hell of a lot of money."

"I am well aware of that, but she is well worth it. She is to marry the Duke of Kingsbridge in the spring, but until then you will find that she will be your most valuable asset."

Sachse nodded. "All right. I'll honor the arrangement you made with her. But there's no need for you to owe me anything. We'll just say it's the estate paying you to keep things going until I got here."

"As you said, it's a large amount of money."

Sachse glanced around, waving his fork in the air. "I

don't need any of this, Warner. I've been working since I was seventeen, putting money away. I've got land and cattle. I'll admit the house I just built isn't as fancy as this, but it's mine. Hard-earned. I hammered a lot of the nails myself. I'm not sure what to make of all this yet, but it's not a comfortable fit."

"Trust Lady Sachse then. When she is finished with you, you'll have no doubt that you were born to it."

Chapter 23

Camilla sat in the library reading, the book on her lap stuffed with slips of paper to mark the pages that contained words she didn't know. If books weren't so precious, if she didn't have such respect for them, she would have circled the words in the book. Instead she'd written them on another piece of paper. But she took no joy in it. Her frustration was mounting as well as her anger again.

Two weeks! Arch had been gone two long weeks. If she'd known he was going to be away for such an extended period of time, she'd have insisted on going with him. She missed him, missed him terribly. How in the world was she going to survive when she was married to another man?

It wasn't only sleeping with him that she missed. She missed his presence, whether they were in the same room or not—simply knowing he was about filled her with peace. She missed the way he pressed a finger to his mouth when he read, the way he always seemed startled when the footman moved in to remove his plate during dinner, as though he couldn't quite get used to the fact that someone was there to tend to his needs.

She missed the way he smelled after his bath, the way he smelled after they made love.

She missed his voice, his hands, his smile, his laugh. She missed everything.

If he missed her as much, why hadn't he hurried back? Whatever could he be doing in London, and why was it taking so dreadfully long?

She looked up at the sound of the butler coming into the room. "The Earl of Sachse is here, madam. He's in the drawing room."

Relief swamped her, gladness filled her. Her anger with him vanished.

"It's about time. I thought he'd never arrive," she said, as she hopped out of the chair, dropped the book into it, and hurried across the room. She squeezed the butler's arm, which caused his eyes to widen. "Tell Cook to begin preparing dinner. I know he'll be hungry. He has such an appetite, you know."

She dashed into the hallway, greeting the footmen and maids that she passed. "The master's home," she sang out. *He's home, he's home, he's home.*

She stopped before a mirror in the entry hall and straightened her hair, pinched her cheeks, and pressed her teeth against her lips to get some color into them. She'd kiss him when she saw him. That would put color in her entire body. In his as well.

She took a deep breath. Why not let him see how glad she was to see him. They'd promised no more secrets.

She fairly waltzed into the drawing room and stumbled to a stop. Archie was nowhere to be seen. The only person in the room was a tall man with dark hair. His back was to her as he studied the portrait over the fireplace, a portrait of the old earl's first wife.

Wearing a black coat that reached down to his calves, he held a broad-brimmed hat similar to one she'd seen in a story about cowboys.

He turned as though suddenly aware of her presence. He wore pointed boots such as she'd never seen. His trousers and shirt were not what a gentleman would wear into a parlor. His black hair was in need of trimming, as was the thick mustache that outlined his mouth. His deep brown eyes seemed to be assessing her as though he should know her.

Something was vaguely familiar about him, and a shiver went down her spine. "May I help you?" she asked.

He tipped his head slightly. "Ma'am. I'm waitin' for the Countess of Sachse."

His voice was deep, but he spoke with a slow drawl. She angled her chin. "I'm the Countess of Sachse. And who might you be?"

Almost lazily, he hiked up one corner of his mouth. "Well, now, from what they're telling me, I'd be the Earl of Sachse." He pointed at the portrait. "Is that my mother?"

She nodded, not certain how she managed to stay and do so. She wanted to run from the room, wanted to find Archie. "Where is . . . where is . . ." What was she to call him now? She cleared her throat. "Where is Mr. Warner?"

"He went home."

"Home?" she repeated.

"Yes, ma'am."

She shook her head. "I don't understand. Is he in his bedchamber then?" Was he waiting for her there, removing his clothes, preparing himself for her greeting.

"No, ma'am. I don't mean this home, I mean the other one. Heatherton, I think he called it. He asked me to give you this."

She stared at the parcel—wrapped in white paper, tied with string—as though it might cause her great harm. "What is it?"

"He didn't say, ma'am."

She took the package from him. She inhaled deeply, remembering who she was and what she was, what this man standing before her was and what he was to her. "You must be tired from your journey. I've asked Cook to prepare dinner. I'll have the butler show you to your chambers. Once you're settled we shall meet for dinner." She took a step back. "Now if you will excuse me, my lord, I must see to this matter." She held up the package.

Before he could answer, she spun on her heel and darted out of the room. She ran. Ran down the hallway, ran up the stairs, ran into her bedchamber, ran to her bed. With trembling hands, she broke the string, tore off the wrapping, opened the box.

A letter. There was a letter. She took it out of the box, only to reveal the most beautiful string of pearls she'd ever seen. She set the box and pearls aside and turned to what mattered to her the most: his letter, his words, his thoughts.

My darling Camilla,

At this point, I suspect you are shaking with anger. I knew when I left that I would not return, but I could not bear to say good-bye, and good-bye was all that was left to us.

The true Earl of Sachse has agreed that you're entitled to the twenty thousand pounds and has instructed Mr. Spellman to make payment posthaste. I fear Mr. Spellman will find the true earl no easier to deal with than he did me.

As for you, my darling, I leave a small gift. Place these pearls against your throat or beneath your pillow, wherever they will bring you the most happiness because happiness is all that I wish for you.

I love you. I always will. Thank you for giving me so many moments to remember.

Yours always,
Arch

Tears washed down her face, splashed onto the paper. He was right. Of course he was right. Good-bye was all that remained to them. Today. A few months from now. It wouldn't have mattered. The pain would have been as great.

She had her duke. She would be a duchess. She would be happy. She would.

If she survived the breaking of her heart.

Following dinner, the Earl of Sachse wanted to sit in the drawing room. He sat in a chair and stared up at the portrait as though he thought he could bring the woman in it back to life.

Camilla watched him, hardly knowing what to say. They'd not spoken during dinner. It hadn't been the welcomed silence that she shared with Archie. Rather it had seemed very forced, as though both simply wanted to get the meal over with and move on to other things.

Finally, after what seemed an eternity, but was probably only a few minutes, he shook his head. "I barely remember her, and I'm not sure if that's a real memory or simply wanting one so bad that I created it just now."

"It's been eighteen years," Camilla said kindly. "You would have been very young."

He leaned forward, planted his elbows on his knees, and clasped his large hands together. Darkly tanned, they bore tiny scars. A workman's hands.

"So my father was a real bastard from what I hear."

"My lord—"

He held up a hand. "I know you got all these rules about what you're supposed to call people, but I'm Tom. Just Tom."

"No, you're the Earl of Sachse." And it appeared he was going to be more of a challenge than Archie had been. At least Archie had understood the history of the peerage and how important it was to Britain. This man was for all intent and purposes . . . *American.* She shuddered with the thought.

"For right now, please just call me Tom, until I get used to this."

She nodded. "All right . . . Tom." She shook her head. "Thomas. May I call you Thomas? Tom seems so . . . common."

"Thomas is fine. It's just this 'lord' business makes me feel like I'm putting on airs. Two weeks ago, I was worried about getting my cattle through the winter. Now I got this dropped in my lap, and I haven't figured out yet if it's good fortune or bad."

"I suppose you had some sort of proof that you're Thomas Warner."

"Other than my name, I had a blanket with a coat of arms on it. Don't know why I kept it all these years."

"You have your father's eyes, but they hold your mother's kindness."

He grinned. "Don't tell that to my cowhands. When I bark, 'jump!' they ask how high."

"I don't imagine you'll be seeing much of your . . . cowhands now."

"That's something to be worked out."

She cleared her throat. "I'll assist you in finding someone to help teach you about your duties and our ways. I'll be getting married in the spring and won't be available."

"That's what Warner told me. I like him. He's a good man."

"Yes, he is."

"Right fond of you."

"As I am of him."

He seemed to be thinking something over, his mustache moving slightly. "So if you're fond of Warner, and he's fond of you, who's this fella you're marrying?"

"The Duke of Kingsbridge."

Thomas sat there, waiting, as though he expected her to say more.

"He's a duke," she added, "so I shall be a duchess."

"And that'll make you happy?" he asked.

"Of course, it'll make me happy." She came up out of the chair and glared at him. "What do you know anyway? You know nothing of the peerage, being raised in America as you were. What was the countess thinking to take you there? You don't understand that a duchess is respected, loved—" A sob, a horrible sound escaped from her throat. She sank to the chair, tears blurring her vision. "Why didn't he say good-bye?"

Tom crossed over to her and knelt before her. "There, there, darlin', don't cry."

"But why didn't Archie say good-bye?"

"Men just aren't any good at saying how they feel."

"Archie is. He's very good at it. We weren't supposed to keep any secrets from each other. He knew they'd found you, and he didn't tell me."

He held her hands. In spite of the scars, they were good hands for holding. "What would be different if he'd told you?"

"I wouldn't hurt so badly." She sniffed. "She loved you, you know? Your mother. She was trying to protect you. Your father was a horrible man. He wasn't really a bastard, though, because he was legitimate."

He laughed, a deep rumble that reminded her so much of Archie. The way the corners of his twinkling eyes wrinkled.

"Darlin', I wasn't referring to his ancestry when I called him a bastard. And I know my mother was probably doing what she thought was best, and maybe it was. But I know that sometimes when a man gets to the end of a long road, and looks back over where he's traveled, he can sometimes wonder if he might be in a better place if he'd taken a different turn farther down the road rather than staying on the one he was traveling. I guess what I'm trying to say is that Warner did what he thought was best. But that don't mean that years from now he won't look back and wonder if he shouldn't have taken a different turn."

She studied him. "Not only men. Women, too, look back and wonder."

And sometimes in looking back, a woman could realize that her dreams had changed.

Chapter 24

It amazed Arch how quickly he'd settled into the routine of his old life. He was once again simply Archibald Warner. Untitled. Common. Plain. Mr. Warner to his students.

He was teaching again—as his father had taught before him. In the same classroom he'd used before he'd gone on his grand adventure. That was how he now thought of the time when he was away. As his grand adventure. His eyes had been opened, and as his father had said, once opened, when again closed, the mind still saw what the eyes had viewed.

His father had possessed a myriad of sayings. In retrospect, Arch was beginning to wonder what his father had seen, had experienced that allowed him to have such insight in order to realize that not everything a man learned was appreciated. And that there were some things he was better off not knowing.

Arch stood before his desk, listening as a young man stutteringly read one of Shakespeare's sonnets, obviously having difficulty not because he didn't know the words but because he couldn't decipher the meaning of the passage.

Arch thought of Camilla reading her first sentence. It was more difficult to read when the words coming together weren't what was expected, and thus made no sense. It confused the mind.

"Mr. Warner?"

A young gentleman on the back row was waving his hand as though his arm were caught in a heavy gale.

"Don't interrupt, Mr. Newman."

"But, Mr. Warner, sir—"

"You'll have your chance when Mr. Ford is finished."

"But Lady Sachse is here, sir."

Arch felt as though the boy had bludgeoned him. He jerked his gaze toward the window, but the sunlight created a glare. If he couldn't see out, how did the boy?

His student was no doubt playing a prank or sadly mistaken. Still Arch walked to the window for a clearer view and sighted the lady in question. He felt as though his ribs were caving in, and his heart was fighting for freedom. He could see her carriage parked a distance behind her as she strolled elegantly over the lawn.

What in the world was she doing there? It had been over a month since he'd left her, a month of trying to forget her, a month of fighting to remember every little detail about her.

"Can we go see her, sir?"

"No, Mr. Newman, you may not. You are, however, responsible for maintaining order in this classroom until I return."

He told himself not to hurry, not to give the impression that he was anxious to see her, but his feet seemed to be moving independently of his mind. Which he supposed was a good thing as he wanted a private moment with her before others were rushing out to greet her. She was a heroine of sorts around there. She'd sent the twenty thousand pounds he'd given her to the school, with a note that it was to be invested, the additional amount it earned to be used for scholarships for those who couldn't afford to attend the school otherwise.

Obviously, with her upcoming marriage to the duke, she no longer had a need for the provision he'd made for her, and while he was well acquainted with her generous nature and knew the school was grateful for the endowment, he'd preferred thinking that he'd managed to do something for *her*, something no one else had done.

As he neared, his feet finally slowed, perhaps because his heart was thundering so loudly. He'd not forgotten how lovely she was, but to see her in person rather than only in his dreams was bittersweet. He wondered how he should address her: my lady or Your Grace.

He dipped his gaze to her hands, looking for evidence of a ring, of her marriage having taken place but as she was wearing gloves, he couldn't discern the state of her life. He'd hoped if their paths ever crossed again, she'd at least look happy. Instead, she looked at him as though he'd deeply disappointed her.

"Hello," he managed past the knot that had risen in his throat. "I'd never thought to see you again."

"So I gathered," she said. No icy haughtiness wove its way through her voice. Rather she sounded incredibly sad. "We'd made a promise to have no more secrets between us, but you knew when you left for London that they'd found the earl."

"Yes, I thought it best to greet him myself, alone."

"I never took you to be a coward, slinking away in the dead of night without even a proper good-bye."

It had hardly been the dead of night. Still she'd made her point. He considered taking a page from her book, hiding the truth behind a wall of lies so as to protect himself, but in the end, he cared for her too much not to be honest.

"I feared if I went to see you that I wouldn't have the strength not to ask you to marry me, and that would have put you in the awkward position of saying no and me in the dreadful position of having to pretend that I hadn't died on the inside."

"So certain were you that I would say no?"

"Camilla, I can't make you a duchess. I can't even keep you as a countess. Marriage to me would strip you of your title. You would no longer by my lady . . . well, you would be *my* lady but that is hardly the same thing."

"I can't make you a father . . . so there."

She'd delivered her statement with her no-nonsense hard edge she'd used when first he'd met her, but there was a subtle difference to the delivery that he couldn't quite fathom. Not a challenge, but rather an acceptance.

"It is hardly the same thing. I can live quite happily without being a father. As you have stated for as long as I've known you, you have no wish to live without a title."

"I told you that I couldn't live without respect, and yes, there was a time when I associated respect with a title; but that was before you taught me to read. You changed the way that I viewed myself. You gave me a wondrous gift, Archie. And then you broke my heart by not realizing that I was no longer the woman I'd been when first we met. I thought you loved me."

"I do. Not a moment passes that I don't think of you."

"You told me that if I searched for love, to one man I would be the most important person in his world."

That seemed ages ago, another lifetime, when he'd lived with hope in his heart and romance in his soul. "And you are the most important person in my world, but it is a very small world."

"I would rather rule in a small world than not rule at all."

He stared at her, trying to decipher what surely must have been a riddle. "Did I hear you correctly?" he finally dared to ask.

"I can't speak to what you heard, only what I said."

Ah, that was the Camilla he knew, striving to distract him, suddenly fearing that she might be the one to be hurt.

"What of your duke?" he asked.

"Apparently I was mistaken about the aristocracy knowing little of love. He believes it is worth fighting for, so here I am doing battle when I haven't the proper arsenal."

"Oh, my dear Camilla, you not only have the proper arsenal, but victory was yours the moment you stepped upon the field." He dropped down to one knee and took her hand. "Will you honor me and grant me my heart's desire by becoming my wife?"

Tears pooled in her eyes, rolled over onto her cheeks. Releasing a tiny gasp, she nodded before dropping to the ground and winding her arms around his neck. "I thought I'd die when you didn't come back for me."

He rocked her back and forth. "Oh, my darling, forgive me. I thought I was giving you what you wanted."

"Well, you thought wrong." She leaned back, her face awash in tears. "I can't carry a tune to save my life so I doubt that my voice will ever delight you, but I love you with every fiber of my being, and I want you to hold me near for a thousand years."

He cupped her face between his hands. "I shall hold you near for eternity."

With tenderness and heartfelt devotion, he kissed her, tasting the salt of her tears, knowing they were from joy not sorrow or fear. He wondered how he'd ever thought that he could live the remainder of his life without her by his side. What a sad and lonely existence it would have been.

Suddenly it was as though he were once again whole and complete. She was the reason his heart beat and his lungs drew in air. As though the world agreed, he heard shouts, claps, and laughter.

Drawing back, he discovered that the boys from his classroom surrounded them.

"Lookee! Mr. Warner was kissing Lady Sachse!" Mr. Newman shouted, pointing with glee.

"Oh, no," Camilla said, smiling brightly. "Mr. Warner was kissing the soon-to-be Mrs. Warner, and it's a title I shall proudly wear as long as I live."

The people of Heatherton were all a-titter because the Duke and Duchess of Harrington had come to Heatherton for the wedding. Camilla had planned on a small gathering for the ceremony, but once Archie's mother had begun making a list of guests who simply couldn't be overlooked . . . well, by the time she was finished, the entire town received an invitation. The advantages and drawbacks to being married in the village church where Archie had grown up.

Camilla had arrived at the church in the duke's own coach, and she would leave in his open carriage, with her husband at her side. Now she and Rhys stood outside the door waiting to hear the music that would herald her arrival. She wore an elegant white gown with a long train. She held a bouquet of pink roses.

"You look beautiful, Camilla," Rhys said quietly.

She glanced up at him. "Thank you."

"The Marlborough House Set won't be the same without you."

She laughed lightly. "I shan't miss it. Isn't that odd? When there was a time when I so desperately wanted to be part of it."

"I'm certain the Prince of Wales would welcome you should you decide to mingle in London."

"Undoubtedly. His gift to us included a note saying almost precisely the same thing. I was always welcome. But it's no longer what will make me happy. Nor would it make Archie happy. I love him so much, Rhys." She placed her hand on his arm. "I never realized why you and Lydia risked so much to be together. Until now. Nothing is more important to me than the man who waits for me inside the church."

"I daresay there is nothing more important to him than you."

"I only hope that he won't come to regret that he won't have children."

His face split into a devilish grin. "There is an old wives' tale I once heard that passing beneath an arch can cure many an ill. I venture to guess that tonight you'll be beneath an *arch*."

"Oh, you naughty man, even to suggest such a thing." Had any other man spoken to her thusly, she would have been offended, but she and Rhys had a long and intimate history, and although she'd never visited his bed, she knew many of the women who had.

Looking away, she felt the heat suffuse her face. She suspected that he was quite right. She would indeed be beneath Arch tonight.

Hearing the music vibrating through the organ pipes, she took a deep breath and placed her hand on Rhys's offered arm.

"Are you ready, Countess?" he asked.

It was strange to hear him address her with a title for the last time. Once she exchanged vows with Archie, she would once again be a commoner, although she suspected that he'd never view her as common.

"I am ready to shed myself of all the trappings of rank," she said without remorse. "I've never been more happy or sure of the path that I'm about to follow."

"He is a fortunate man, Camilla. If I were not madly in love with my wife, I would envy him."

She pinched his arm. "Envy him anyway."

His laughter accompanied them into the church, then fell silent as the immensity of the occasion dawned upon them both. The church was packed to the rafters, and she thought that even the nonreligious were in attendance. But she barely noticed the crowd once her gaze fell on Archie, waiting for her. Winston stood beside him to serve as best man.

But all she could think was that she was getting married to the one man who could truly make her happy. He was so handsome standing there that he took her breath, and she was hardly aware that she walked beside another man up the aisle.

In truth, she was hardly aware of walking. She felt as though she'd fallen into a dream, but she knew that she'd never awaken from it. That with Archie, if they never had anything beyond this, still they would have *everything*.

"Who gives this woman?" the minister asked.

"I, the Duke of Harrington, do," Rhys said.

Then Rhys was gone, and she found herself beside Archie, her hand nestled in his.

"Are you sure?" he asked quietly.

"I am sure that I love you. I am sure that I wish to spend the remainder of my life with you. Beyond that, I am sure of nothing."

"You've given me all that I ask." He turned to the minister and gave a nod.

"Dearly beloved . . ."

The words flowed forth with resonance and purpose. The ceremony seemed at once brief and too lengthy, vows exchanged, a simple gold band placed upon her finger, a tender kiss pressed to her lips. And then the words that it seemed she'd waited forever to hear.

"It is my honor to present to you Mr. and Mrs. Archibald Warner."

It was a night of celebration. Tables surrounded Archie's house—the one where his mother had lived. Now she was living with Nancy and Owen, so her older son and his wife could have some time alone.

Camilla was more than ready for that time alone. But

first there had been well wishes from everyone in the town, shaking hands, offering them the best.

Winston had been the first in line, taking her in his arms, bending her back, and planting a kiss on her mouth. She'd actually laughed when at last he'd straightened her.

"I suppose your mouth does that whenever you cross paths with a pretty girl," she'd admonished.

"No. Only when my brother marries a woman of whom I heartily approve." He'd kissed her lightly on the cheek. "Make him happy."

"I will," she'd promised. "And I'll begin searching for a wife for you."

He'd looked horrified. "No thanks. Marriage isn't for me."

Nancy's daughters had given their Auntie Camilla a kiss. Camilla had loved the new title: auntie. She wondered why she'd ever set her sights on the title of duchess. It seemed so unimportant somehow.

She'd danced with Archie, Rhys, Winston, and two dozen other men. She'd laughed, been toasted, and watched as her husband had looked upon her as though no other woman existed.

And when she thought her feet wouldn't be able to endure another round of dancing, Archie lifted her into his arms. "Let's take the merriment inside, shall we?" he whispered.

Although she heard the shouts and cheers from those who had yet to leave, she merely nestled her head into the crook of his shoulder and wound her arms around his neck as he carried her into the house and up the stairs to the room they would share from this night forth.

Someone had turned down the blankets—his mother she suspected—and left the light in a lamp burning.

"Shall I try to find Frannie?" he asked as he set her on her feet.

"No." Frannie had come with her, as had Lillian, and though neither could earn what they had when they worked for a countess, it seemed each felt being with her made up the difference. She couldn't have been more glad because she hadn't been sure how she'd make it without them. "You can undress me."

He pulled her into his arms. "I don't know if I can wait that long. To have you near this entire month while preparations were going on for the wedding and *not* have you in my bed nearly drove me mad."

Before she could reply that it had been the same for her, near madness, his mouth was on hers, cutting off anything she might have wanted to say . . . and nothing she had to say seemed important any longer. All that mattered were the sensations coiling tightly within her preparing to be unleashed. Oh, it seemed an eternity had passed since she felt the hardness of his body pressed up against hers. She was suddenly craving him, and she wanted to shout for the joy of it, because he stirred within her sensations that before him had been foreign, because his touch was like magic.

Even through the many layers of her clothing, she could feel the heat of his hands, the impatience, the power that would cause her to soar to unlimited heights.

He trailed his hot mouth along her throat. "Oh, Camilla, how I've missed you."

"Mrs. Warner," she rasped.

"What?"

"I'm Mrs. Warner. Call me it. Just once."

He leaned back until she could meet his gaze. He skimmed his gloved fingers around her face. "I love you, Mrs. Warner."

Tears stung her eyes. "I love being Mrs. Warner."

"That's good, because I plan for you to be Mrs. Warner for a great many years." He stripped off his gloves and dropped them to the floor. "Now let's see if I can figure out how to get you out of all this."

It didn't seem long at all before she was lying on the bed, completely nude, and saying, "I always knew you were a smart man."

Then he was stretching out beside her, his clothes shed more quickly and easily than hers. She placed her bare hand against his naked chest, heard him catch his breath, felt the muscles beneath her hand tighten and quiver. He wrapped his hand around hers, brought her hand to his lips, his eyes never straying from hers. "We will have a lifetime to go slowly; but I need you, Camilla, and I need you now."

Nothing, not even reading, made her feel as powerful as the desperation that laced his voice. She'd never felt more wanted, more essential, more desired. It was a heady and potent sensation. Yet as desperately as he seemed to need her, she needed him equally as much. "I need you, too, Arch."

The urgency in his voice, the readiness of his body, his quivering muscles gave her the impression that he would quickly slake his desires and then see to hers, but it was as though having voiced his needs, learning that she had needs as well, that his fires had been banked.

He ran his hand along her side, down to her thigh, her calf, then back up, his gaze following the path of his hand. He met her eyes, gave her a smile, a kiss. The press of his lips to hers was brief, yet filled with promise. His mouth grazed her cheek, her chin, then took a leisurely journey along her throat.

Growling low, Arch dipped his tongue into the hollow at her throat. Rolling slightly, she bowed her body against his, to urge him on, to encourage him to hurry.

"Not so fast, my darling," he whispered.

Now that he was so close, was able to feast on her flesh, he seemed in no hurry to finish the meal. She threaded her fingers through his hair, pressed her palm to his cheek. Tomorrow she would watch him shave, and the day after that, and the one that followed. Without guilt, without shame, without worrying that anyone would learn of her behavior, she would watch him awake, brush his hair, dress. She could share all aspects of his life, openly and in public, that before she'd only shared in secret.

There would be no more secrets, not between them, not around them. They could be open and honest and the knowledge was incredibly liberating.

His hands worked their magic over her breast, cupping, kneading, reshaping. She loved the feel of his hands reacquainting themselves with her body. He lowered his mouth to her breast, his tongue circling, creating a familiar path. He closed his mouth over her turgid nipple and suckled gently.

"Archie." She dug her fingers against his scalp, holding him in place, relishing the feel of the roughness of his tongue.

He kissed the underside of her breast, the valley between them, then gave attention to her other breast. She stroked her hands over his shoulders and back, rubbed her feet along his calves. She kissed his throat, his neck, his chest. She took satisfaction from his growls, his harsh breathing, his tense muscles, and his dew-coated skin.

How could he have thought she'd truly give any of this up for a dukedom?

They became a tangle of arms, legs, and bodies sliding one over the other. Touching, teasing . . . *now* . . . *not quite yet* . . . *a bit longer* . . . *I can't wait* . . .

When they came together it was as though they'd never been apart. And yet at the same time, it was new and different. These weren't stolen moments, secretive moments. These were their moments, the first of many to be shared during all the nights to come.

They rode the wave of passion together, and when it crested, she thought nothing had ever been so glorious.

It was long moments before she came back to herself,

aware of the weight of his body on hers. She loved the feel of it. Loved everything about this man.

He eased off her and brought her up against his side, holding her close, his hand idly stroking her arm.

"I've missed this," he said quietly. "Holding you. Having you near."

"I'm so incredibly happy, Arch. I never thought I would be. Not like this."

She raised herself up, leaned over, and kissed him. She was Mrs. Warner now. She'd never cherished a title more.

Epilogue

Eight years later

"Papa, when I grow up will I be as beautiful as Mummy?"

Arch glanced over at Venetia sitting on a blanket, the wide boughs of the tree spread out above her creating shade to protect her fair skin from the summer sun. Although she was only six, it was quite obvious that she'd not only inherited her mother's features, but her mother's intelligence as well.

Resting on an elbow, he reached over and tweaked her nose, which caused her to giggle. "You are as beautiful as Mummy now."

"And me, Papa? Am I beautiful like Mummy?"

This question from four-year-old Helena. He tweaked her nose also, which made her release a bout of irresistible chortling. "Undoubtedly."

"And me?" two-year-old Anna asked.

"Of course," he said, pretending to snatch away her little button nose, which caused her eyes to sparkle.

Then, because she wasn't talking yet, but he was certain she was equally curious, he tickled his infant daughter's tummy. A large toothless grin appeared, and her chubby legs began kicking at the air. "And you, too, little one."

"And will Roman be as handsome as you when he grows up?" Venetia asked.

"More so, I should think."

He glanced toward the distance where his son—the first of their children to prove that Camilla wasn't barren—was playing cricket with his friends. After Helena was born, Arch and Camilla had stopped taking holiday in places with warmer climes. After Anna, Camilla had removed the pearl necklace from beneath her pillow. With this latest addition to the family, it seemed that the only way Camilla would no longer have children was if Arch stopped removing his trousers before going to bed.

And that wasn't likely to happen. No indeed, not in the least.

He watched as his wife strolled toward him, having gone to get a closer view of the cricket match while the girls napped following their picnic. Greeting people along the way, she smiled brightly. The breeze carried her laughter, and he thought he'd never known a happier person. Or one more involved with the community.

Through her efforts the Haywood School for Boys had become the Haywood School of Etiquette and Advancement. It taught boys *and* girls now, and not only the fundamentals. It taught the ambitious how to fit in with the elite.

"The world is changing, and a new class of people is emerging. The aristocracy is welcoming wealthy Americans into its ranks. Wealthy Brits can't be far behind, and there is a good deal one must know in order not to appear foolish."

She jokingly referred to her etiquette program as "Fooling Them All." She never joked about her reading program for adults, "Catching Up."

She was an outstanding example of what a person could achieve if she set her mind to it. She frequently spoke to groups about the need to provide educational programs not only to the poor but to those who'd been overlooked for one reason or another, not only to children, but to adults as well. Using herself as an example, she proclaimed, "An adult's inability to read is not the fault of the individual, but it is rather the fault of England. How can we as a nation eliminate financial poverty if we do not first battle educational poverty?"

Arch had never been more proud of her than he was when she petitioned Parliament, urging them to pass an act that would allow for free education.

She worked tirelessly to improve the educational system, and while she was often frustrated by how slowly the wheels of progress turned, he couldn't help but believe she was making some impact. If nothing else, she was able to loosen the tightest purse strings when it came to raising money for her causes. He suspected it was because she'd once been privy to a good many secrets. And she had no shame when it came to the foundations she believed in and using whatever methods necessary to improve the plight of the uneducated.

When she was near enough, the older girls popped up and ran to her. She managed to get her arms around all three. "Hello, my little angels. Did you enjoy your naps?"

"Not really," Venetia said. "But will you read to us now?"

"In a bit," she promised.

Taking the baby into his arms, Arch pushed himself to his feet as Camilla herded the girls back to the blanket. Once they were situated, she turned to him.

"I can't understand the rules of cricket regardless of how close I stand to the game," she said, clearly agitated that the sport seemed beyond her comprehension. So little was.

"I suppose it only matters that the players understand them," he said.

"I suppose." With a loving smile, she took their youngest daughter from him, turned around, and placed her back against his chest. He wrapped his arms around her waist, drawing her nearer, and rested his chin on her shoulder, bringing her scent and warmth closer to him.

No, indeed, he wouldn't be going to bed without removing his trousers anytime in the near future.

"Do you ever regret not marrying your duke?" he asked quietly.

Leaning her head to the side, she glanced back at him. "Why would I want a duke when I could have a prince?"

But seeing all the love for him reflected in her eyes, he didn't feel much like a prince. Rather he felt like a king.

Courting Rituals

O ne of the things that I enjoy about writing historical romance is the opportunity I have to discover little tidbits of history and use them to add flavor to the story. I have always been fascinated by the Victorian courting rituals and entertainment. What did people do a hundred and twenty-five years ago to have fun?

In *An Invitation to Seduction*, Richard and Kitty played lawn tennis and went yachting. In *Love With a Scandalous Lord*, Rhys and Lydia played croquet and attended a performance at Albert Hall. In *To Marry an Heiress*, Devon and Georgina rode through Hyde Park.

For *As an Earl Desires*, I wanted something that I hadn't used before. I had thought to have my characters riding a bicycle, but the bicycles of the 1870s were "high wheels" which only men could ride, because the design with the oversized front wheel didn't accommodate a lady's attire. And very often, the rider took a tumble because the machine wasn't well balanced.

So what would a gentleman suggest if he wished to lure the young lady away from her chaperone so that he might have an opportunity to woo her with his charms unobserved—and if he were very lucky, receive a kiss while no one was watching?

Why he took her rinking!

Or as we think of it today, skating. James L. Plimpton is recognized as the father of modern roller-skating because he designed a skate that allowed the wearer to more easily make turns. Because I couldn't find enough information on skating, I contacted the National Museum of Roller Skating. Deborah L. Wallis, Director and Curator, answered my questions about the design of the skate and how it would have been tied to the shoe in 1879. She also told me that in 1875, Plimpton visited England and afterward, the popularity of skating as a sport rose within that country.

So it lent itself well to being the "something different" that I was looking for. While rinks were often built so people had somewhere to skate—hence the term rinking—many couples would skate in the park. While the terrain wasn't as smooth, it was easier to escape the chaperones who were seldom able to keep up. And "a little harmless flirtation" could ensue.

Resources:

Pleasures and Pastimes in Victorian Britain by Pamela Horn

www.rollerskatingmuseum.com